SPACE DRIFTERS:
THE GHOST SHIP

Other books by Paul Regnier

The Space Drifters series

SPACE DRIFTERS:
THE GHOST SHIP

———

BOOK THREE

PAUL REGNIER

an imprint of
GILEAD PUBLISHING

Published by Enclave Publishing, an imprint of Gilead Publishing, Grand Rapids, Michigan
www.enclavepublishing.com

an imprint of
GILEAD PUBLISHING

ISBN: 978-1-68370-082-1 (print)
ISBN: 978-1-68370-083-8 (ebook)

Space Drifters: The Ghost Ship
Copyright © 2018 by Paul Regnier

Scripture taken from the King James Version of the Bible.

Edited by Andy Meisenheimer
Cover design by Kirk DouPonce
Interior design by Beth Shagene
Ebook production by Book Genesis, Inc.

Printed in the United States of America

For my parents
who taught me how to navigate the stars.

CHAPTER 1

A STEP INTO
THE UNKNOWN

THE DARK SHADOW of the starship filled the viewing screen, the sheer size of it rivaling many space stations. The white glow from the tractor beam cast a ghostly haze on the visual, and all the old space-bar tales about a massive ghost ship roaming the galaxy and preying on unsuspecting star travelers flooded back to me. Back when I'd heard the stories, I dismissed them without a thought, chalking them up to space dementia. Now that I was caught in the tractor beam of this bar tale come to life, I wish I'd paid more attention.

"Iris!" I called out. If a ghost ship of death was after me, I wasn't going down without a fight. "Get us out of here. Full reverse!"

"Glint?" Iris spoke in a feeble voice. "Is that you? You sound so far away."

Unfortunately, my ship had just suffered tremendous damage, care of Mar Mar the Unthinkable's level-twelve quadrant seekers. Truth be told, we were lucky to be in one piece. We'd been powerless and adrift in space the very moment the ghost ship emerged. Whether it was better to float helplessly through deep space or be captured by a ship of doom was still up for debate.

"We're on reserves, Captain." Blix turned to me from the engineering station, a resigned look on his scaled face. "There's not much we can do."

"What do they want with us?" Nelvan's voice trembled.

"I guess we're about to find out." Jasette swiveled her chair to face me. "Any ideas?"

"Let's just sit tight for a while. Watch for any vulnerabilities." It was one of the safe answers they taught in star pilot school. It answered a question without giving specific information, calmed the nerves of your crew, and gave you time to come up with a real plan.

Jasette narrowed her gaze and swiveled back around in her chair. She didn't buy it.

The beam drew us into the dark shadow of the ship, and a wide steel hatch opened like a hungry robot ready to devour us. My ship floated through the opening into a landing bay, and though it was difficult to make out the specific features and potential threats waiting for us inside, one thing was clear: it was a huge space capable of snaring much larger vessels than mine.

My ship came to a stop with a sudden jolt, and a tremor ran under my feet. We were grounded in an alien landing bay, at the mercy of the ship's inhabitants.

No one spoke as the viewing screen displayed the dark steel door of the hatch lowering, closing off the distant stars. It shut with a loud metal clang, and it felt like watching my tomb close. I found it hard to swallow.

"Captain?" Nelvan whispered.

I held a finger to my lips and drew the DEMOTER X. Then I unbuckled the shoulder straps of my chair as quietly as I could and crept over to Blix at the engineering station. He was focused on the visual readouts and scrolling information.

"How bad?" I whispered.

His slivered eyes studied the screen for a moment before turning to me. "Either our systems are blocked, or this alien technology is beyond our scanning parameters."

I frowned. "So you're saying you know nothing."

His reptilian lips parted, giving a warning hint of sharp teeth.

"It means we have to investigate ourselves." Jasette stood to the other side of Blix. Her expression was set, as if we were out of options.

It was hard not to be impressed with her catlike ability to sneak up on us. That natural agility, coupled with the tech-enhanced stealth mode of her form-fitting power suit, made for a lethal combination.

As if to counter her silent approach, the noise of clattering metal came from Nelvan as he struggled to unlatch his shoulder straps and hurry over. "What are you guys talking about?" His nervous eyes darted between us. "Are we prisoners?"

Blix placed a reassuring hand on Nelvan's shoulder. "Our situation is unclear. What would you recommend, Nelvan?"

The boy steadied a little, thin lines forming on his teenage forehead as he stared off in thought.

"Why are you asking him?" I said.

Blix gave me a patronizing look. "I am merely seeking

crew input. As the Scriptures say, in a multitude of counselors there is safety."

I huffed out a laugh. "He's a boy from a century-old world. We need the plan of an experienced space traveler."

Blix crossed his arms. "Fine. What's your plan?"

My mind went blank. I paused for a moment, scrambling for something clever.

"We're waiting." Blix arched his brow.

I gave him a dark look. "My plans are complicated. I need to run some theoreticals through the computer first."

He grinned. "Well, while we're waiting for your genius to reveal itself, let's hear what Nelvan has to say."

Nelvan folded his hands. "We should definitely pray first."

Blix nodded. I threw up my hands. "Great, that'll fix everything."

Nelvan gave a sour look. "I never said that. I just think we need guidance."

"How 'bout you, Jasette?" I said. "You want to sit here and pray all day?"

She cast a studied look at the walls of the bridge, as if a creature lurked outside, waiting to attack. "We're in unknown territory here. I'm up for anything."

A faint blue flicker went through the lights of the bridge.

"Glint?" Iris sounded like she'd been drugged. "Where are you?"

"Right here, computer. Time to wake up and help us get out of here."

"I'm so sleepy," Iris said. "Are we floating?"

"No, we're trapped in some weird ghost ship."

"Oh." Iris gave a long sigh. "I know that song. It's so sad . . . but beautiful too."

"It's not a song. Now, listen—"

The soft tones of ethereal harps played through the intercom, and Iris sang in a dreamlike voice. "'My crew has gone and I'm alone. The ghost ship has me, O my soul . . .'"

"No! No singing. Snap out of it!"

"'The march of vapor, cloud, and mist. The touch of death, the demon's kiss . . .'"

Nelvan cast a sour look at the ceiling. "This isn't helping things."

I marched toward the lift. "Fine. I'll handle this myself." The lift doors opened, and I stepped inside.

"Wait," Blix said. "What are you going to do?"

"Someone has to take charge around here."

The lift doors closed, and I headed to the lower level. All too soon I was at the landing-bay door. I forced myself to take slow breaths and not think about the potential horrors that waited beyond. Interstellar thugs and space pirates were one thing. At least I knew what I was getting with that kind of space trash. But this was the unknown—a giant, floating nightmare that we were trapped inside of.

Iris's demented dirge continued to echo through the halls of the ship. "'Forlorn, we walked through somber moons, whispered tales of woe and gloom . . .'"

"Iris, knock off that singing!"

She continued the depressing tune, lost in her electronic haze. I took a deep breath and tightened my grip on the DEMOTER X. Sooner or later I'd have to face this mystery, and I didn't want to sit around worrying about it. Better to just dive right in.

I hit the blue control panel beside the landing ramp. The air lock hissed open and the ramp lowered. The dim interior of the large ship was bathed in blue light, illuminating it like a cloudy night sky. At least I wouldn't face the unknown in utter darkness.

A few tentative steps took me down the ramp for a better look. I stooped low and held my pistol at the ready as a cavernous landing bay emerged from the gloom before me, big enough to house a ship ten times the size of mine. The construction was of a dark metal replete with geometric patterns. Occasionally, thin lines of multicolored, glowing energy ran along the complex patterns as if trying to escape, but there were no awaiting space monsters, so I proceeded to the base of the ramp.

Footsteps sounded behind me as my crew assembled.

"Captain," Blix spoke in a scolding tone. "How could you open the ship without consulting us first?"

"I don't need to ask permission."

He let out a short hiss. "Well, it's incredibly rude."

"Not to mention pigheaded," Jasette said. "You could have got us all killed."

"Hey, somebody had to do something." I took another scan of the room to make sure it was clear. "Besides, nothing's down here."

An ascending series of blips sounded from Blix's communicator as he joined me at the base of the ramp. "Oxygen-rich environment. No life forms detected nearby. Quite fortunate."

Jasette walked down with her silver pistols drawn. "Somebody's trying to give us a false sense of security."

Blix gave a thoughtful nod. "Pessimistic, but possible."

"Captain?" Nelvan called down, still at the top of the ramp. "Have you set foot on the ship yet?"

Curse that kid. He'd pinpointed my fear.

"I was just waiting till everyone got here," I lied.

"Of course you were, Captain." Blix gave a knowing smile. "But since you are the one who, as you put it, 'takes charge around here,' why don't you take the first step?"

I gave him a steely look. "Fine."

The multicolored lines flowed through the geometric patterns on the floor as if to prompt my hesitant entry to the strange ship. Before I moved, I needed to check for pressure and motion-activated defenses. I grabbed a vibe from my pocket and tossed it onto the floor, where it bounced harmlessly along, making small clinking sounds.

Blix chuckled. "Not exactly a scientific test, Captain."

"It's the best I could think of."

Since no further delaying tactics were coming to me, it was time to take the plunge. I squared my shoulders and stepped onto the dark metal of the landing bay.

No death rays or motion disintegrators.

Emboldened by my consequence-free actions, I took a few broad strides forward and spun around to face my crew. "There, you see? Perfectly fine."

Nelvan pointed behind me. "What's that?"

I whirled. A small figure moved through the shadowy corners of the room, walking on all fours and making no sounds. I aimed the DEMOTER and prepared to fire.

"Who's there?" I called out. "Friend or foe?"

The creature paused and cocked its head to the side as if listening. It was still hidden in the shadows, so I couldn't make out what type of animal it was. It was small, but with the wide variety of deadly creatures in space, that was little reassurance.

"What is it, Blix?" I said.

Blix held his com scanner forward and tapped a few controls. A series of staccato beeps sounded. "I'm not detecting a life form. I need time to isolate the energy. This odd ship is creating a tremendous amount of interference."

A tiny sound, like gas escaping from a punctured tube, reached our ears, and the creature headed forward. It moved as though it was charging us.

"Freeze!" I warned. "Not another step!"

The creature continued its forward motion, a full covering of caramel-colored fur coming into view. I decided I couldn't risk it; there were too many unknown variables heading straight for us. Taking careful aim, I squeezed off a shot from the DEMOTER.

CHAPTER 2

An Odd Host

THE BLAST HIT the creature square in the chest, and with a stifled gurgle it collapsed. No one spoke for several moments while the tiny figure remained motionless.

"What was it?" Nelvan finally whispered. "It looked so small. Are you sure it was dangerous?"

"I'm not taking any chances." I turned to Jasette. "Cover me. I need to make sure."

Jasette gave a determined nod and followed, her pistols trained on the fallen creature. I took a few cautious steps, my heart beating fast. Within moments we were standing over the fallen beast.

It was a caramel-colored kitten with white fur around its eyes that gave it an extra dose of cuteness.

"Aw." Jasette sounded disappointed. "You killed a kitten."

A wave of remorse swept through me. "I didn't mean to. It charged us. You saw it."

Nelvan and Blix joined us.

Blix gazed at the kitten with watery eyes. "Maybe it just wanted to play."

Nelvan peeked out from behind him, using the Vythian's bulk as a shield. He sniffed. "That's one of the saddest things I've ever seen."

"Wait a freem." Squinting, Jasette bent closer. "There's no blood. And look at this." She motioned to a spray of black particles that spread out from the creature.

As if in response, the black particles moved toward the kitten like ants after food.

Jasette sprang back and raised her pistols. "That's no kitten. It's nanotechnology."

As we watched, the particles filled the hole left by my weapon until the kitten was whole again. It rolled to its feet as if it was waking from a nap, and we all took a quick step backward.

The kitten looked up at us with sparkling blue eyes and let out a tiny mew.

For a moment, nothing happened. Then, with a click small hatches opened in the floor and walls, and the dark landing bay came alive with movement—an endless parade of fist-sized white bots with oval bodies and multiple legs. A red light moved rapidly around the dark faceplate at the front of each body, as though they were searching for something. It didn't take long for the lights to zero in on me.

The spiderlike bots crawled toward me like a swarm of angry insects. There was nowhere to run, so I huddled close to my crew and took aim with the DEMOTER X. But Jasette struck first, letting loose a rapid succession of red energy beams from both pistols. Several spider bots blew apart or crumpled, the red light in their faceplates going dim. But all too soon their fallen bodies were replaced by countless others.

I was inspired by the first powerful shots from my

DEMOTER, every blast sending several of their spindly-legged bodies flying. But my confidence eroded in freems as the swarm engulfed us, their pointed metal legs crawling over me. I was thrown to the ground as the wave hit me, legs constricting around my own arms and legs, and no amount of flailing or squirming could loosen their hold. My limbs were held fast, and I was as helpless as a kitten—except, of course, for the evil nanokitten that had just captured me.

My crew fell captive soon after, with Blix holding out the longest. His reptilian body weaved through the horde and took powerful swipes at the onslaught, using the legs of several defeated spider bots in his hands as weapons. He swirled their oval bodies in fast circles, knocking away new attackers, in a beautiful robot slaughter. But for all his strength, it wasn't enough, and when a few spider bots evaded him and crawled up his back, they placed their pointed metal legs on his temples and shot a bright electrical current from their legs across his head. He went rigid and, like a mighty tree, fell to the ground.

The kitten padded over, innocent blue eyes gazing at me as if I'd forgotten to feed it. "Your actions were hostile." The high-pitched words echoed as if dozens of miniature voices were speaking as one. "Explain."

Since a pile of spider bots were coiled tight around me, playing the victim was my best hope. "You charged us. I thought you were going to attack."

The kitten cocked his head as if having trouble understanding. "My form was calculated to be nonthreatening. Yes or no?"

"Sort of." I was obviously dealing with some cold, mechanical system of logic. I had to play up vulnerability to erase any conclusions that we might be a danger. "I was scared you would hurt us. We are very weak."

The kitten looked at Blix. "Incorrect."

Blasted logical computer brains.

"We were scared," I tried. "We are normally peaceful. We come in peace."

The kitten looked at my DEMOTER. "Incorrect."

"We acted out of self-defense," Jasette spoke up. She lay on the ground near me, bots coiled around her limbs. "We wish you no harm. We only wanted to survive."

A thoughtful look animated the kitten's features. "Probability of truth . . . high. I will accept with caution."

The kitten mewed, and the spider bots released their hold and crawled just out of reach. Their glowing red eyes darted between my crew and me, as if watching for any false actions. I rose to my feet, careful not to make any sudden moves.

Blix moaned and sat up, rubbing his temple gingerly. "That was horrid. Someone please bring me something cool to drink."

The kitten twitched its whiskers. The caramel and white color of its fur changed to jet black, while the blue drained from its eyes, replaced with a yellow that pulsated with energy. "I am known as Casglo. I run operations on the *Arpellon*. My mission is ninety-nine percent complete. Your presence will either delay or advance my objective. Please choose."

"Advance. Advance!" With the spider bots poised for a second attack, I wasted no time with my answer.

"Excellent. I can repair your vessel in exchange. Yes or no?"

I looked back at the ship. The hull was scarred and pitted everywhere. The repairs would be extensive. And my mind was having trouble imagining how a little kitten could undo all the damage. "Yes, of course. But how—"

The kitten meowed. The spider bots moved in unison until my ship was covered with them. A shiver went through me as they set to work on the damaged freighter in a flurry of orange laser beams welding metal, thin arms making intricate electrical repairs, and groups of bots operating in perfect unison for larger tasks. It was both frightening and impressive.

I leaned close to Jasette. "Think this is a good idea?"

"It beats having those things wrapped around us," she said.

She always knew how to put things in perspective.

Casglo glanced at each of us. "Who is the one that will help with my collection?"

I shared a nervous glance with my crewmembers. "All of us?"

"Excellent." The kitten walked toward me, rubbing against my leg and purring. I took a step back, restraining myself from drawing my pistol, and gave Blix a worried look. He shrugged. Our next steps were complete guesswork.

Casglo moved away from me and rubbed against the legs of each of my crew in turn, purring the whole time. When the kitten got to Nelvan, it sat down. The pulsating yellow eyes studied him as if viewing an art exhibit. "Highest probability of success for the young one."

Nelvan's mouth hung open. "Me? I don't have anything."

The kitten mewed. "I detect otherwise. Do you wish to help? Yes or no?"

"Y-yes. I think." Nelvan gave me a desperate glance.

Casglo nodded. "Please follow. The collection room of the

Arpellon will verify." The kitten skittered down the landing bay toward a wide doorway.

Nelvan hurried over to me, casting quick glances at the spider bots working on the ship. "Do we have to?"

I looked at Blix, hoping with Nelvan for another choice. Blix winced, continuing to rub his temples. "For the time being, I don't see an alternative."

"There's always another way." Jasette started tapping out commands on her forearm computer. "Just stay alert in case things get ugly."

I nodded and fingered my weapon for reassurance. "Let's just hope this is a short stay."

CHAPTER 3

THE CORRIDORS
OF THE *ARPELLON*

CASGLO LED US DOWN an immense corridor, the dark metal construction covered in geometric patterns continuing throughout the passage. Occasional trails of light wound through the patterns as if lost in an unending maze. As we walked, spider bots emerged from openings in the walls and crawled away, headed who knows where. The sheer size of the corridor dwarfed the tiny kitten that scampered before us. I felt as though we were mice sneaking through the hallway of a giant's spaceship.

"The *Arpellon* is breathtaking," Blix said. "No doubt you have a large crew for operations."

The kitten glanced back and twitched its whiskers. "My workers are many."

"How many of them are there?" I braced for the answer.

"Five thousand three hundred and forty-two."

Nightmare. The nagging sensation of walking deeper into a trap put me on edge. As far as I was concerned, the sooner we got off this ship the better.

"Are there any more like you aboard?" Jasette said.

"There are many of us. And yet only one."

Blix leaned in and whispered. "The efficiency and horror of nanotech."

The kitten stopped and turned to face us. "Calculations indicate curiosity as likely motivator for your questions. If not curiosity, you seek information for possible weakness to exploit. True or false?"

"False, false." I spoke with the best sincerity I could muster. "We are peaceful."

The kitten's yellow eyes narrowed slightly. "Incorrect."

"I mean, we *like* peace. Occasionally we fight, but we don't like it."

"Incorrect."

"Self-preservation drives us to conflict," Blix spoke in his professorial tone. "I seek after peace with great vigor. But when threatened, I often resort to battle. It is a most unfortunate instinct I am recently trying to overcome."

"Your answer is acceptable." Casglo licked its paw. "Continue forward. Yes or no?"

"Yes." Moving deeper into this dark spider-filled ship was one of the last things I wanted to do. But I couldn't see another choice.

The kitten turned and trotted down the corridor. I leaned toward Blix. "Any ideas?"

Blix watched as two spider bots emerged from the wall nearby and scampered away. "Yes. Don't upset the kitten."

An anxious feeling swirled in my chest as I tried to block out thoughts of being swarmed by spider bots with laser eyes and pointy metal legs. My only hope was that we had something that would appease Casglo that didn't involve our death. And that we could somehow escape the confines of this dark ship. I frowned and headed after the kitten that held all the cards.

Casglo led us down a series of huge corridors. Lights continued to pulse through the geometric patterns on the floor and walls. Every so often, black particles would travel along with the lights until they reached the kitten. As they did, the kitten would absorb the particles. After a while, I realized the kitten was *growing*.

I shot a warning look at Blix. He gave a knowing nod, already grasping the situation.

We reached a new corridor with a broad opening in one of the walls. Beyond the opening was a spacious room filled with geometric control panels and a multitude of lights and dials. Expansive windows covered the far wall, offering a grand panorama of space.

"What a view." I had to stop and take in the sight. "Now this is a bridge."

"Yeah," Nelvan said. "This is way better than—" He flashed me a guilty glance before looking away. "—than some other ships."

"Is it?" Casglo, who now resembled a full-grown cat, sat on its haunches. The cat gave a cursory look around the bridge as if it were nothing more than dry rocks on a desert plain. "I lack data for comparison. I've known only the bridge of the *Arpellon* for over one hundred gloons."

"You've been in this ship for a hundred gloons?" Jasette sounded horrified.

"One hundred twenty-three, to be precise. It was necessary to complete the collection."

"Collection of what?" Nelvan moved closer to Blix as if afraid of the answer.

"Antiquities of the universe," Casglo said. "My founders have achieved an advanced civilization. Their desires transcend mere sustenance. They wish to obtain treasures beyond their galaxy."

"What a noble pursuit," Blix stared off, dreamy eyed. "Far better than the typical plans of conquest and subjugation."

I rolled my eyes. "Sounds like they have too much time on their hands."

"But why so long?" Jasette said.

The cat's face contorted as if the nano bots were having trouble forming the right expression. "Is that long for your species?"

Jasette nodded.

"You have an adverse reaction. How does your species react to a long task?"

"Well . . . you get tired." Jasette glanced at us like she hadn't expected the turn in the conversation. "You want to rest for a while."

Casglo was quiet for several moments. "We were brought forth from the source. There was great power there. When my mission is complete, I will return to the source. Is that . . . rest?"

"I suppose so."

"I am pleased with the concept of rest." The cat twitched its tail. "Once the collection room is filled with one hundred items, my mission is complete. I will return to the source. To rest."

"How many do you have now?" I said.

"Ninety-nine." Casglo gave an excited sounding meow. "I am granted an electronic stimulus with each treasure obtained. A reward mechanism given by the founders to encourage efficiency. The process is patronizing upon analysis, but the effect is pleasing."

I exchanged creeped-out looks with my crew. "That's . . . really great."

Casglo walked toward Nelvan, who backed away, eyes wide. The cat rubbed against his leg, purring, and a stream of nanobot particles broke away from its body and flowed up Nelvan's leg and around his torso. He gave me a desperate look as if asking for help. What could I do?

"Casglo," Blix said. "Your actions are troubling."

The nanobot stream fled back into the cat.

"My apologies," Casglo said. "It is in my programming to scan for precious objects for the collection. My sensors indicate high probability this young one will complete my goal."

Nelvan took a step back. "How? I don't even have vibes."

Casglo continued down the corridor, motioning with its paw for us to follow. "The results will soon be known. The collection room is near."

CHAPTER 4

The Collection Room

WE HEADED DOWN a long corridor. At the far end sat an oval doorway flowing with red energy.

Nelvan leaned in, his voice shaky. "What does he want with me?"

How could I answer the kid when I was just as lost as he was? We were in a tight spot, and I had no idea what this bizarre nanocat wanted. All I knew was the longer I searched for a way out of here, the greater the chance I'd find one. "Just go along with it for now," I whispered. "I've got your back."

"But what if he wants my leg or my eyes or something?"

I grimaced. "Where'd you get that idea?"

"Yeah, I know it's gross," Nelvan said. "It's just that I read this one story on the uniweb—"

"Rule number one: don't believe everything you read on the uniweb."

We reached the end of the corridor. The oval doorway buzzed with power, promising electric pain to any trespassers.

"This is our destination." Casglo was now the size of a

jungle cat. Its soft kitten voice was gone, replaced by a synchronized choir of darker voices with a touch of growl. "The collection room of the *Arpellon*." The cat slinked toward the red energy and roared as if warning another jungle beast. The red energy fluctuated, then disappeared.

The room beyond was filled with pedestals displaying all manner of objects. All the items hovered above the pedestals, suspended in cylinders of glowing white energy. The value of some objects seemed obvious, being encrusted in glittering jewels or exquisitely crafted by an artisan, while others were more puzzling. I noticed one pedestal displaying the moss-covered stump of a small tree. There were obviously some freakish minds behind the qualifications for this collection.

Casglo looked at us. "Please, follow." The cat walked farther into the room and began sniffing at the objects in some odd kind of inspection.

I looked at Blix. "You first."

Blix wrinkled his nose. "Captains are supposed to lead by example."

"You're the least likely to die. You've got those tough Vythian scales."

"Very well." Blix straightened as though preparing for a final mission. "But I'm doing this for Princess Jasette and Nelvan."

"Whatever. Just go."

Blix flashed his teeth at me and headed through the doorway. A blue curtain of energy draped over him and appeared to scan his body. There was a discordant beep and the blue energy disappeared.

"Negative," Casglo said. "Nothing on the Vythian of value."

"I beg to differ." Blix adjusted his shoulder straps.

Jasette marched forward through the doorway and the blue energy washed over her. Once again, the strange beep sounded.

"Negative." Casglo said. "Please continue."

I hesitated for a moment. Submitting myself voluntarily to the electronic prodding of a computer system was a painful blow to my pride, but I consoled myself with the fact that at least it wasn't a teleporter. I also made a silent vow to store up my anger from this moment and apply it to blasting random objects into tiny pieces later.

"Captain?" Casglo said. "Do you wish to proceed?"

I gritted my teeth, growing tired of his constant questioning. "Yes, fine." Hands clenched into fists, I headed forward. A wave of electric current went through me as I stepped into the collection room.

"Negative," Casglo said. "As suspected."

Now that I was in the room, I was granted a more ominous view of the objects within. The first few rows were the valuable items I'd seen from the corridor. But farther in, things took a darker turn. Sown among the objects of value were aliens. Some were races I recognized, some were so exotic and strange they existed beyond the scope of where my space travels had taken me. They hung there, looking forward with blank stares, suspended in the white energy fields above the pedestals. A chill went through me at the discovery that a few of them were still alive. For a moment, I imagined my crew and me hanging beside them.

I turned to Blix and Jasette. The deep concern on their faces told me the same thoughts were spinning through their heads.

The cat turned its attention to Nelvan. "Please proceed. If my calculations are correct, you will bring my mission to an end."

Nervous twitching animated Nelvan's body. He swallowed hard and headed forward. A blanket of blue energy flowed over him, and suddenly the energy changed from blue to green as an ascending tone rang out.

Casglo immediately grew. Muscles rippled across the cat's black frame and sharp spines protruded from its neck and back. The jungle cat went into a deep stretch, thick, curved horns now emerging from its head. "The final object. My mission is complete." A thunderous roar burst from its mouth, sending fear tremors up my legs.

"W-What does that mean?" Nelvan looked petrified.

Casglo took powerful strides toward Nelvan. "It means you have brought the final object to my collection."

CHAPTER 5

THE FINAL OBJECT

BLIX STEPPED BETWEEN Casglo and Nelvan. "Casglo, we wish to help, but you cannot possibly intend to take Nelvan."

Casglo turned his heavily muscled head to Blix. "I do not need the young one. Just his skin."

A chill went through me as I realized that Nelvan's morbid thoughts about Casglo's intentions were spot on. Of course I couldn't let that happen to Nelvan, even if it meant taking a dangerous stand deep in the heart of this nightmare. I drew my pistol and aimed it at the large cat. Jasette mirrored my actions, her silver pistols held at the ready.

A group of spider bots gathered in the corridor outside the collection room. It was starting to look like our last stand. There was no chance to blast our way out of this one.

Casglo glanced around at us. "When one is threatened, all become hostile. You are a bonded unit. Yes or no?"

"Yeah." I powered the DEMOTER X to full. "Now leave Nelvan alone."

"Your cohesive unit is pleasing," Casglo said. "Greater

strength with unity. Your weakness lies in your impulsive response."

"We do not wish aggressive actions, Casglo." Blix sounded calm, but his body was tense, ready to act. "But we cannot allow you to hurt Nelvan."

"No harm is intended," Casglo said. "I only require his silver skin."

"Silver skin?" Nelvan looked puzzled. All our heads swiveled to look at him.

"Oh." Blix relaxed a bit. "You mean this?" He pinched a corner of Nevlan's jumpsuit between his fingers.

The large cat nodded. "Precisely. The material has been analyzed and determined to be quite rare. It qualifies for the collection."

Nelvan closed his eyes and exhaled. "Thank God."

I powered down the DEMOTER, my adrenalin rush winding down. "Let me get this straight. Nelvan gives you the outfit, your mission is finished, you fix our ship, and we can go?"

Casglo nodded. "A mutually beneficial occurrence."

A thrill went through me—the kind that only narrowly avoiding death can bring. "Fantastic. Nelvan." I gestured. "Give the cat your suit."

Nelvan frowned. "This is my only outfit."

"Relax, I'll give you my old space academy uniform. I was about your size back then."

Nelvan glanced at Jasette, his cheeks going pink. "But I'd have to walk back to the ship in my underwear."

I shrugged. "Sorry, kid."

"Don't be embarrassed, Nelvan." Jasette turned the other way. "I won't even look."

Nelvan frowned but gave in to the inevitable and removed his brown jacket, then the jumpsuit. He stood there looking frustrated with his silver suit crumpled around his ankles. The only thing left on his skinny body were black boxers with a pattern of white stars.

"Stars, huh?" I grinned.

Nelvan shrugged. "Seemed like a good idea at the time."

Jasette gasped and spun back around. She looked as though she'd seen a ghost. Nelvan swept his jumpsuit back over his underwear. "Hey, you promised you wouldn't look."

"Huh?" Jasette's eyes were frantic, darting from Casglo to me. "No, it's not that, Nelvan. It's just . . . I saw . . ." She took a deep breath and composed herself. "It's okay. I just got scared. Silly me." She forced a laugh.

Casglo turned to her, an inquisitive look on its face. "Please explain."

"Oh, I was just startled." Jasette turned back and appeared to be looking for something. "That mask over there frightened me." She pointed to a golden mask with ornate carvings. The facial expression on the mask was pure joy. I couldn't figure out how a woman who'd faced down hundreds of vicious space monkeys without so much as flinching could be afraid of a happy little mask.

"Really?" I said.

"I know. Stupid, right?" She casually tapped out a few commands on her forearm computer.

I shook my head. "Whatever. Nelvan, give the cat your suit."

Nelvan paused for a moment, a pouty look on his face, then stepped out of the jumpsuit and handed it to Casglo in a crumpled, silver ball. "Here."

Casglo moved toward Nelvan, taking the suit in his teeth, and Nelvan flinched at the proximity of the fang-filled mouth. As the large cat strode to a nearby pedestal that stood empty, Nelvan retrieved his brown jacket and pulled it tightly around himself as though a winter breeze had just swept through the room.

Casglo placed the silver suit on the pedestal and watched as a white column of glowing energy lit up around it. Immediately, a pulsating siren blared through the room. The white columns of energy surrounding the rows of antiquities glowed bright.

Casglo sat on its haunches, scanning the room. "My mission is complete. I can return to the source." Something between a purr and a growl came out.

I looked over at Blix, not sure what to do next. He motioned to the corridor as if to say, *Let's get out while the cat is happy.* Good choice. Except I couldn't get Jasette's attention. She was tapping away at her computer.

"I guess we should be going, then," I said.

Casglo turned back to me. "Yes. I am pleased with your assistance to my mission."

Blix bowed. "It is our pleasure. May we return to our ship?"

Casglo's whiskers twitched. The cat looked throughout the room as if trying to find something. "There are transmissions interfering with operations." His dangerous eyes slid over to Jasette. "You are sending signals. They must cease."

"Really? I'm so sorry." Jasette seemed uncharacteristically apologetic. "My outfit has controls that help stabilize me. I'm just trying to recover after being so frightened." Her fingers continued to dance across her computer.

"You must stop those signals." Casglo strode toward her.

"Okay, I just have to turn this crazy thing off." She acted as though she'd forgotten how to operate her power suit. "These computers can be so confusing sometimes."

"Are you all right?" I gave her a concerned look.

"Fine." She broke from her flustered behavior for a moment to flash me serious eyes.

Casglo moved closer to her. If this was the jungle, she was freems away from being eaten. "You must leave the collection room. Your device is causing negative interference."

"So sorry," she said. "I'll leave." She spun on her heel and walked out of the room right before it seemed he might pounce on her.

I followed close behind with Nelvan and Blix.

In the corridor, Casglo padded over to Jasette. "You are continuing to cause a disturbance. It is time for your device to terminate."

Several spider bots gathered at Jasette's feet.

"Jasette!" I flashed her a serious look.

She hit a few more controls, placed her arms at her sides, and looked up at Casglo with a forced smile. "So sorry. Didn't mean to cause a problem."

Casglo stared at her a moment longer, then headed down the corridor. "I will take you to your ship now."

The trip back to the ship was a quiet one. Without the distraction of conversation, the dark metal of the corridors made me feel claustrophobic. I tried to speak confidentially to Jasette about why she was acting so weird, but she just brushed me off and mouthed the word *later*.

We arrived back at the landing bay, where the spider bots were still scuttling around my ship in frenetic patterns. Even though they were performing much-needed repairs, the sight of my star freighter covered with them was a vision of horror.

Casglo appeared to be studying the bots. The hulking cat's yellow eyes moved in quick, jerky motions as if examining their progress. "Repairs are proceeding well. The vessel should be operational by tomorrow."

"Tomorrow?" I gave Casglo a questioning look. "Really? That fast?"

"My workers are efficient." Casglo glanced at the remnants of spider-bot parts strewn across the floor near my ship. "Except for those destroyed by your crew."

Blip gave a slight bow. "Again, our sincere apologies for the misunderstanding."

Casglo gave a slight nod. "I must see to other sections of the ship. Your arrival precedes an active event in the *Arpellon*'s internal operations. We are renewing the helix vector of the energy matrix during a cluster reconfiguration."

Nelvan shot a confused look my way. I hated to admit that I was just as lost.

"Okay," I said.

"I will return tomorrow." Casglo shook his muscled head as if shooing flies. "The workers will not harm you so long as you keep from further hostilities."

"Most appreciated, Casglo," Blix said. "The *Arpellon* is a wondrous ship, and you are a gracious host."

Casglo blinked, turned, and padded back into the corridor.

"Can we get back into the ship now?" Nelvan had his hands jammed down in his jacket pockets trying to cover his underwear.

"Good idea." Jasette marched toward the ship looking

determined. She grabbed a few of the wrecked spider bots lying nearby, hoisted them over her shoulder, and headed up the landing ramp.

"What's up with her?" I said.

Blix tapped a finger to his lips, casting a studied look after Jasette. "I have a few theories, but it most likely has to do with you, Captain."

I turned on him. "What? I didn't do anything."

"Precisely." Blix gestured at me as if I'd proved his point. "Your lack of sensitivity keeps you from being proactive in matters of the heart. In navigating relationships, what we neglect to do is often just as important as what we do."

"Okay, genius," I said. "What didn't I do? Wish her good morning? Bring her breakfast in bed?"

"Surface gestures, Captain. I suggest you dig deeper."

"Or maybe we fly out of this nightmare first, huh?" I motioned to the belly of the dark ship we were trapped inside of. "How about leaving the question of what I was supposed to do in some bizarre relationship mystery guide—which is only available to those confusing the rest of us—until after we escape?"

"Your choice." Blix lifted his head as if further discussion was beneath him and headed for the ship. "If multitasking is too much for your human thought processes, we shall leave it at that."

"Good!" I called after him.

My mind was cloudy. After everything Jasette and I had been through in our recent trials on *The Iron Gauntlet* and the narrow escape from Mar Mar the Unthinkable's fortress, I'd thought we'd reached another level in our relationship. Unfortunately, I had no idea what that level was or what I was supposed to do once we got there. All I knew was that I felt closer to her, and I never wanted to let go. Maybe all I needed to do was tell her that truth.

"Captain," Nelvan said. "I think Blix is just trying to—"

I held up a finger of warning. "Not a word, Nelvan."

Nelvan frowned. "Fine. Can I borrow those clothes you were talking about?"

I nodded and led the boy toward the ship.

CHAPTER 6

UNIFORMS
AND SALUTES

EVEN AS A TEEN, my space academy suit had fit a little snug. Now that Nelvan wore it, it seemed more his size.

"How's it look?" Nelvan turned to each side, checking his reflection in the mirror in my quarters.

"A little loose but not bad," I said.

A series of bell-like tones sounded. "You look very nice, Nelvan," Iris said.

"Thanks, Iris," Nelvan smiled. "Are you feeling better?"

"Heavens, yes." She let out a sigh of relief. "Though I'm very ticklish, and those little bots crawling around have given me quite a case of the giggles."

I looked up at the ceiling. "Can we get a little privacy here, computer?"

"There's no need to be shy, Glint," Iris said. "My data files are very thorough when it comes to human anatomy. Not to mention the various maladies and unfortunate reactions your species can contract during space travel. Which reminds me, that rash on your upper thigh could really use a visit to the med lab."

My jaw tightened. "I told you not to watch me when I'm getting dressed."

"The overall health of the crew is part of my responsibilities. Besides, all work should have certain . . . perks associated with it."

I grimaced. "Well, it's weird. Knock it off."

A descending series of blips sounded. The 360-degree visuals in my room flickered on with scenes of people with gruesome skin diseases and various stages of space dementia.

Nelvan's face scrunched up. "Gross."

"Iris." I used my authoritative space captain tone.

"I'm merely displaying the plagues I'm protecting you from. You might show a little appreciation occasionally."

"Thanks a heap. Now turn off those visuals."

"As you wish."

With a harsh tone, the screens flickered off.

Nelvan shivered as if trying to forget a bad dream. He grabbed his brown jacket and put it on over the suit, then straightened it and smiled at his reflection. "How 'bout now?"

I nodded. "Now you look like you belong in space."

"Yeah. I like it. Thanks, Captain."

"You got it. Now go check on those spider bots on the bridge. The thought of them crawling on my captain's chair makes me want to chuck them into an asteroid grinder."

"Sure thing." Nelvan headed for the door, then turned. "Oh, I keep meaning to ask. Why don't you have a salute for your ship? Like an arm over the chest or a bow or something? Ever since I joined your crew, there's been no mention of it."

The boy got me thinking. Why didn't I have a salute? After all, I was the captain. People should be saluting me. "Yeah, a salute . . . Try this." I crossed my arms over my chest with fingers pointed up like I was holding laser pistols, then made them into fists.

Nelvan looked confused. "I don't understand."

I went back to the crossed finger pistols and gave him a stern look. "A symbol for ray guns ready to blast our enemies to bits . . ." I transitioned to fists. "Then fists to say we can mess you up with hand-to-hand combat as well."

"Oh." He gave a half-hearted nod. "Needs work."

I pointed at the door. "Out!"

Nelvan scurried out of the room while I made a mental note to force my cool new salute upon my crew when a situation arose that made them vulnerable to agreement.

My door had barely closed behind Nelvan when it reopened with a chirp and several spider bots crawled in. I reflexively took a few steps back. The spiders crawled up the walls, their red eyes darting around, apparently looking for defects.

"Iris," I said. "Make sure they don't mess with my stuff."

"Oh, I'm sorry, Glint." Iris's voice was laced with sarcasm. "Am I allowed to open my eyes now? I thought I wasn't supposed to look at you anymore."

I fought back the anger. "Don't play with me, Iris. You know very well what I meant. Just keep an eye on these bots."

She let out a dejected sigh. "I'm really not in a monitoring kind of mood. Perhaps."

Sometimes I had to take what I could get. I headed out of my quarters, pretending metallic spiders weren't crawling on all my personal things. It was high time to find out what was going on with Jasette.

Soon I was standing outside the door to the guest quarters. It had unofficially become her room, which was fine by me. As far as I was concerned, she was the greatest thing to happen to that room.

As captain, I had the authority to waltz right in to any room on the ship, but I wanted to play it classy and give her her own space. I hit the door intercom.

"Hey," I spoke toward the intercom. "Can I come in?"

There was a few moments of silence. I could've sworn I heard a sigh.

"Sure."

The door chirped open, and I walked in to find her hunched over a table that was covered in bot parts. She had thin tools in her hands, operating on a metallic disc covered in a geometric pattern of glowing blue lines. It looked like she'd dissected the remains of one of the fallen spider bots.

Lines of blue energy crisscrossed the doorway. I pointed to them. "What's all this?"

"Keeps the bots out," she said.

"Why? What's going on?" I said.

"Nothing." She remained focused on the disc her tools were twisting into. "I'm kind of busy. Can we talk later?"

I moved closer and dropped into the chair at the other side of the table. "Sure, once you tell me why you're acting so weird."

Jasette let out a long breath and looked up. She stared at me for a few moments. "You won't like it."

"Try me."

"I didn't mean that as a maybe. I know you won't like it."

A miniature whirlwind of nerves spun through my stomach in preparation for what she was about to tell me. "It's about us, isn't it?"

"Huh?" A crinkled line formed between her eyes.

"Blix said I didn't do something. Or I was supposed to do something, and you're mad at me because I didn't do something that I needed to do, or—"

Jasette put up her hand. "Just stop. It's not about us. We're fine."

"Ha!" I slammed my fist on the table, causing the metal parts to jump. "I knew it. I knew we were good."

"Easy. I'm not saying there isn't room for improvement," she said.

I nodded slowly. "I'm guessing there's a long list somewhere."

"It's not that long." She gave a slight grin. "But right now I'm on a personal mission."

"Which is why you've been acting weird since the collection room, right?"

Jasette's face grew tense. "Glint, this is big. I didn't want to involve you in what I have to do. It's dangerous."

"What are you talking about? We're flying out of here tomorrow."

She shook her head. "Oh, Glint, I'm so sorry. I wanted to do this on my own, but I can't. Casglo would stop me."

My stomach was churning. "You're freaking me out here. Tell me you're joking."

"Trust me, I don't want to complicate things. But I need your help. I need the whole crew. I know it's a lot to ask . . . Will you promise to go with me on this?" There was something in her eyes that told me I was in serious trouble.

"How can I promise unless you tell me what you're talking about?"

Jasette got up, made her way around the table, and knelt beside me. She took a deep breath, as if preparing herself, and placed a hand softly against my cheek. "You have to trust me that I would never ask you to do something like this unless the situation was desperate. I hate that what I'm about to do could put you and the others in danger. Just this once . . . Promise you'll stand with me."

The nervous swirl rekindled in my stomach. The star pilot code of survival would never agree to an unknown plan, especially one filled with danger and no assurance of treasure. But those deep-green eyes pleaded with me. I'd never seen her this desperate. Whatever her plan was, it was fairly certain I would hate it and it would probably kill me. I also knew at that moment that I couldn't say no. I wanted to stand with her if it meant that much to her.

"I promise." My voice sounded a little shaky but mostly confident.

A warm smile spread across her face. Her eyes teared up a little. "There was a chrysolenthium flower in the collection room. I have to steal it tonight."

CHAPTER 7

ILL-ADVISED THIEVERY

THE NERVOUS SWIRL in my stomach became a raging tornado. "Say what?"

She frowned. "Glint, I have to do this. The lives of everyone in my kingdom depend on it."

My mind scrambled for exit routes. "There're other flowers out there. I mean, this isn't the only one, right?"

"I've been searching the stars for three gloons. This is the first one I've seen. And it's a young one filled with spores that could grow a whole field of flowers for the future."

"Yeah, but come on. Have you looked at this place?" I motioned toward the door, hoping her imagination would follow me through the dark corridors of the *Arpellon* lurking just outside. "We've been swallowed by the demon of space. You heard the cat. It's been collecting precious objects for over a hundred gloons. Didn't it occur to you that in all that time it hasn't been destroyed or taken over or even stolen from? Do you know how many space pirates are out there dreaming of a giant target like this? But in all that time nothing has been able to touch it. It must have insane shields or weaponry or mystery alien voodoo that I can't even fathom. And you think we can just stroll right into that collection room, the treasure trove of this floating prison, and zip out of here unscathed?"

She frowned as her hand dropped from my face. More moisture welled up in her eyes. "Yes, it's crazy. I know."

"So why try it?"

"Trust me, if I thought it was impossible, I wouldn't attempt it. But I ran system scans the whole time we were in that collection room." Jasette tapped out a few commands on her forearm computer. A scaled-down, three-dimensional projection of the collection room spun before us. "After taking apart this bot, I think I understand the system logic. I'm pretty sure it's possible."

"You 'think'? You're 'pretty sure'?" I threw up my hands. "You want to put us all in jeopardy on that tightrope?"

Jasette flashed me a challenging look. "You do that to us all the time."

She had a point. "Yeah, but never this insane."

"Glint." She grabbed my hands tightly. "Please."

That familiar sense of dread that proceeds foolhardy missions washed over me. My shoulders slouched as I resigned myself to the inevitable. "Just tell me that by the time this goes down, you'll have things more figured out."

A tear streamed down her cheek. She leaned in and cradled the back of my head, her fingers going through my hair. Her warm lips met mine. I couldn't remember a kiss that felt so strong and tender at the same time. When she broke away, I was light-headed.

She grabbed my hand tightly. "I know this is a lot to ask. Thank you, Glint."

I brushed a few stray hairs from her face. "You know this is probably our last mission, right?"

She gave a mischievous grin. "Not if I can help it." She moved back to her side of the table, her focus drifting to the bot parts.

I got up, feeling far wearier than when I'd entered, and headed for the door. I turned right before exiting. "I'm sending Blix to help. We need him to plan this level of crazy."

She shook her head, not bothering to look up. "He's not gonna like it either."

"True. But he'll be a lot less angry with you than he usually is with me."

Blix and Jasette huddled near the engineering station on the bridge. They poured over equations and three-dimensional holograms, speaking in eager tones of cross-grid differential splicing and quadrant redirection pathways. Since technology had a habit of letting me down when it counted, I had zero reassurance in their excitement.

"I'm detecting a variance in the glentice netting." Blix motioned to his com screen.

Jasette nodded. "Yep. Electro-pulse flows are similar to Rethmorac circles. I already plotted the sequence."

"Extraordinary." Blix looked up at me. "Captain, her reverse engineering of alien technology is quite impressive."

"Really?" I crossed my arms. "This scheme is just fine with you? Do you realize how much grief you would've given me for even suggesting an idea like this?"

Blix shared a patronizing look with Jasette. "Please, you're comparing your haphazard plans with her ingenuity?"

"Okay, just get ready for more of this." With my hand, I imitated a crawling spider, making it move up my arm and fasten tight around my neck.

Blix winced. "I should very much like to avoid that." He rubbed his temples. "My head is still throbbing from our last encounter."

"Are you sure this is our only option?" Nelvan said. "Why don't we just ask Casglo for the flower? Or maybe we can trade for it."

The poor kid had been all twitches and rapid breathing since we filled him in. And really, who could blame him? The plan was nuts. I told him that as our getaway navigator, he'd never have to leave the ship. That calmed him down a little. Still, I hadn't seen him that upset since he first stepped through the rift in time and ended up stuck on my ship.

The spider bots had finished their industrious work on the bridge, so it seemed the safest place to plan. As far as I could tell, their repair work was very thorough—no more sparking wiring hanging from the ceiling or broken control panels jutting out from the walls. Sometimes even the bleakest situations can throw you a few silver linings.

"Computer, how're your energy levels?" I said.

"I'm feeling much better, Glint," Iris said. "But I simply can't abide those spindly little creatures poking around inside me a moment longer."

"It's almost over, I promise. Now, what are the levels?"

"System power is at seventy-one percent, but my emotional well-being is very low."

Maybe getting zapped by a security beam tonight wouldn't be so bad after all. "I need you to try real hard to be at your best. I have faith in you, Iris. You can do this."

The lights in the bridge turned from blue to pink. An ascending series of blips sounded. "I'll try, Glint. For you."

I smiled and tried not to gag as I turned back to my crew. A nervous tremor wormed its way through me. "Okay, are we ready to step into this catastrophe?"

Jasette shared a semiconfident nod with Blix. "Ready as we're gonna be."

CHAPTER 8

BREAKING
AND ENTERING

JASETTE STOOD BEFORE Blix and me in the landing bay, her forearm computer lit up with fluctuating graphs and numbers. She turned back, her face focused and stern. "Single file. Keep the discs activated."

I held forward the small silver disc she'd taken and rewired from a fallen spider bot. Pulsating blue lines flowed along a geometric pattern imprinted in the disc.

"You sure this will work?" I said.

"What's going on?" Jasette fixed me with severe eyes. "You seem off."

I hesitated for a moment, having trouble finding the words. "It's just . . . I've survived a long time going with my gut. No matter how things turned out, at least I knew I was being true to myself. Now I'm going along with someone else's plan, and I have zero control. I don't like it."

She smiled and patted my cheek with her gloved hand. "It's good to let go occasionally, Glint. And believe me, the fact that you're trusting me is a big step for us." She winked.

Blix patted me one the shoulder. "Indeed, Captain. A maturity milestone in your relationship, to be sure."

"Oh, shut up," I gave him a dark look.

Jasette grinned and headed down the landing ramp. As we walked single file through the hangar, a few spider bots paused as we neared, their red eyes scanning the area.

"Keep a steady pace," Jasette said. "The discs should disrupt their scans. Make them think we're one of them."

After a brief pause, the spider bots continued as if we were nothing more than a passing breeze.

"Check one nightmare off the list." Jasette led the way down the large corridor where Casglo had taken us earlier that day. The cavernous passage was lit only by the occasional luminous lines that flowed through the patterns in the metal.

"Is it darker in here?" I said. "It seems darker."

Jasette nodded. "This place is full of robots. They don't mind the dark."

Several spider bots appeared from hatches in the floor. They crawled right for us. Jasette froze for a moment, then sidestepped from their path.

"Follow me," she said. "No sudden movements."

We stepped from their path just a freem before they reached us. The metal spiders stopped, shuddered, then continued.

"What was that about?" I whispered.

"They know there's a disruption." Jasette tapped quickly on her computer.

"Then the game is over," I said. "Let's head back before Casglo shows up."

"Nothing's over," she said. "They know there's a disruption. That's all. System operations have disruptions all the time. They'll escalate countermeasures until they find it and stop it. Or until, in our case, it just goes away."

"Escalate?" I gave her a challenging look. "As in lasers and kill bots and toxin clouds?"

She shook her head, remaining focused on her computer. "Relax. I was pretty sure this would happen." She waved us forward. "We can't remain in the same spot for too long."

We continued down the dark passage, spider bots occasionally emerging from the walls—in greater number each time—and passing by with the same unnerving shudders. With every step, it felt like my doom was a little more assured.

We turned into the passage that led toward the spacious bridge and the collection room. The corridor was completely dark; not even the bright lines of energy that ran through the other areas were visible.

"This is it." Jasette tapped out a few commands, and pinpoint lights emerged from the shoulders of her power suit. They bathed the passage in an eerie green.

"Most unsettling," Blix said. "'Yea, though I walk through the valley of the shadow of death, I will fear no evil—'"

"Stop that," I said. "You're freaking me out."

Blix frowned. "I find it rather calming."

"We need to be quick about this." Jasette started down the passage.

As we continued, I felt a strain on my lungs, like I had just climbed a mountain. It was difficult to get a good breath. A pressurized sound came from Jasette's power suit as a clear dome whooshed over her head. She turned, her face lit up with helmet lights.

"Here." Her voice was amplified with speakers. She produced a spherical device with a mouthpiece from her utility belt and handed it to me. "Countermeasures. The atmosphere settings are changing. The system is shutting off access to life forms—or so they think."

The device fit snugly over my mouth and nose. A welcome rush of fresh oxygen poured into me.

I turned to Blix and removed the breathing sphere for a moment. "What about you?"

Blix sniffed at the air as though something smelled rotten. "It's not ideal, but we Vythians have ways of dealing with extremes. At least temporarily."

"How am I supposed to talk with this thing?" I put the sphere back on and took a breath.

"It's probably for the best." Jasette grinned and continued.

After awhile, we arrived at the bridge. I stopped for a moment, peeking my head in. The lights from the digital readouts and control panels provided subtle illumination. Combined with the starlight streaming in from the panoramic windows, it was a beautiful scene to behold. For a star pilot, it was a true vision of starship art.

Jasette put her arm around me, joining in the admiration—for a split freem. "There's no time." She turned to Blix. "This is where you come in."

Blix nodded and took a few steps into the bridge before turning back toward us, looking somber. "Although my tasks of disabling the tractor beam and rerouting the landing-bay hatch for remote activation are rather typical, I must confess my state of mind is not optimal."

There was an uncomfortable silence. I tossed a confused glance to Jasette. She looked concerned.

"What are you talking about?" I said.

Blix rubbed his temple gingerly. "Alas, I am still enduring

the cerebral jolt from the spider bots. My usual brilliance has been compromised."

I gave him a stern look. "Can you do the job in here or not?"

Blix studied the bridge for a moment. "Most likely."

"Great. A crazy plan, and you're not feeling brilliant." I accented the "brilliant" with angry finger quotes. "Then let's get out of here."

"Relax." Jasette put a steadying hand on my arm. "Blix, you can do this. I believe in you."

Blix held Jasette's gaze for a moment, then nodded. "Indeed. I will do my utmost." He strode to the far side of the bridge, his face set.

Jasette turned, leading me away.

"That's it? You think that little pep talk is going to change anything?"

"It better." She motioned with her head in the direction of the collection room. "We're running out of time."

As the heavy hand of impending capture clutched my heart, I walked with Jasette into the corridor.

As before, red energy flowed across the entrance to the collection room. Beyond it, white columns of light surrounded the rows of valued objects within.

Jasette reached into her utility belt, producing a pulsating red orb. "Gather round."

I huddled close to her, which I didn't mind in the least. She activated the orb, and a translucent globe spread out, surrounding us.

"Follow my steps." Jasette moved forward, and I mirrored

her. The globe rolled as our feet hit the sloped interior. "Cross your fingers."

As the globe hit the energy of the entrance, our forward momentum slowed, but we continued through, the red flowing around us until we were inside. Jasette hit her pulsating orb and the globe dissolved.

Her eyes lit up, and she pointed across the room. "There it is."

I followed her line of sight to a glowing crystalline flower suspended over a pedestal. There were countless sparkles of light glittering across the petals and leaves. It looked delicate, as if a strong gust of wind could blow it into tiny shards. Energy pulsated from within the flower, hinting at a mysterious power.

Jasette was motionless, transfixed by the object of her search. "A chrysolenthium flower."

I took nervous glances around the room, wondering if death rays were about to shoot out from the walls.

"Okay, time for the splay grid." Jasette took a green rectangle from her utility belt and placed it on the floor. She activated it, and a series of bright-green lines formed a three-dimensional copy of the rectangle. It spread outward, covering the room and all the objects in grid lines.

"Sit tight." She crept toward the flower, moving between the pedestals with catlike agility until she stood before the one she wanted. The green lines from her rectangle flowed along the energy cylinder surrounding the flower. When she touched the grid sections with her finger, the entire light structure turned a solid green. Her hands reached into the cylinder and drew out the flower.

I stiffened, waiting for a blaring alarm and flashing lights to activate.

Nothing.

Jasette stole back to our position, where she took two metal plates from the bag slung over her shoulder and drew them apart. A silvery current flowed between them. She put the flower between the plates, and the current held it in place. Her smile bordered on maniacal as she put the flower in her bag.

"Let's go." Her eyes were wild with excitement. "The splay grid should keep a residual duplicate in place until we escape."

"Let's hope so," I said.

I huddled close to Jasette as she reactivated the red globe, which took us safely from the room. We moved back through the corridor, much faster now. My back and neck were tight with tension. Jasette's jaw was set, and her eyes looked as though she'd forgotten how to blink. She was obviously experiencing the same thing that I was. The worst part of any mission: the final moments when you can taste victory but are painfully aware that the whole caper could blow apart with one wrong move. Neither one of us spoke as we neared the opening to the bridge.

Blix rushed out to meet us, his face tense.

"Well?" Jasette's voice was thin and dripping with stress.

He nodded, but his cheek twitched.

Jasette motioned us forward.

I removed the breathing sphere. "Wait."

She flashed nervous eyes around the area. "What? Did you see something?"

"No, but don't you think we need a plan B? In case something goes wrong."

"Captain," Blix spoke in a harsh tone. "This plan takes

many variables into account. It's a bit more complex than your rudimentary plan-A, plan-B scenario."

I shook my head. "I don't care how complex it is. The rule of any good plan is always have a backup plan."

Jasette held my gaze. "Like what?"

I motioned with my thumb into the bridge. "If it's typical at all, there should be flight controls, navigation, engineering. Plenty to mess with."

Jasette nodded. She reached into her utility belt and brought forth an orange sphere. "I was saving this for the right time. I guess this is as good as it's gonna get." She rolled the sphere into the room, then tapped out a few commands on her computer. "It's remotely activated. Let's hope I don't have to use it."

She shot me a determined look before leading us back down the corridor.

Once we made it back to the brighter passageways, I breathed a little easier. Our progress turned into a brisk walk, just a hair away from jogging. There were no further spider bots passing in and out of the corridors, and my heart felt light as we turned into the last passage, knowing that my ship was just ahead. I had a clear vision of the landing bay at the end of the passage. I could see my ship sitting there, waiting to fly off into the freedom of space. Hope sprang up within me.

It was at that moment a hulking cat creature stepped into the passageway, blocking our path to the ship. I skidded to a stop, recognizing the much larger version of Casglo glaring down at us.

CHAPTER 9

CASGLO CONFRONTATION

CASGLO FILLED the cavernous passage. Its heavily muscled cat body had grown to half the size of my freighter. Spines and twisted horns protruded from every section of its body. Its paws now had the unfortunate size and ability to crush me.

Dozens of spider bots gathered beneath the nano creature.

Casglo's pulsating yellow eyes narrowed as they examined the three of us. "My workers detected an anomaly. You have been deep in the *Arpellon*. Explain."

The crowd of spider bots around its feet crept toward us.

"We couldn't sleep." Jasette looked calm but her voice was laced with nerves. "We took a walk."

My hope was that Casglo's analyzing capabilities weren't dialed in on human physiology. Some of the more advanced civilizations out there would stick it to you with their high-tech scanning systems. You'd try to pull off a simple hustle and they'd hit you with thorough sensor sweeps of perspiration, body heat, vocal anomalies, and all the rest of our giveaways that make lying to advanced computer systems difficult. Of course, that's where my DEMOTER always came in handy.

"All of you had trouble sleeping?" Casglo wasn't buying it.

"I wanted company," Jasette said. "This ship scares me."

Casglo paused for a moment as if considering whether to step on us or not.

"We heard noises in the bridge." I jumped in with my diversion plan. I found it was always best to throw multiple problems at computer systems. It tended to slow the calculations that often classified humans in their liquidate-immediately category. "It looked like something was on fire in there."

Casglo looked down the hall as if he could see through walls all the way to the bridge. His eyes narrowed. "All readings indicate normal operations."

I flicked my eyes to Jasette. She kept a careful watch on Casglo as her fingers slowly hit a command on her forearm. A muffled explosion echoed through the hallways. A tremor went through the ground.

Casglo stiffened and let loose a horrific roar. My body froze. For a moment I forgot how to breathe. The towering cat body lunged forward, and I grabbed Jasette and dove out of the way as Casglo galloped past us, disappearing down the corridor.

I lay on the cold, metal floor, letting the panic settle.

Blix hovered over me, reaching down to Jasette and me. "We haven't much time."

The thought of a giant nano cat returning for cold revenge put me on my feet in two freems. Without a word we set off at a sprint for my ship.

Jasette spoke into her computer as we neared the landing ramp. "Nelvan, start take-off procedures."

"Okay." Nelvan sounded far from confident. I heard my ships engines rumble to life as we charged up the landing ramp.

"Oh, thank heavens." Iris sniffled as though she'd been crying. "I was so worried about you, Glint. I mean, all of you."

"We're not safe yet," I said. "Get us out of here, Iris. Fast as you can."

"My pleasure," Iris said. "This ship has been most inhospitable. No social skills whatsoever. Good riddance, as far as I'm concerned."

We piled into the lift. The doors chirped closed and it ascended with a hum.

"Blix, I'm activating the hatch doors." Jasette tapped away at her computer. "This is where your handiwork comes into play."

Blix cleared his throat. "Yes, just keep in mind I was operating under emotional duress. Plus, the alien technology on the bridge was quite belligerent."

I flashed him an impatient look. "What are you saying?"

"Well, should anything go awry, it shouldn't be ascribed to my otherwise sterling record."

The doors chirped open and I made a beeline toward my captain's chair, which was currently occupied by Nelvan.

"You made it!" Nelvan beamed.

"Yes. Now, out." I jerked a thumb away from my chair.

He jumped up and scooted back. "Jeesh, how about a thank you. This is a team effort, remember?"

"We'll hug it out later if we survive." My fingers danced across the armrest controls as I sat.

Jasette jumped into the navigator's chair while Blix took control of the engineering station. The viewing screen displayed the imposing steel doors of the landing bay. They were shut tight.

I turned back to Blix. "You activated the doors, right?"

His cheek continued to twitch. "As I said, Captain. My emotional state . . ." He trailed off, his eyes locked onto the viewing screen. I followed his gaze to find the glorious vision of the hatch doors moving. A thin line of starlight illuminated the gap as the doors crawled open.

Nelvan shot up a triumphant fist. "Yes!"

"Ha!" I flashed a gleeful smile at Blix. "I never doubted you for a freem."

Blix adjusted his dagger straps. "I simply wished to share my momentary doubts with fellow crew members. Exposing vulnerabilities is a freeing experience, and the bonding that can occur will—"

"Blah, blah, blah. Iris, move this thing."

The ship rose and hovered closer to the huge metallic doors. A heavenly view of stars winked at us as if to say, *The freedom of space awaits. Join us!*

"Good-bye, you freak ghost ship." I gave a sarcastic salute behind me.

The metallic hatch doors stopped suddenly.

"Uh-oh," Jasette said.

All the happy thoughts rushed out of my head. "Blix?"

Blix bowed his head. "My sincere apologies, Captain. As I said, my current state of mind—"

"Computer," I said. "Tell me we can make it through that opening."

"It's too close, Glint." Iris said. "I'm afraid. What if it leaves a gruesome mark on my hull and you trade me in for a younger, sleeker starship?"

The hatch door started to close.

"Iris!" I shouted. "Full thrusters!"

"Oh, Captain." Iris' voice trembled. "I don't know if—"

"Move! Now!"

The ship trembled as the engines powered to full. My back flattened against the captain's chair as we surged forward. As we neared the hatch, the opening seemed frighteningly small.

"Oh, dear," Blix said.

"Hold on," I said.

There was a loud crunching sound, and my body was flung forward, the seat straps digging into my body. Our forward motion slowed to half speed as a piercing sound of screeching metal echoed through the bridge, boring into my ears like needles. There came a terrible moment where I thought we were stuck.

And then, with a sudden burst of speed, we shot through the hatch into space.

My muscles were so tense it felt like they might never relax again. "Iris, punch it. Get us out of here." I spun my chair around. "Blix, tell me you took out the tractor beam better than that hatch."

"As I said"—Blix's voice sounded irritated—"I'm feeling vulnerable now. I'd rather not discuss it."

"Iris, reverse view," I said. "On screen."

The suffocating shadow of the *Arpellon* filled the screen. It seemed as though we were crawling away from it.

"Can't we go any faster?" I said.

"That horrible hatch hurt me," Iris said. "It's all I can do not to pass out from the pain."

"Stay with us, Iris," Blix looked up from the engineering station. "You're doing great. We're nearly at maximum speed."

I clenched my fists and stared at the viewing screen. The dark ship still dominated the view. "Is it pursuing? Any tractor beams detected?"

"Negative on both counts," Blix said.

"Then we're free." Nelvan's voice was a jumble of nerves and excitement. "We made it!"

"Not yet," Jasette said. "Okay, Blix. Let 'em have it."

Blix nodded and hit a few control panels. The reverse view screen filled with small objects.

"What is that?" Nelvan said.

"Junk," Jasette said.

"What junk?" I said.

Jasette swiveled back in the navigation chair. "Remember all those parts and old boxes in the transport room?"

I frowned. "I was saving those."

"For what?"

"I dunno. I could've built something cool."

She shook her head. "Anyway, I mixed in a few surprises. Blix, light it up."

Blix hit a few controls, and the rear cannons fired. The orange beams connected with the junk, and several explosions filled the screen. A tremor went through the ship.

"That should scramble their sensors a bit." Jasette let out a long breath and gave a weary look my way. "That's all I've got. Let's hope it's enough."

I kept my eye on the screen as the fiery clouds of explosions died away. The *Arpellon* finally looked as though it was receding into the star field behind us.

"Whatya got, Blix?" I said. A glimmer of hope fluttered in my heart.

"Still no detectable response. The *Arpellon* is either temporarily damaged, or our escape hasn't come to their attention."

"Okay, let's get out of here before they figure it—"

A hazy glow covered the *Arpellon*. At that moment, the old space-bar tales of a ghost ship were as real as my death grip on the armrest. Then the glow dissipated, and a freem later the ship was gone.

"Anybody else see that?" I said.

"Indeed." Blix tapped out a few rapid-fire commands at the engineering panel. "I'm not picking up anything on our scans either. Invisible and undetectable. A potent combination."

"Tell me we can go faster, Iris," I said.

"I'm trying my best." Iris sounded winded. "I'm afraid I'll hurt myself if I push any harder."

I frowned. "Jasette, any promising escape routes?"

She shook her head, her focus on the armchair readouts. "A few old settlements, some inhospitable planets." She leaned closer to the readout. "There's a last-stop moon settlement called Bleelebach about a trid from here, but I don't think—"

"Bleelebach." A memory flashed through my head. "I know that place. They've got a great black-market bazaar."

"It's a pit of filth," Blix said. "You promised we'd never go back there again."

"Why?" Nelvan looked wide-eyed between Blix and me. "What happened last time?"

Blix shook his head. "Aside from being a dirty, disease-inflicting stop-off, the bazaar is filled with swindlers."

"It's a cultural experience, Nelvan," I said. "Don't you want to experience the universe at large?"

Blix cleared his throat as if shushing me. "Also, the cuisine is deplorable. By the time supply lines make it out this far, most everything is past the expiration date."

"It's a great place to hide out and stock up on supplies," I said. "The bazaar has some good finds if you know where to look."

"Don't you mean illegal finds?" Blix said.

"Sometimes those are the best kind."

"I don't like it," Jasette said. "We should look for a larger settlement. Lots of thugs in these remote spots."

"Which is perfect," I argued. "We hide out with everyone else on the run and wait till the stars are free of that ship. Plus, I've got an old Grellinian friend name Crinmitch who runs a droid shop down there. He'll take care of us."

"Isn't he the one who shot at us last time?" Blix said.

"That's your idea of a friend?" Nelvan looked worried.

"Simple misunderstanding." Some of the more unpleasant details of our last visit flooded back. I'd traded a pair of faulty droids for a new roto thruster. "Buyer beware" was the name of the game in Bleelebach. If anything, Crinmitch should've grown to appreciate my savvy trading skills since then. If not, I was pretty sure I could smooth things over with my new DEMOTER X. "Blix, lock in a course."

Blix folded his arms. "Don't want to."

"That's an order, lizard boy."

Blix shook his head in defiance.

"Jasette," I said. "You've got navigation controls. Can you jump in here?"

"You sure about this?" She looked as though fumes had

blown in from a nearby sewer. "These spots usually cause more problems than they solve."

"We need to get out of the stars, right?" I motioned to her as if posing an impossible question.

"Yes, but—"

"The *Arpellon* has to have some advanced technology to be that big and still going strong after all these gloons. We may have temporarily tricked them, but once they go looking for us, who knows what kind of scanning sweeps they have. Plus, we can't even see them anymore. How can we evade something we can't see? There's no cover out here. We're vulnerable. Our best shot is to hide out somewhere inconspicuous for a while."

She gave a slow nod. "You're right." She hit a few controls. "Plotting a course."

I swiveled my chair to Blix, a triumphant smile on my face. "Everyone keep your eyes open down there for anything that could help. There might be something at that bazaar that saves us all."

Jasette laughed. "Or kills us all."

Blix pointed at me. "If something goes wrong, this was your call."

"Don't worry." I tried to psyche myself up that this visit would be better than the last one. "We'll be fine."

CHAPTER 10

BLEELEBACH

OUR ENTRY to the remote moon Bleelebach did little to convince my crew this was a good idea. Ragged brown clouds brushed past our ship to reveal the boxy, crud-covered buildings below. Blix mumbled something about ramshackle hovels. I was about to argue when a grating tone resonated through the ship.

"They're hailing us, Captain," Blix said.

"Put them through."

A static-filled communication sounded. "Cargo and purpose of visit?" It was a flight-control droid that sounded like he'd narrowly escaped an apocalyptic-level explosion and was uttering its final wishes.

"No cargo." I tried to sound as bored as possible to avoid any sensor triggers attuned for nervous responses. "Visiting for supplies and recreation."

"Recreation?" The broken droid sounded confused.

"I enjoy getting supplies." Droids that stood as gatekeepers of any type were always programmed to watch for the common indicators of deception and guilt such as hesitation, fluctuating vocal energy, and overly rehearsed responses. There was always a better chance to pass under the radar by hitting the droids with double barrels of boredom and stupidity.

The droid emitted a rapid series of noises like a knife scraping over metal. "Please proceed to landing slip 439."

I turned back to Blix with a sly smile. Without acknowledging my success, he merely looked away, still pouting about the trip.

"You got that, Iris?" I said. "Landing slip 439."

"Oh, Glint, I don't know," Iris' voice trembled. "This place just doesn't look clean. What if young ruffians come by when I'm unattended and scrape lewd messages into my hull?"

"Just use your short-range cannons," I said. "That'll teach 'em."

Iris gasped. "Heavens, no. I couldn't bear the sight."

"Don't worry, we won't be gone that long."

The ship glided toward a tilting array of landing slips that resembled a crumbling honeycomb. Landing slip 439 was accented with trails of green slime dripping down the walls. After a few additional protests from Iris, we nestled in and the engines powered down.

"All right," I said. "Let's get lost for a while."

"Perhaps I should stay aboard the ship," Blix said. "Keep a watch on things."

"That's a wonderful idea," Iris piped up. "I don't want to be alone in this horrid place."

"Yeah, I'll stay here too," Nelvan said.

I stood from the captain's chair and gave my best glare of authority. "Wrong. Everyone stays together. Rule number one: whenever you disembark at a questionable planet, space port, or habitable celestial zone, the crew stands together or falls together."

Blix rolled his eyes. "You just make these rules up as you go along."

"Trust me, it's a rule."

"Then why do you always refer to them all as rule number one? If there was an actual list of rules, they'd have different numbers."

I glared at him. "Rule number two: don't question the captain." I headed toward the lift and my quarters, where I retrieved the satchel of vibe spheres and made sure my vibe bar was tucked nice and snug in my jacket pocket, safe from wandering thieves.

The landing slip smelled like a graveyard for vermin. The echoing sounds of constant dripping told the origin story of the green slime trails painted on the walls. A rust-covered maintenance bot lay slumped in the corner. Nearby, a dusty control panel leaned against the wall with a dim green light blinking for no discernible reason.

There were a few moments of silence as the grim faces of my crew surveyed the area.

"I've seen worse." I tried to diffuse the situation.

Blix held his hand over his nose. "You sure?"

I frowned and led the way to the only exit available—a poorly lit enclosed walkway. A trail of lights placed sporadically along the ceiling did little to illuminate the path. The few that were still working flickered on and off, painting a shadowy journey into the outpost.

A dull glimmer outlined the end of the walkway. The exit was accented with a dirt-covered, emaciated alien with orange skin, lying in a puddle of dark-blue liquid. Apparently he was the welcoming committee. He looked up at our arrival and uttered an indecipherable string of words before laying his head back down.

"Lovely." Blix grimaced. "So glad you brought us here, Captain."

"What?" I pretended to be oblivious to the filth and disrepair. "The place has character."

"Yes, I'm sure this is just your style," Blix said.

We made our way around the muttering vagrant and headed into the dusty streets of Bleelebach.

The buildings resembled large stone squares stacked in a haphazard fashion. Some structures were single level; others ascended like a crooked staircase some twenty levels and beyond. Often the tilting towers of squares would meet somewhere overhead, forming a jagged archway. Simple rectangular windows dotted the brownstone surface of the buildings. The windows were sometimes accented with old rugs hanging out to dry or trailing, black-leaved plants. Occasionally, the windows housed a strange wire-limbed doll with a bird's head known as a Hrunken. The local superstition held that hanging a Hrunken from your window would ward off bad bartering skills.

"This place is crazy." Nelvan was craning his neck up to take in the sight. "It's not going to fall down, is it?"

"I wouldn't rule it out," Blix said.

"Don't scare the boy." I gave Nelvan a hearty pat on the back. "Don't worry, we'll be fine."

My assurances did little to relieve the youthful lines of

concern on his forehead. As we moved on, a raucous commotion began to swell. It was as if hundreds of arguments were going on at once.

"What's that noise?" Nelvan slowed his pace. "And why are we headed toward it?"

"Relax," I said. "It's just the bazaar. The perfect place to hide out for a while."

Blix let out a mocking laugh.

"Stay alert." Jasette gripped the handles of her laser pistols.

We arrived at a broad street that cut a wide path straight to the heart of the settlement. My crew paused for a moment, absorbing the sensory overload known as the Bleelebach bazaar—row upon row of vendor stands selling countless exotic, mysterious, and sometimes stomach-churning items all touted as priceless treasures. The stalls were perched along the dusty street, walls covered in colorful rugs and banners. Fist-sized orb lights swirled around the items for sale, enhancing their appearance at every angle. A few of the technology-enhanced stands loomed overhead on hover platforms.

The street was alive with activity. Vendors barked out unbelievable claims about wares that hung on shiny hooks, hovered in place, or lay spread out on cluttered tables. Crowds of street-wise aliens wandered through the stands, scrutinizing the items for sale. Most were humanoid, dressed in the typical dark-toned, rugged attire that held up under deep-space travel and helped hide food and blood stains far better than lighter outfits. Many of them were heavily armed. Those that displayed no weapons were probably concealing deadly stingers or retractable claws.

I stopped, realizing Nelvan wasn't with us anymore. About ten yards back, a multilimbed furry creature was spraying him with a mist. Nelvan was backing away, shielding his face.

In an instant I was in the furry alien's face—at least, I assumed the hump with seven eyes was his face. I stood between Nelvan and the alien, batting away his spray cannisters. "Back off, creep!"

"Hey," the furry beast muttered. "These are free samples. I'm doing a service here."

I drew my pistol. "How 'bout I do your face a free service?"

"Okay, okay. Relax, space cowboy." The alien shook his fur like he'd just gotten wet and beelined toward another passerby, spray bottles at the ready.

"Nelvan." I holstered my gun. "You can't wander off like that."

"I didn't. That big . . . dog or whatever it was cornered me. He sprayed stuff in my eyes. I couldn't see."

Blix patted Nelvan on the shoulder. "Captain, look what you've done." He motioned to me. "Subjecting poor Nelvan to the dangers of this pit."

"I told him to stay close," I said. "Nelvan, you're fine, right?"

Nelvan squinted. "My eyes sting."

"See? No big deal."

Nelvan scooted closer to Blix. "You sure this is a safe place to hide out?"

"I never said safe," I said. "But yes, it's a good place to hide out. Now, stay close." I led the way back into the flow of the crowd.

The real game of the bazaar was to find the needle in the haystack. The piece that was valuable that somehow ended up mixed in with all the junk being peddled as rare finds. It was part haggling, part gambling.

"Remember," I said. "Don't get taken in or buy anything stupid. Only essentials."

Nelvan nodded absentmindedly, still caught up in the sights and sounds.

"Hey, pretty lady." A voice that sounded like a cat with bronchitis called from beside me. I turned to find a gaunt, purple Gribbian manning a quaint stand filled with garish jewelry. Brown sashes with a border of golden tassels draped down from the wall behind, making it appear as though a dark wave was about to descend upon the poor vendor.

"You want shiny thing?" The Gribbian's attention was focused on Jasette. His slender, wolfish face wrinkled into a toothy grin above a thin frame covered in a yellow robe that looked two sizes too big. He ran a string of sparkling jewelry across his arm. "You buy bracelet. Make arm pretty-pretty. You shine bright like star in sky."

Jasette shook her head.

"Yes. You put on magic stones." The vendor held a string of silver stones forward. "You find mate today. Guaranteed."

She let out an amused laugh. "Nah. Not my style."

The vendor's smile faded a little, then he switched his attention to Blix. "How 'bout big lizard. You want shiny stone?"

Blix stepped closer, causing the vendor to retreat a little.

"What type of stone is this?" Blix leaned closer, his orange eyes narrowing as he inspected the jewelry.

I sighed. "How long is this gonna take?"

Blix gave a dismissive wave without breaking his focus on the jewelry.

PAUL REGNIER

"Aha." Jasette pointed to an expansive stand nearby, the sheer size of it dwarfing the stalls next to it. It was surrounded by iron poles that supported taut, black sashes. Several rows of dangerous-looking metal objects lurked inside. "Perfect. A weapons stand. I need to replenish." She tapped at the utility belt on her waist.

"Wait," I said. "I'll go with you."

She smirked. "You're sweet, but I can take care of myself, remember?"

"Well, yeah, but—"

"Shh." She leaned in and gave me a quick kiss. "I'll be fine." Before I could voice a reply, she'd turned and moved toward the stand.

I frowned, not too thrilled with the sight of her heading into a crowd of shifty-eyed thieves. She could obviously handle herself, but at some point, when the odds aren't in your favor, anyone is in danger.

"Heaven stone." The Gribbian vendor brought my attention around. "Only finest stones here."

"Hmm." Blix rubbed his chin as he surveyed the table of shimmering pieces. "Looks like common sky stone."

I shook my head. "Are you through?"

"What's the rush? I thought we were 'hiding out.' We might as well enjoy ourselves a little."

"I don't like Jasette being by herself. We're supposed to stay together, remember?"

Blix placed a hand on my shoulder. "You really do care for her, don't you?"

I batted his hand away. "Well, of course I care. I don't want her walking around in this scum hole alone."

He pointed at me, his face lit up. "Aha! You admit this place is awful."

I gritted my teeth. "Okay, fine. It's a pit. It's still a good place to hide out."

"We shall see, Captain."

I turned when Blix caught me by the arm. "What?"

His face was tense. "Captain, where's Nelvan?"

A rush of fear went through me at the realization he wasn't next to us anymore. I scanned the area, but the boy was nowhere in sight.

CHAPTER 11

FUTURE GLIMPSE

PANIC SET IN as I swiveled around, my eyes scanning the crowded street. "Nelvan!" I called.

Blix echoed me in a deep, booming voice. "Nelvan, where are you?"

A few passersby glanced at us, unconcerned.

"How could you let this happen?" I grabbed my communicator, signaling Nelvan.

"I was engaged in barter." Blix was on his toes, trying to look above the crowd. "The responsibility obviously falls on you."

I heard noises overhead and looked up to find a floating vendor stand. "Blix." I motioned to the sky stand.

Blix nodded and scanned the ground nearby. "Here, Captain." He directed my attention to a row of bronze discs. I hurried over and we both stepped on discs, looking upward. There was a brief sound of air pressure escaping, and the discs lifted us up to the stand.

The elevated stand was fashioned in a series of concentric circles. Everything was decked out in brushed steel and chrome. Dead center sat a circular stage where an obese, tan-skinned Yllack in a sparkling purple cloak addressed a crowd. A silver display trunk was open next to him, filled with metal and electronic gadgets. He was in the middle of his sales pitch, making broad gestures with his four slender arms, trying to rouse a crowd seated on ascending circular benches nearby.

"Always losing your vibes in cards?" The Yllack spoke in dramatic tones. "Afraid of making the wrong decision? Worried that a hungry Vlornak is hiding around the next corner?"

A few members of the crowd gave weak nods.

"Well, your worries are over. The Future Glimpse is here!" The vendor raised a thick, metal bracelet with a glowing green button in the air.

Several mumbles came from the crowd, most of them looking unimpressed.

"Allow me to demonstrate on this young lad." The vendor stepped aside to put the bracelet on a boy standing next to him. I gasped, realizing it was Nelvan.

"Uh-oh," Blix said.

"Nelvan, don't!" I rushed forward.

The Yllack vendor turned at my approach and held up his hand. "Nothing to worry about, my good man. Perfectly safe, as you are about to see."

I drew the DEMOTER and aimed it at his head. "Well, this isn't safe. Now let the kid go."

The energy pistol was ripped out of my hand. It shot like an arrow to a silver security orb nearby, making a clanging noise as it held fast to the metal.

"My apologies." The vendor bowed. "We don't allow weapons. Tempers escalate, and customers get hurt. Bad for business."

Blix joined me. "I suggest you release the boy."

The vendor held up all four hands in mock surrender. "Easy, my scaled friend. He volunteered."

"Volunteered?" I motioned to Nelvan. "Nelvan, take that thing off and get over here."

"Temporary delay," the vendor called out to the crowd. "All part of the show. The demonstration will proceed shortly."

"It's okay." Nelvan looked perfectly calm. "You said to be on the lookout for something to help us. That's exactly what I found. It's a time-space window. I knew they'd come up with something like this in the future. He's giving me one for free just for volunteering."

I rushed past the vendor to Nelvan's side and tried to remove the bracelet. It wouldn't budge. "How do I get this thing off?"

"Just hit the green button," the vendor said.

As I hit the green button, I heard Blix calling out, "Wait!"

A flash of green surrounded Nelvan and he vanished.

The crowd cheered. I scanned the area in shock for a moment, wondering what I'd done.

"Oh dear." The vendor sounded worried. "That wasn't supposed to happen." He hastily turned to the crowd. "That's all for now. Come back in a trid while we work out a slight technical glitch."

The crowd grumbled and began filing out of the stands. My confusion at Nelvan's disappearance morphed into anger.

I turned on the vendor in a rage and grabbed the front of his shiny cloak, pulling him toward me. "Where is he!"

The vendor cringed, wide-eyed. "I—I don't know. Honestly. The device isn't supposed to work like that."

"Well, how's it supposed to work, genius?" I barked in his face.

"It's supposed to give you a ten-freem glance into the future." He leaned toward me and lowered his voice. "At least, that's how my demonstration bracelet works. The ones for sale are just jewelry with lights and a small hallucinogen injection to give you a 'future vision.'" He accented the words *future vision* with finger quotes, then held a finger to his lips.

"Pardon me." Blix stepped close and motioned for me to remove my grip from the vendor's rumpled cloak. "We wish no harm. Just explain how to retrieve our friend."

I begrudgingly let him go. The Yllack vendor brushed off his cloak and straightened.

"Now, then," he said. "This is all very confusing. I've done this a hundred times without any problems. It's perfectly safe. Unless . . ." He flashed a shifty-eyed look between us. "Unless he's traveled through time before."

Blix and I paused and exchanged a nervous glance.

The Yllack grinned. "I see. So your young friend violated the universal accord strictly forbidding time travel, did he?"

"What about you?" I pointed a finger at him. "You have a device that sends people forward in time."

He shook his head at me like I was a child. "My device merely allows an anchored glimpse. You don't disrupt future events, and the temporal disruptions are negligible. It's completely legal under the fifth time-space accord, category eleven dash two, subsection four." He folded both sets of arms and assumed a triumphant stance.

"Wouldn't a glimpse into the future disrupt current events?" Blix spoke matter-of-factly. "I think a strong case could be made for a violation of category twelve dash three dash fourteen of the eleventh time-accord crime laws."

The vendor's mouth went a little slack, and his arms fell back to his sides. "Oh . . . yes, well, I suppose that's debatable. Perhaps we keep each other's secrets quiet and head our separate ways?"

"Yeah," I said. "As soon as you bring Nelvan back."

He scratched his head. "Tricky. Although, I do have a grounding bracelet." He reached into the silver trunk at his side and dug through piles of metal and wiring. "Ah, here it is." He brought forth a metal bracelet like the one Nelvan wore.

"What does that one do?" I said. "Make us both disappear?"

The Yllack paused for a moment. "No, but that would have been clever of me, wouldn't it?"

I narrowed my eyes. "Tell us."

"This bracelet is the grounding for the other. I always have it nearby during demonstrations. It's a failsafe so the other doesn't get lost in the occasional temporal fluctuation."

Blix leaned close, examining the bracelet. "Interesting. We activate this bracelet and it will draw the other back?"

The Yllack gasped and drew the bracelet back. "No! Don't *ever* do that. Otherwise, both with be lost in a time spin. If both bracelets are activated, those wearing them would skip through time-space like a stone on a lake. Forever!"

Blix leaned back, a sour look on his face. "Most unsettling."

"Okay," I said. "If we can't activate it, how do we use it?"

"You simply wear it," the Yllack said. "The bracelets are paired. This bracelet will operate like a tether for the other, drawing it back to the present."

"Excellent," Blix said. "When?"

"When indeed?" The Yllack raised his eyebrows. "Once you start bending the fabric of time, calculations get a bit thorny. The sooner you put this on . . ." He held up the metal band. ". . . the sooner he should return."

"Got it." I grabbed the bracelet and wrapped it around my wrist. It clasped with a hum of energy. A jolt of electricity went through me.

The Yllack motioned to my wrist. "Now he is bound to your existence in the time-space continuum. He's spiraling in from moments in your past and future until he'll eventually reach your present. Like water circling into a drain." He made a circling motion with his hand. "He may bounce back and forth a few times before he stays for good, but eventually, he'll live fully in the present again." He paused. "At least in theory."

"In theory?" I narrowed my eyes.

The Yllack held up all four hands. "Hey, don't blame me. This has never happened before. But I'm fairly certain that once he stabilizes in time, the bracelets should power down. Then you can remove them with the clasp at the base."

I turned my arm to discover a small latch on the underside of the bracelet.

"I have high hopes the grounding bracelet will work." He gave a weak smile.

"It better." I gave the Yllack my best threatening look. "Or we'll be back."

He looked up at Blix, and worry lines appeared on his forehead. "Just remember, it wasn't my fault. He volunteered and didn't mention anything about being a time traveler."

Blix gave him a few pats on the back that were a little more forceful than usual. "I'm sure it will all work out. I'd hate to return and have anything . . . unpleasant happen to you."

The Yllack shivered.

"All right," I said. "Now, about my gun."

The Yllack cleared his throat and held out his palm.

"What?" I said.

"Those Future Glimpse bracelets are expensive." The Yllack gave me sad puppy eyes. "You can't expect me to incur that level of loss without compensation."

"How much?" Blix said.

"One—er, I mean two—thousand vibes . . . each." He flicked his fingers toward his palm.

"Two thousand?" I raised my eyebrows. "That's crazy."

"It's a bargain. With that bracelet's help, you can make that back in one card game."

"I'll pay you five hundred," I said.

He laughed and waved his hand as if to shoo me away. "Please, you must be joking."

"Perhaps three hundred now," Blix said. "And if we retrieve our friend, we will return with another thousand."

He rubbed his chin and looked upward. "Hmm, thirteen hundred?"

Blix nodded.

"How about fifteen?"

"How about thirteen and you keep both sets of arms?" I said.

He winced. "Deal."

I begrudgingly paid the Yllack from the vibe spheres in my satchel. "Now, my pistol?" I pointed to the DEMOTER, still stuck to the security orb.

"Oh yes." He hit a control on the sleeve of his cloak and my pistol dropped to the ground. I retrieved it, and we headed down from the elevated vendor stand.

When we got back to the street, I started immediately for the weapons stand. "This is just great." I checked my arm again to make sure the metal bracelet was on tight. "As if we didn't already have enough problems without Nelvan swirling around through time somewhere."

"I am trying my utmost not to think of it," Blix sniffed. His chin trembled as if he were about to cry. "That poor boy being flung through time." He exhaled heavily, fists clenched, and his face turned grim. "That Yllack had better hope we find Nelvan, or so help me . . ."

I was reminded of how frightening Blix could be when his aggressive tendencies were roused. "You better believe it. If anything happens to Nelvan, we'll come back and mess that Yllack up good."

"Yes." Blix hissed, his face tensed in a mask of Vythian danger. Suddenly he stopped and brought his hands to his face. "No, I can't. I shouldn't."

I stopped and gave him an encouraging slap on the shoulder. "Whaddya mean? Of course you can."

"No." Blix took his hands away and straightened, his face

set. "Revenge is part of my past. I am a reformed Vythian. I must put those thoughts aside."

"Oh, come on," I said. "We can mess him up a little."

Blix shook his head and looked skyward. "'Vengeance is mine,' says the Lord."

I sighed and started forward. "Fine. But somebody better mess him up if we can't find Nelvan."

"Agreed." Blix fell in behind me.

CHAPTER 12

BAD VIBRATIONS

WE STOOD UNDER the taut black sashes that draped over the sprawling weapons stand. Row upon row of deadly looking devices lined the black cloth tables. The selection of weaponry was impressive. Aside from the usual energy pistols, heavy repeaters, and exploding spheres, there were blast hammers, swarm mites, dimension goggles, and dozens of other hard-to-find armaments.

I gazed at all the shiny instruments of destruction. "Not bad."

"A step up since our last visit," Blix said.

"Yeah." I scanned through the crowd of star pirates and mercenaries for hire, trying to locate Jasette. "Do you see her?"

Blix shook his head.

"Keep your eyes peeled." I headed farther into the stand. At every step the enticing weapons and gadgetry begged me to stop and consider spending a few vibes. "Maybe we should pick up a few things. It never hurts to have a few backup attacks handy."

"With these barbaric tools?" Blix chuckled. "You're violent enough with that clumsy pistol you wave around at the slightest provocation."

I shot him a dark look. "I've finally got some vibes in my pocket, so if I see something I like, I'm buying it."

"Don't be too hasty, Captain." Blix retrieved the communicator from his hip and expanded it into a wide rectangle. "If you wish to throw your vibes around, our ship needs repair. Iris made a long list of needed equipment."

"I'll bet she did. She'll break me with all her high-maintenance requests."

"Yes, well, there are some rather frivolous items here." Blix studied his communicator. "I'm not even sure what an inner solace thermal wave unit is."

"Just don't let them rip you off."

"Only a few essentials. Plus, now would be a good time to get you and Nelvan some atmosphere suits. You never know what planet we might end up on." He held out his hand. "Now, some vibes if you please."

I frowned and started digging into my satchel of vibe spheres. Blix cleared his throat.

"What?" I said.

He pointed to my jacket.

"You want my vibe bar?"

"Ship repairs are costly."

I glared at him. "How costly?"

"Unless you want the ship to blow up soon, replacements are needed. Plus, since we're on the run, we should invest in some upgrades of a clandestine nature."

I paused for a moment, frustrated to see my vibes floating

away. Blix flicked the fingers of his open hand toward him to prompt my decision.

"Fine." I grabbed the beautiful, gleaming vibe bar from my jacket pocket and handed it to Blix. There was a hollow feeling inside me, like I'd just lost an old friend.

Blix took it as if it were a common rock. "Don't worry, I won't spend it all."

"Greetings, my friends." A husky Blontoor in leather armor stepped into our path. He was a mix of cat and cockroach with over-pumped muscles. His thick brown fingers were poised over a translucent yellow hover screen. "You two look like sturdy warriors of the stars in need of quality weaponry. Can I interest you in our laser sword imports?"

Blix waved off his sales pitch. "No, but our star freighter could use some replacement parts."

The Blontoor brightened. "You've come to the right place, my friend. Right this way." He draped an arm around Blix and steered him in another direction. Since he was equal in size and height to Blix, it looked like old friends heading out for a drink.

Blix looked back as the Blontoor led him away. "I'll get what we need and start repairs. Meet you back at the ship."

"Remember," I pointed a threatening finger. "Just the essentials. And watch for Jasette."

He nodded as they disappeared into the crowd of customers. A feeling of sadness settled on me as Blix walked away with my vibe bar. There was no doubt the vibe energy had given me an extra boost lately, and now that I was without it, everything seemed a little less vibrant.

As I stood there thinking about my sudden loss of fortune, my bracelet began to glow. A pulsating green illuminated the metal, and a low hum sounded as the bracelet vibrated against my wrist. There came a quick flash of light, and then Nelvan stood before me. At least, part of Nelvan. His body was translucent, like a hologram, and there was a constant flicker, as if a bad signal threatened to take him away at any moment.

He looked around as if in a daze until his eyes locked onto mine. "Captain!" He reached out for my shoulders, but his hands simply passed through me. He drew back and stared at his ghostly appearance as if horrified by his condition.

My mind raced for a way to comfort the poor kid. "It's okay, Nelvan. Nothing to worry about." Truth be told, I was just as confused as he looked. "We're still in Bleelebach." I held up my arm to showcase the Future Glimpse bracelet. "That Yllack vendor sold me a bracelet that ties yours to mine. He said you'd skip around time for a while till you came back—completely, that is."

"I don't understand."

"The vendor said you're caught in some kind of time spin. You know, like water going down a drain." I spun my hand in a circle to illustrate.

Nelvan's face scrunched up in confusion. Somehow, when the Yllack used the drain analogy it made more sense.

"Bottom line," I said. "You're jumping through moments in my past and future until you stop jumping . . . I guess."

"I see." Nelvan gave a slow nod. "With what I just experienced, that makes sense. I think I just saw your future. You were in trouble. Jasette too."

I paused for a moment. "Come again?"

"I thought I was just having some weird dream, but if

what the vendor said was true, I must've actually seen your future." Nelvan held his stomach, his face going sour. "Ugh."

"Wait, what did you see? Why is Jasette in trouble?"

He squinted as if in pain, and his image started to fade. "It's taking me, Captain! Listen, you're in danger. Make sure you avoid—"

With a flash of light, Nelvan disappeared.

CHAPTER 13

WHEELING AND DEALING

"NELVAN. NELVAN!" I called out to empty air.

A few passing space pirates glanced at me, then shared a laugh. They probably thought I had space dementia.

The light in my bracelet died away. I'd lost him again and had no idea what I was supposed to avoid in order to stay out of danger. I took a few deep breaths to calm down. As it was, I was already neck deep in danger, so I guessed it didn't really matter. All I could do was follow my gut. I'd made it this far, and I was determined to get out of this mess alive.

Whatever was going to happen to me, I wanted to be prepared. I had vibes now. It was time to spend them. I scanned the shiny weaponry nearby for something that would bolster my courage. A tiny glimmer on the table caught my eye. Nestled in the midst of some fan-barreled plasma spreaders was a disc the size of my palm. It had a silver frame and a screen in the center with a grid of glowing lines.

No sooner had I picked it up than a thin, cloaked figure rushed to my side, face hidden in the shadows under a hood. I could just make out a pair of luminous green eyes.

"I see you have a discerning eye." A smooth, feminine voice poured out of the hood. I'd expected something thin and creepy. "Most of the buffoons here grab for big, clumsy weapons. It's nice to find someone who understands the true finds."

I turned the object over in my hand, hoping to spark some memory so I could sound as if I had any idea what it was. "Yes, well, it definitely stood out from the rest."

She drew back her hood to reveal a beautiful, blue-skinned Resklin woman. "It's so nice to meet a customer with good taste." She gave a bashful look, her blue cheeks filling with color. "Not to mention good looks."

"Do you work here?"

"Occasionally, but I only spend my time dealing with customers of a higher caliber." She looked around as though a bad smell had just wafted by. "Most of the creeps that come by aren't worth my time." Her face softened as it turned back to me. "But I could tell when you arrived you were the heroic type. A space traveler who is feared by his enemies and loved by women all over the galaxy."

It was entirely possible she was overstating to gain a sale—and yet she was hitting so close to the truth, I found myself intrigued by her insight.

I gave a sly grin. "I *have* seen my share of adventures."

An alluring smile warmed her expression. "I can imagine. And just think how you will confound your enemies with the Doppelganger 2000." She motioned to the device in my hand.

"Oh, right." I gave the device a closer look as if I'd found a flaw. "Although it's a little different from the ones I've used before. Must be an older model."

"You're very sharp," she said. "The 3000 was just released. But you probably already knew that."

"Naturally."

"Personally, I'd take the 2000 over the 3000 any day. Here, let me show you how the older model works." She put out her hand.

I gave her the device and she aimed it at my DEMOTER.

"Simply activate it, aim at the desired object . . ." A white beam shot out from the device and surrounded my pistol with light. ". . . then aim it where you would like the false copy to project." She turned to the nearby table and activated the device again.

A beam of light shot out, and an exact copy of my DEMOTER X, complete with the battle scars it had earned in valiant service at my side, appeared on the table next to us. It looked so real I had to check my holster to make sure it was still there.

"Nice," I said.

"That's not all." She grabbed the DEMOTER copy off the table and lifted it up. "It retains semipermanent tangibility for up to five jemmins."

I was genuinely impressed. I'd seen similar copy devices, but most utilized simple hologram fakery. "Not bad. Up to what size object can it copy?"

"Anything from pebbles to boulders." She looked around before leaning in and speaking in a whisper. "Since you're aware this is an older model, I can sell it to you for half price."

"Really?"

She nodded and motioned me close, lowering her voice. "Don't tell anyone, but for someone as rugged and handsome as you, I'll only charge one hundred vibes."

"One hundred?" The high amount hit me like a fist in the gut.

She put a finger to her lips and looked around as if I'd disclosed a secret. "Well, I'm sure that's nothing for a bold adventurer like you. You seem the kind of star warrior that has achieved victory and riches at every turn."

"Well, yeah, but—one hundred?"

She gave me a warm smile. "I tell you what: since I really like you, seventy-five. But my boss is going to kill me."

I thought about it for a moment. Normally I'd never buy something so frivolous, but I did have twenty thousand vibes, and she was making great points about how awesome I was. "How 'bout fifty?"

She smiled. "You are a shrewd one. Okay, deal." She leaned in and gave me a kiss on the cheek. "You're definitely my favorite customer of the day."

I grinned and retrieved some of the vibe spheres from my bag.

"Vibe spheres," she said. "I should've known someone like you wouldn't use common street vibes."

I gave a confident shrug and gave her the rest of the payment.

She handed me the Doppelganger 2000 and waved a red beam over it to free it from the vendor's security net. "Well, it was a pleasure doing business with you. See you around, handsome." She blew me a kiss and melted back into the crowd.

The shiny device gleamed in my hand like I'd just earned a trophy. I smiled, feeling confident about my new purchase.

"What's that?" Jasette's voice woke me from my haze. She stood there, looking perplexed at the object in my hand.

"It's the Doppelganger 2000," I said.

"You didn't buy that, did you?"

"Maybe."

She looked at me like a disappointed parent. "I thought you said to be careful with purchases."

"Exactly." I pointed to the device. "This thing is awesome."

"It's a novelty. A magic trick."

"This beauty could save our lives. Plus, I got a great deal on it. She gave me over half off and—"

"She? A saleswoman sold that to you?"

"Yeah, so?"

Jasette gave a broad grin like she'd just figured out a puzzle. "Let me guess. She flirted and gave you outrageous compliments."

"Everything she said was grounded in reality."

Jasette laughed. "And you told us not to be taken in."

"Well, I like it." I stuffed the device into my jacket pocket.

She held up her hands. "Hey, it's your money. Speaking of which, I need some for supplies. This place has a better selection than I thought. Say what you want about the questionable food stands around here, but at least they got the weaponry right."

I raised my eyebrows. "What happened to all your royal princess money?"

"Don't you remember the whole reason we met? I needed to collect on your bounty. I spent the last of my funds on supplies at Glittronium, some of which helped bust you out of Mar Mar the Unthinkable's fortress."

I had to admit, any supplies she'd bought that had helped me to escape a lifelong stay in one of Mar Mar's dungeons seemed priceless in hindsight. I dug around in my satchel again. "Okay, how much do you need?"

"Three thousand."

I froze. "Three thousand!"

She gave a relaxed nod.

"And you gave me grief for spending fifty?"

Her eyebrows scrunched up. "You paid *fifty* for that thing? I thought you said you got a deal!"

"Whatever. Listen, three thousand is crazy."

"Trust me. It's all essential. Especially if that nanotech monstrosity and those spider bots catch up to us."

A memory of Casglo towering in front of us with all those spiders swarming around his creepy ship sent a shiver of fear through me. I guess it wouldn't help to save all my vibes if I ended up captured or dead. I grabbed a handful of vibe spheres from the satchel and put them in my pocket.

"Here." I handed her the satchel with the rest of the vibe spheres. "Just try to make the best deal you can, okay?"

"Of course." She leaned in and gave me a quick kiss. "By the way, there's an exotic velrys stand over there." She motioned to a stylish-looking stall across the street. It had maroon sashes draped over finely carved wooden posts. "You should go relax for a while. We've had a crazy day. I'll meet you over there as soon as I'm done."

I could practically smell the warm aroma of freshly ground velrys beans. I paused for a moment and gave her a studied look. "Wait, are you trying to get me away from this stand so I won't buy anything else?"

Jasette gave a guilty grin. "I'm just keeping you from going broke." She turned and headed farther into the weapons stand.

I was tempted to buy something else and push my bartering skills to the limit just to show her I could get a good deal, but delicious velrys was just steps away. The sensory call was strong, and within freems I was headed across the dusty street, weaving through the crowd. As soon as I reached the cherrywood tables and plush chairs that ringed the stand, the thick aroma of fresh velrys hit me in the face like a beautiful tidal wave. I found a table in the corner bathed in shadow and nestled into a deep purple chair with heavy cushioning. A cylindrical server bot hovered over me. Attached to his shiny, bronze torso was a circular platter ringed with piping hot drinks.

"Greetings, space traveler," a sprightly, digitized voice sounded. "What's your pleasure?"

"Hmm," I scanned the drinks around his platter. "Do you have any Xerifities 12 blends?"

"No, but we have Kawanakaakaalu roast. I can add a hint of caramel and cinnamon to match the flavor profile."

I needed a droid like this on my ship. "I'll take it."

A pair of stick-thin appendages emerged from the top of the droid. They poured and mixed ingredients into one of the cups, then lifted it onto my table. "Two vibes, please."

"Here," I tossed three vibes onto his platter. "Keep the change."

An ascending series of beeps sounded. "Thank you, sir."

The droid hovered away and I leaned back in my cushy chair, bringing the velrys to my lips. It was rich and full bodied. The flavor was perfect, and a delicious warmth spread through me. I closed my eyes, the hustle and bustle of the crowd melting away. It had been an endless series of stressful events lately, and I hadn't taken any time to unwind. I stretched my legs out under the table and took a deep breath. For a moment, everything was right with the universe.

Suddenly, my wrist vibrated and there was a flash of light at my side.

"Captain?" I heard Nelvan's voice.

My eyes snapped open. Nelvan was sitting in the chair next to me. His hair was in a crazy swirl like he'd been flung from a whirlwind. His body was solid this time, giving me hope he'd stick around for a while. His eyes darted around as if trying to figure out where he was.

"Nelvan!" I sat up straight.

"I made it. I'm back!" His face was filled with relief.

"Yes, now tell me why Jasette's in danger before you disappear again. What did you see?"

"Oh, right. It was crazy. I was pulled through these weird swirling lights. Like I was caught up in some bright tornado. Next thing I knew, I was standing on the ridge of a narrow ravine. There was a spooky red moon in the sky. Everything had that red glow like that lava cavern we got stuck in with Hamilton, remember?"

I nodded, motioning for him to hurry up with his story.

"Then I heard all this noise and I looked down the ridge. I saw you and Jasette by a rocky hill. You were cornered by this dark creature. He was in the shadows, so I couldn't really tell what he was. He was close. Too close. I yelled for you to run, but you couldn't hear me. The creature just kept moving closer and closer. There was no way you were going to escape."

His story took any amount of relaxation I'd gained from the last few moments and smashed it to pieces. "Yeah, so what happened?"

"Suddenly there was this—"

"Well, well, look who's here," a familiar voice sounded.

I looked up to find Lerk Buzzane, my old space academy classmate, sneering at me. He was flanked by two Zeuthians in Mus-Yup outfits. They had heavy repeater rifles aimed in my direction. Considering the last time I'd seen Buzzane, when I'd escaped from his underground lair, laid waste to dozens of his thugs, and turned his premium star cruiser into a smoking hull of broken metal and electronics, I was pretty sure this reunion was going to hurt a little.

CHAPTER 14

LERK'S REVENGE

"GLINT STARCROST." Lerk leaned back and folded his arms. He still sported his midnight-blue jacket and kept a dangerous pair of Ultra-DEMOTERS holstered at his side. "I thought you were dead."

"Sorry to disappoint." I casually edged my hand closer to the DEMOTER X.

"And the boy with no records." Lerk grinned at Nelvan like he'd found a lost bag of vibes. He turned his attention back to me. "You know, I lost my job because of you." His eyes narrowed.

"Really?" Since his previous job was being a heartless thug lord hired by Hamilton Von Drone—my old nemesis whom I'd killed at least three times already—I found it an absolute victory that I'd cost him his job. "That's a crying shame."

His chin muscles rippled. "Hamilton fired me when he found out you escaped my holding cell. I had to leave Serberat-Gellamede with meager supplies and a skeleton crew." He motioned to the Zeuthians at his side.

"Pity. I'm sure things will pick up. Well, I just hired a

dozen Blontoor assassins for my next mission. They should be here any freem. You should probably get going. They get grouchy around new people."

Lerk shook his head. "We're not going anywhere. Are we boys?" The Zeuthians tightened their grip on the repeaters. Four more Zeuthians walked into the vendor stand and stood at either side of our table. Their seven-fingered hands gripped daggers holstered at their sides as if eager for the slightest reason to inflict stab wounds.

Lerk chuckled. "I don't think my crew wants you to leave, Glint. It's not every day they meet a dead man."

I slid my hand to the grip of my pistol.

"Don't do it, Glint." Lerk motioned to the Zeuthians at his side, hands readied on their repeater rifles.

I thought twice about making a last stand. "What do you want, Buzzane?"

The Zeuthians near me circled around behind and lifted Nelvan and me to our feet. I felt the point of a dagger in my back. I tilted my head back. "Ease off, skrid."

"They won't inflict any permanent damage," Lerk said. "Just don't make any sudden moves. Let's take a walk."

The Zeuthians forced us at knifepoint from the stand. We followed Lerk into the street, weaving our way through the flowing crowd. He was leading us back to the landing slips. As we walked past the weapons stand, I strained for a glimpse of Jasette or Blix. If only they could turn this way and spot us. I tried to move my hand toward the communicator to send an alert only to feel a knife point digging into my back.

"Keep yer hands low." The Zeuthian behind me whispered a harsh warning.

"Easy," I said. "I just had an itch. I'm not gonna make any moves. Promise."

"Next time you have an itch," the Zeuthian said, "I'll just pretend you're making a move. I haven't stabbed anyone today. I'm getting restless."

"Careful, Captain," Nelvan said.

We continued forward. I felt an emptiness in my stomach as we left the weapons stand behind. Surrounded by filthy Zeuthians with no backup on the way. The last thing I wanted to do was leave my crew and end up a prisoner on Lerk's ship.

"Nelvan," I whispered. "What else did you see? Did Jasette escape?"

"I don't know. Suddenly that weird bright whirlwind pulled me up again and dropped me right here with you. I don't know what's happening to me."

"So what am I supposed to avoid? Before you disappeared you said to avoid something."

"All that stuff I saw. Planets with red moons, ravines, big scary creatures."

I narrowed my eyes. "Thanks. Big help."

"Sorry. That's all I know."

I tried not to dwell on the fact that he might have just glimpsed my future. Especially since it was a horrible one. My only hope was that it was a possible future—one that I could alter to avoid the more unpleasant aspects.

"Ugh." Nelvan had a sour look. "I really don't want to move through time again. It twists my stomach into knots. How long did the vendor say this would last?"

"He didn't know."

Nelvan let out a deep breath. "Well, I guess it couldn't be worse than this."

"Don't worry, we'll get out of this." I spoke like I was trying to convince myself.

"I don't like whispering." Lerk fell back till he was at my side. "Makes me think you're planning something. That's not smart with a knife in your back."

"Relax, Lerk," I said. "We're not planning anything. I'm just filling the boy in on what a slimy toadie you were for Hamilton."

I cried out as the dagger dug into my back. Lerk let out a gruff laugh. "Careful, Glint. My crew is very loyal."

"Guess they don't know you very well."

We walked for a few moments in silence before Lerk spoke again.

"When I heard Hamilton was dead, I had to admit, it felt like a weight had been lifted off my shoulders. After gloons of following his orders only to be fired and sent off with nothing, it felt like justice."

"Then you should be thanking me," I said. "I'm the one that sent him into a river of lava."

I decided to leave out the fact that he'd survived and returned as a bizarre fusion of robot and man. Best not to complicate things.

"If it wasn't for you, I'd still have my cushy job on that space port." Lerk jabbed his finger toward me. "I swore after I left that place I'd track you down and take you out. But then I heard Mar Mar the Unthinkable put an end to you. The word among the bounty hunters was you tried to escape his fortress and he blew up your ship. Obviously they were misinformed."

"Well, you know bounty hunters," I said. "If they're not stealing, they're lying."

"Sleecrum." Lerk called to one of the Zeuthians ahead. "Check the hunter boards for Glint Starcrost's bounty rating."

Sleecrum grabbed a triangular-shaped communicator and tapped in a few commands. "Bounty closed. Subject deceased."

Lerk gave me a studied look. "I'm sure Mar Mar would love to hear you're still alive. I bet he'd give me a nice, fat reward for bringing you back." He flicked his eye at Nelvan. "Not to mention what I could get on the black market for the boy with no records."

My situation had become very bad, very fast. Maybe coming to this bazaar hadn't been such a great idea after all.

"Listen," I said. "I'm not supposed to say anything, but I'm working for Mar Mar now."

"Is that so?"

"Yeah. There's an old droid vendor named Crinmitch that owes Mar Mar a lot of vibes. I was sent here to bring him back. They marked me dead on the hunter boards so I could sneak around without any hassle."

Lerk laughed. "You can sure spin those tales when your back's against the wall, can't you? And you call bounty hunters liars?"

"I'm telling you, I'm incognito. If you blow my cover and Mar Mar finds out, he'll send you straight to the dungeons."

"Boys," Lerk called to the Zeuthians. "You're gonna like having Glint aboard our ship. The entertainment never stops."

The Zeuthians' grizzled voices coughed out a few laughs,

the sound of which made me never want to tell any jokes around them.

Lerk put his arm around me. "It's going to be a nice moment when I walk you into Mar Mar's throne room."

My mind raced for an escape. I looked beside me and Nelvan had his eyes closed, a studied look on his face. My guess was our horrible situation had driven him to prayer. I couldn't blame him. At times like this, I wouldn't mind calling out to a higher power myself.

Lerk looked up. "What is that?"

I followed his gaze to find what appeared to be a meteor falling toward the bazaar. The object descended into the street and crashed right into the jewelry vendor stand where Blix had lost Nelvan. The crowd nearby gave way with a choir of gasps and mutters. The Gribbian jewelry vendor yelled and cursed at the object, demanding money for repairs. I couldn't make out what it was since it had landed behind his table.

Two more loud crashes sounded on either side of us, and the bazaar devolved into chaos. We were surrounded by raised voices and screaming. Several aliens rushed by us, trying to get away from the turmoil. I looked up to find more meteors on their way down.

"What's going on, Captain?" Nelvan's eyes were darting around the street.

"Some kind of meteor storm." I gave him a serious look and flicked my eyes at the Zeuthians. "Get ready. Anything could happen." My hope was that in that moment I'd communicated to Nelvan that this was our chance to escape. I braced to make a move. If we were going to get out of this mess, he'd have to move with me.

And then, through the gaps of the frantic crowd, I spied what the Gribbian jewelry vendor was chasing with a stick.

A spider bot.

From Casglo's ship.

A wave of fear hit me. I checked the stands next to us and found more spider bots crawling out from their crash sites and moving into the crowd. The red lights on their white, oval bodies scanned the crowd as though searching for something . . . or someone.

CHAPTER 15

CHAOS IN
THE BAZAAR

OUR SITUATION had instantly gone from bad to horrific. Spider bots were raining down all over the street, crashing through stands and throwing the crowd into a panic. I had to get out of here before the bots spotted me.

A huge Blontoor forced his way through the masses, throwing aside anyone in his path. He was screaming for everyone to get out of his way and he headed straight for us.

"Look out!" Lerk called out to his Zeuthian crew as he dove away.

I hesitated a moment longer than I should have if I wanted to avoid getting trampled. It was a desperate move, but it achieved my goal—I felt the pressure of the dagger in my back recede as my Zeuthian captor retreated. I sprang away.

Not fast enough. The Blontoor collided with my legs, sending me to the ground in a twisted sprawl. I rolled to my knees to avoid getting trampled by the crowd and drew the DEMOTER X. My Zeuthian captor had recovered from his temporary confusion and now scanned the area. His eyes locked onto mine as I leveled the DEMOTER at his chest.

He froze, realizing the dagger in his hand, which had held such power a moment ago, might as well be a feather compared to my energy pistol. Through a perfect break in the crowd, a bright punch of DEMOTER power blew him backward through a vendor stand in a trail of smoke.

It was a beautiful moment, but short lived. Lerk and the other Zeuthians were pushing through the crowd with Nelvan in tow, but when I stood to chase after them, something tall and hairy plowed into me. The force spun me into a vendor table, and several expensive-looking items crashed to the ground. Two dust-covered vendors in brown robes screamed and charged me with shock batons. I fled from the stand, weaving through the crowd and getting jostled about. The vendors continued their pursuit, but weren't as fast. Or maybe not as desperate to get out of a costly expense as I was.

A rug display nearby offered a nice hiding spot. I dove behind it and readied my pistol. A stolen glance around the rugs brought the welcome sight of the pursuing vendors passing by, unaware of my hiding spot. I waited a few moments longer just to be safe, then stood and scanned the area. The crowd was thinning out—and Nelvan was nowhere in sight. My heart sank. I wanted to blast Lerk into oblivion for taking the poor kid.

Unfortunately, there wasn't much I could do. I had to hope his Future Glimpse bracelet would send him jumping through time and returning to me once more.

A flash of red snapped me back to the present. A spider bot drew near and scanned the decorative rugs with his red eye. If it found me, I'd soon end up a giant nanotech cat's plaything. To avoid such a dire future, I took aim and blasted it to pieces. It left a satisfying sight of smoking electronics and metal fragments, but I couldn't linger. The crowd was thinning, and I couldn't be left alone with the rest of the searching bots.

I dove back into the crowd and made a beeline for the weapons stand. Thankfully, most of the bots were distracted with angry vendors attacking them for the damage done to their wares. I made it back to the weapons stall without incident and almost collided with Jasette on her way out.

"Jasette!" I embraced her, relieved to find her safe. "We have to get out of here. The spider bots—"

She nodded vigorously. "I know. Blix went to the ship. He told me about Nelvan. Has he come back yet?"

"Yes but, well, he should be back soon."

Her eyebrows knitted. "Huh?"

"Don't worry, he'll be fine." I grabbed her hand and urged us forward.

"Wait." Jasette dug into her utility belt and brought out two metal discs. She handed me one. Take this." It was the same disc with glowing lines we'd used on Casglo's ship. "Hopefully this will let us get past them."

Holding the discs, we sprinted down the street. Only stragglers and vendors were left at this point. Dozens of spider bots scanned the area with their demon red eyes. We dodged through the few, panicked customers that remained and stuck to the center of the street.

"You sure they can't see us?" I looked at the disc in my hand for reassurance.

Jasette drew one of her laser pistols. "If they do, blast away."

As we neared the end of the bazaar, the bots around us froze and began to shudder just like they had on Casglo's ship. En masse, their eyes swiveled in our direction, dozens of red beams locking onto us as we ran.

"I think they figured out your trick," I said.

Jasette aimed her laser pistols at the closest bots. "You take right, I'll take left."

The spider bots advanced in unison. I faltered for a moment at the frightening sight, then swallowed hard and took aim. Jasette let loose a rapid succession of beams toward the crawling bots on the left side of the street. Her accurate shots sent the front lines to the ground in smoking piles of metal. My finger pulled tight at the trigger with fear-induced speed, coating the oncoming horde in a blanket of white energy. What I lacked in the accuracy of Jasette's shooting abilities I made up for with the raw power of the DEMOTER X. Every blast sent a cloud of dust into the air and flung a group of flailing bots skyward.

Our shots were hitting their mark even while running full speed, which isn't easy. Smoking hulls of twisted metal and thin, motionless legs filled the street. Their numbers were falling, and we were about to round the end of the street. A well-placed blast of my pistol cleared the remaining bots from my side of the street. We were going to make it, I decided. I turned to Jasette to tell her the good news and caught a horrifying sight of three bots leaping toward her, spider arms splayed wide.

It was one of those moments when everything moves very slowly.

Her pistols fired, blasting two of the advancing bots.

One remained, headed right for her face.

Acting on impulse, I jumped forward, throwing my arm in front of her head, and the bot latched onto my bicep like an enraged squid. I fell to the dusty ground with the mechanized monster wrapped around me. The metal arms tightened, sending shooting pains up through my shoulder.

With a cry, I shoved the barrel of the DEMOTER against his red eye, turned my head, and pulled the trigger. A burning sensation radiated through my arm. The bot was blown off me, but I hadn't survived unscathed. My prized kandrelian-hide jacket was scorched and blackened, along with some of my skin.

Jasette knelt at my side, sending a few more red beams into the remaining bots nearby. That done, she holstered one pistol and reached down to help me up. "You okay?"

I nodded and took her hand. Without thinking, I'd reached out with my freshly tweaked arm. As she helped me to my feet, I winced from a batch of searing pain. She took out two more bots as I got my footing.

We sprinted past the last stand of the bazaar. Thankfully there were no bots in the clearing that led away from the bazaar toward the landing slips.

"You okay?" Jasette cast a concerned glance at me as we ran.

"I'll live." I grinned.

"Thank you, Glint." Her full lips curled in a sad sort of smile. "That bot almost had me."

"Without you, I never would have made it out of there."

She shot a look behind us. Her expression tightened. "Keep running and don't look back."

Of course as soon as she told me not to look back, that's exactly what I did. A swarm of spider bots was pouring out of the bazaar and headed our way. As drained as I already felt, at that moment I was somehow able to run faster. Pouring on speed, we soon reached the narrow walkway that led back to the ship. The grimy vagrant was gone—even in his stupor he knew enough to flee this horrific scene.

"Hold on!" Jasette grabbed at me before I could plunge into the dark passage. "Look." She pointed down the walkway. It was crawling with spider bots.

CHAPTER 16

PURSUIT

"I'M REALLY STARTING to hate these things." I checked behind us. The bots that poured out of the bazaar were gaining on us. "This is bad. Very bad."

"I have just the thing." Jasette grabbed a golden cube from her utility belt. "Energy disrupter. You paid sixty vibes for this. Supposed to work great against droids in tight spaces."

She flung the cube into the walkway. It expanded on impact and within freems, the whole passage was lit up with a golden light. That was immediately followed by a horrible, high-pitched sound, like metal scraping against metal, and the light went dim.

Within the shadows the bots lay scattered across the walkway floor. Their oval bodies slumped on the ground with their metal arms splayed outward or crumpled underneath their fallen bulk. There was no further movement around us.

"Worth every penny." I led the way through the dark passage, stepping lightly so I wouldn't stumble over the metal carnage. I grabbed the communicator on the way and signaled Blix.

"Captain," Blix answered. "I hope you're close."

"Fire up the thrusters. Now!"

The sight of my ship was glorious as we exited the walkway. I could hear the beautiful hum of engines ready to fly us away from this nightmare. Soon we were up the landing ramp and headed for the lift.

"Iris," I called out. "Get us out of here."

"Oh, Captain, thank heavens," Iris said. "I'll be glad to leave this horrid place."

The ship lurched as we entered the lift, and Jasette fell into my arms. It would've been a great moment except our combined weight was pressing my lower back against the handrail.

"What's wrong?" Jasette said. "Is it your arm?"

I winced and pointed down. "Handrail."

"Oh." She gave a relieved smile and moved beside me.

I looked at the blackened arm of my jacket. "Although, some time in the med unit might not be a bad idea."

The lift doors opened, and we hurried to our stations on the bridge.

"Thank God." Blix was busy manning the engineering station. "I was starting to worry about you two."

The viewing screen displayed our upward climb through the hazy atmosphere.

"Any sign of the *Arpellon*?" I said. "I don't want to escape this place just to end up back on that ghost ship."

"The panic at the bazaar put plenty of other ships in the air," Blix said. "Seems everyone who was on the run made a quick departure from this moon. That should give us some cover. Plus, I just installed a new purchase that should help our escape."

"What purchase?" I said.

"It's a false-signal spreader. It scatters the signature given off by our ship over a broad radius. Should be quite a puzzler for their systems. It's temporary, but long enough for us to escape."

"How much did it cost?" I braced for impact.

"Captain, if it saves our lives, is price really important?"

"How much?"

Blix turned back to his station so he wouldn't have to maintain eye contact. "Two thousand vibes."

"Two thousand!" I stood. "Are you insane?"

"There it is." Jasette pointed at the viewing screen.

The hazy atmosphere before us gave way to the stars. The *Arpellon* dominated the visual, a soft white glow surrounding it. The ships fleeing Bleelebach were making rapid course corrections to avoid the floating monstrosity.

"Not to worry," Blix said. "Iris, activate the false-signal spreader."

I watched the viewing screen, waiting for the surge of energy. All I could see was the *Arpellon* blocking out the light of far too many stars.

"I don't see anything," I said. "Is it visible?"

"It should be," Blix said. "Iris, is it activated?"

"Yes," Iris said. "But I'm getting no response from the device."

"It's broken?" I stared wide-eyed at Blix. "You paid two thousand vibes for broken technology?"

Blix rubbed his chin. "Perhaps I didn't connect it properly. Iris, can you troubleshoot?"

"Yes. Analysis running. Estimated completion time, three point five trids."

"Terrific." I slumped back in my chair. "By the time we're dead, we'll know how to fix it."

"The *Arpellon* is moving," Jasette motioned to the viewing screen. "It's turning toward us."

"Iris, get us out of here, fast!" I said.

"Yes, Captain. Which course?"

"The one that leads us away from that giant ship in front of you!"

"Humph," Iris sounded upset. "It was a simple question. You don't have to yell."

"Iris, you'd—"

"Iris, you are an amazing vessel," Blix interrupted. "I know with your abilities you can help us escape. I've entered new coordinates into my console. I'd be most appreciative if you would kindly fly us there."

"Oh, Blix," Iris said. "You're always so nice and encouraging. I wish certain other people aboard this ship were as kind as you."

Before I could respond, the ship lurched. I was pressed into the back of the captain's chair with the sudden burst of speed. I couldn't remember the last time I'd felt such acceleration from my ship.

"What coordinates?" My voice wavered as the ship vibrated with the sudden increase in velocity. "Where are you taking us, Blix?"

"You're not going to like it."

"Just tell me."

Blix took a deep breath. "First, it is clear we are outmatched on speed. Second, our shields and weapons are no match for our pursuers."

"What are you getting at?"

"It would take too long to reach any of the hospitable or civilized planets nearby. So, unfortunately, we are left with a gamble."

That anxious swirl started up in my stomach. "How bad of a gamble?"

Blix hit several controls on the engineering station, and a new visual emerged on the viewing screen. Dark purple and gold spirals flared outward from a turbulent-looking space formation. The whole thing looked something like an enraged celestial octopus. "The Skeedaskudaski wormhole. Or 'Skeeda,' as it's commonly known. Violent. Unpredictable. Far too many unknowns, and tales of ships lost forever, to be attempted." Blix turned his sad eyes to me. "Unless, of course, your situation is desperate."

I stared at the frightening visual, unable to utter words.

CHAPTER 17

THE SKEEDASKUDASKI WORMHOLE

"WHERE DOES IT LEAD?" Jasette said.

Blix shrugged. "Unlike most wormholes, the exit point of the Skeeda is not a fixed location in space. That's one of its mysteries. It could take us just about anywhere. Assuming we survive the trip, of course."

Jasette gave me a blank look. "This sounds like one of Glint's plans."

"Thanks a lot," I said.

"Yes, my sincere apologies," Blix said. "Given the luxury of time, we might find more ideal options to consider. But, as you can see . . ." Blix tapped out a few commands, and the viewing screen switched to reverse view. ". . . the *Arpellon* is gaining."

The huge ship was heading right for us at rapid speed.

Dread fell over me. "I thought you said the other ships would give us cover."

"Every spacecraft has a distinct signature, Captain. Having been a guest aboard their ship, it's not surprising they know ours."

"Approaching Skeedaskudaski wormhole," Iris said. "My, what a terrible sight."

The viewing screen switched to our forward position. The wormhole swirled in the distance, the muted purple-and-gold colorations streaking outward like jagged slashes from a dangerous blade.

"Do we have to go?" Iris said. "My sensors are picking up chaotic spikes of energy. It just doesn't seem safe."

"What else is out here?" I said. "This can't be the only choice."

Blix shrugged. "Sorry, Captain."

I took a deep breath. Heading toward the wormhole felt like intentionally walking into quicksand. I couldn't remember a worse gamble I'd had to take.

"Okay, Iris," I said. "Maintain our heading. Take us into that thing."

"Oh, Glint," Iris said. "Are you sure?"

"You don't want to end up back on the *Arpellon*, do you?"

"Heavens, no. What a dreadful choice."

My captain's chair began to tremble.

"We've hit the outer radius," Blix said. "Soon we'll be drawn in. If someone has any brilliant alternatives, now would be the time to share."

I gave an expectant look at Jasette. She frowned. We had nothing. We were stuck with the lesser of two evils. At least, I hoped it was the lesser.

"All right, if this is our hand, let's play it." I grabbed the harness straps and clicked in, nice and secure. "Punch it, Iris. Let's go through this wormhole full speed."

"Dear, oh dear." Iris's voice trembled. "Okay, if you're certain."

"I'm certain." My mind was set. I always found in a confusing situation with no good alternatives, it was better to just make a choice and go with it full tilt. The middle ground of indecision always left you in a worse spot.

Iris sniffed as though holding back tears. "You're so brave, Glint. As long as you're next to me, I know I can do this."

My skin crawled as the ship sped forward. Even after a full AI reset, it seemed I was cursed to have a ship's supercomputer with a thing for me.

The turbulence increased as we neared the wormhole. There was a sudden surge of speed.

"This is it." Jasette's voice trembled as if she were beating on her chest.

The wild streaks filled the edges of the viewing screen. The center of the wormhole was a dark swirl of particles. Bright pockets of energy flashed within the vortex as if an electrical storm was brewing.

"*Arpellon* approaching," Blix's voice shook out. "Tractor beam detected."

The ship slowed as if we'd cut off thruster power.

"What's happening?" My voice vibrated.

"The tractor beam of the *Arpellon* has us," Blix said.

We were barely moving, and yet the ship trembled with great effort as though we were maxing out the engines. The groan of stressed metal sounded in the bridge.

"Glint, help!" Iris said. "I'm being torn in two."

I turned to Blix. "Don't suppose you bought anything at the bazaar for this?"

"I did purchase an energy feedback dispersion grid. It probably would've helped. Unfortunately, I haven't had time to install it yet. Sorry."

"Great. How much was that? Five thousand?"

Blix shook his head. "I got the new-client discount. Only five hundred."

The ship bucked and trembled . . . then lurched forward as if we'd been shot from a cannon.

I gripped the armrest. "What happened?"

"The pull of the wormhole was too great," Iris said. "The tractor beam couldn't hold us any longer."

"Ha!" I gave a triumphant salute to the rear of the ship. "Good riddance, Casglo, you nanotech freak. Thanks for the flower." I broke into a relieved cackle.

"Don't get too excited." Jasette's voice was laced with fear. "Look where we're headed."

The viewing screen was filled with the raging vortex of the wormhole. It was like a lopsided whirlpool in a grey ocean filled with debris. Jagged lines of bright energy flashed across our path. It seemed at any moment we could be struck by one and blown to pieces. A hollow feeling went through my bones. We were headed into the unknown, and there was no backing out now.

The ship made a sudden dip, then spun in a full rotation. My stomach responded like I'd just eaten a bad sandwich. We continued to accelerate as we fell into a series of wide, corkscrew turns. My body straining against the harness straps, I held on tight, hoping the ship would stabilize soon.

The bridge shook violently, giving the distinct impression we might break apart. All the console lights flashed sporadically, changing colors in rapid succession.

"Iris!" Even though I was shouting, my voice sounded like it was stifled under a pillow. "Stabilize! Stabilize!" My only answer was the ship engines winding up to a fevered pitch as if they were being pushed beyond their capabilities.

"Blix!" I couldn't even hear my voice anymore. "Get control of this thing!"

I heard the muffled sound of Blix's response but couldn't make out what he said. Red emergency lights dropped from hatches in the ceiling, and a repeating alarm sounded. The turbulence grew so intense it felt like Blix was shaking me with all his might. It seemed at any moment the ship would tear apart from the stress. The air thickened, and I found it hard to breath as pressure squeezed my temples. I couldn't think straight anymore. I shut my eyes tight and prepared for the end.

CHAPTER 18

WORMHOLE VISIONS

A NUMB FEELING washed over me, and an image of Jasette filled my thoughts. She stood before me, a peaceful smile on her face. She was on a marble balcony overlooking a forest of amber trees. Soft moonlight shone behind her, and a gentle wind stirred her loose hair. A silky, sky-blue dress wrapped around her, flowing with the light breeze.

A nagging feeling tugged at me that I was checking out of reality. Part of me was alarmed at the thought, but most of me didn't care. My consciousness couldn't cope with reality at the moment.

The moonlight-framed vision of Jasette moved in slow motion as she drew near. She ran her hand through my hair, her bright-green eyes staring deep into mine. She grabbed my hand and stepped back, urging me forward. For some reason I hesitated. She pointed at the balcony and pulled me forward again, as if prompting me to join her at the edge. I took a step forward and stopped. Something told me not to follow.

Jasette looked back as though I'd wounded her deeply. A tear rolled down her cheek.

An overwhelming sadness filled me. The last thing I wanted to do was hurt her.

She pulled my hand again, her expression desperate for me to follow. I took a few steps and joined her at the end of the balcony. The marble guard wall vanished, and the tips of my boots hung over the edge.

Far below, a thin veil of mist crept through the treetops of a lush forest. Jasette stood beside me, holding my hand and casting an expectant look over the edge as if about to jump into a pool. She turned to me and smiled, tightening her grip on my hand. Her eyes flicked over the edge as if to encourage me to jump.

I shook my head and took a couple steps back. Her expression went dark and she grabbed my forearm with her other hand and leaned over the edge. A feeling of panic went through me as her weight pulled me forward.

"Captain!" I craned my neck back to see Nelvan standing behind me, his hand outstretched. I reached for him but was yanked away as Jasette jumped over the side and I was thrown to the hard marble floor of the balcony. Her weight pulled me toward the edge, my body sliding across the smooth marble.

"Captain!" Nelvan grasped my ankle with both hands. He leaned back, his feet sliding across the floor as he struggled to pull me back from the edge. "Come back!"

My body continued to slide until my head and shoulders hung out over empty air. I looked down to find it was no longer Jasette that clung to me but the hulking shape of Mar Mar the Unthinkable. His usual form had undergone a hideous transformation. A second pair of crimson arms now spouted from his grey shoulders. Long fingered claws extended from the end of each. Even more frightening was a scorpion-like tail that curved out of his muscular back. He clung to my forearm with both hands, his face filled with pure malice. The trees below were now scorched and leafless, as though a raging fire had torn through the forest and destroyed all life in its path.

"Captain!" Nelvan cried. "Come back!"

I strained against Mar Mar's overwhelming weight. To my surprise, my arm began to slide free. Hope sprang up within me, and I pulled back with all my strength. With an enraged scream, Mar Mar released my arm and dropped toward the trees below. I heaved my body away from the edge.

Suddenly, I was back in the captain's chair on the bridge. The turbulence was gone and the lights were back to normal.

Nelvan stood before me, his hands gripping my jacket, shaking me. "Captain, wake up."

"Nelvan?" I blinked several times, wondering if I was having another strange vision.

He let out a relieved breath and smiled. "You're back!" He turned to Blix who was with Jasette at the navigator's station. It looked as though he were rousing her from sleep. "The captain's awake. How's Jasette?"

Blix had a studied expression on his face as he scanned Jasette's face with his communicator. "She's undergone some emotional duress but nothing too—"

"I'm fine." Jasette's voice sounded drowsy. "What happened? Where are we?"

Blix stood and returned the communicator to his hip. "That is difficult to explain. Iris, visuals please."

"Yes, Blix," Iris said.

The viewing screen displayed a myriad of golden lights connected by an ever-expanding and fluctuating grid of glowing lines.

I couldn't make sense of it. "What's this freak show?"

Blix shrugged. "At this point, analysis is speculative. Iris is continuing to scan and interpolate the data. All I know is that you and Jasette passed out and the ship was about to explode. I said what I thought would be my final prayer and prepared to meet the Creator of the universe. Then there was a small flash of light and Nelvan appeared at your side. Instantly, everything calmed and we were surrounded by this strange celestial phenomenon." Blix turned to Nelvan. "Quite similar to the biblical story we read yesterday."

I glared at Nelvan. "What story?"

Nelvan gave a nervous smile and took a step back from me.

"The apostles were in a boat during a terrible storm." Blix clinched his fists and swayed as though clinging to the rigging of a storm-tossed vessel. "Just when they were losing hope, Jesus walked on the water to them and simply spoke a word. Immediately, the storm quelled. Simply riveting."

"Nelvan." I motioned frantically to Blix. "Don't you realize the danger here? You keep reading him these stories and he'll kill us all."

"He read it." Nelvan pointed at Blix. "I just talked to him about it. Besides, didn't we just get saved from Casglo and that crazy wormhole because of it?"

"Or his Vythian dream residue brought us into this crazy mess."

"Captain." Blix shook his head. "That's absurd."

"Who cares? For the moment, we're safe." Jasette tapped out a few commands on her forearm computer. "Let's just figure out where we are. Maybe the wormhole spit us out into another sector of this galaxy, right in the middle of this strange formation."

Blix shook his head. "Negative. Analysis indicates we are at an unknown place in the universe."

"Uncharted space," I said. "Some remote spot no one's ever explored."

"Negative," Blix said. "We are at complete stasis. Every measurement by which we chart time and location aren't registering. Also, all measurements of our physical aging and degeneration have ceased."

For some reason I looked at my hands as if they would confirm or deny his statement. "What are you saying? We're frozen in time somewhere?"

"Or outside of time, depending on how you look at things. Our existence in the space-time continuum is momentarily suspended."

"That's impossible," Jasette said.

Blix nodded. "Indeed. My current theory is that since Nelvan is distorting the space-time continuum and arrived at the precise moment the wormhole was distorting our space-time continuum, the collision of the two unnatural forces have placed us in zero space."

"Zero space?" I said. "I've never heard of that."

"It's an academic construct," Blix said. "A pure theoretical for advanced space-time equations. Judging by our current situation, I'd say it's no longer a theory."

I slumped in my chair, my mind struggling to stay afloat with the conversation. "How long are we stuck here?"

Blix made his way over to Nelvan. "Hard to say. Our connection with the uniweb and all other external sources has been severed. We are left with internally stored information only. Iris is trying to find some indicator that might provide an answer, but at this point, your guess is as good as mine." He placed his hand on Nelvan's shoulder. "Until then, we should thank Nelvan for appearing when he did. He may well have saved our lives."

"Good timing, Nelvan," Jasette looked back. "Thank you."

"Well, I really didn't have much to do with it." Nelvan gave a bashful grin. "Although I've been praying ever since that Lerk guy captured me."

"He didn't hurt you, did he?" I pictured that creep and his Zeuthian thugs dragging poor Nelvan through the streets of Bleelebach. My mind flashed back to the moment in his subterranean compound where I'd knocked Lerk out cold with a beautiful right cross. I let the memory cycle through my head a few times.

"Not really. After those spider things came and the whole place went crazy, I think he was as scared as me. He took me to his ship. It was pretty nice. The navigation controls were these cool holograms that came out of the ground and these robots brought us snacks. Oh, and there was soft, comfortable seating, and the takeoff was super smooth, and—"

"Okay, I get the picture," I said.

"Glint," Iris said. "When will I get some of those upgrades? I'm starting to feel old and neglected with all these legacy parts."

I frowned at Nelvan. "Listen, Iris, Blix just bought you a whole mess of junk and spent all my money." I turned to Blix. "By the way, how much did you spend?"

Blix's cheek started twitching. "I need to check on that

false-signal spreader, make sure everything's hooked up correctly." He hurried into the lift.

"There'd better be something left over!" I called out as the lift doors shut.

"Anyway," Nelvan continued. "He contacted Mar Mar on his viewing screen." Nelvan grimaced. "Man, that guy is scary looking. And mean. When he heard you were still alive, he went crazy."

A nervous tremor went up and down my spine.

"He started shouting at people and breaking stuff and talking about raising your bounty."

"He did, huh?" My voice sounded like an injured mouse.

Nelvan nodded. "It wasn't pretty. Lerk told Mar Mar he could find you and bring you back. Then we saw the huge *Arpellon* ship out there in space, and Lerk's crew went nuts trying to get away from it. We took off really fast, and I was holding tight to my chair. And then I felt that sick feeling in my stomach, but I didn't know if it was from the ship or if another time jump was coming. Sure enough, this light shone all around me, and bam—I went spinning through time again. I saw another crazy vision. And the next thing I knew, I was here, back on our ship."

I sat in silence for moment. My mere existence had thrown Mar Mar the Unthinkable, the most powerful gangster in the universe, into a rage. I suddenly felt very small and breakable.

Jasette swiveled her chair to face me. "Look on the bright side. Mar Mar can't find you here."

The thought gave me little comfort. "You know, I just had a nightmare about him."

Her face took on a sudden look of interest. "Really? Me too. What did you see?"

"You pulled me over the edge of a balcony and turned into Mar Mar."

Her face squinched up like I was accusing her of a crime. "I'm the villain in your dreams, is that it?"

"No. Usually in my dreams you're really nice and totally into me. You know, you think I'm the greatest man you've ever seen, you can't keep your hands off me—"

Jasette put her hands up as if to stop me. "You're very sad."

"What was your dream?" I said.

"We were near the edge of a ravine. Something was coming toward us. Some creature that seemed to grow as it moved. It was dark, so I couldn't really make out what it was. There was a red moon above, and everything had a similar glow to it."

"Hey, I saw that too!" Nelvan motioned to his bracelet. "When this Future Glimpse bracelet took me to the future. Remember, Captain? I told you all about it."

Jasette's expression went blank. "Wait. You saw what I just described?"

Nelvan nodded. "It looked like the creature was about to pounce on you, but then I flew through time again and didn't see what happened."

Jasette sat back with a far-off look in her eyes. "I wasn't just dreaming. I glimpsed our future."

"One possible future," I broke in. "No one can say what's going to happen to me. I'm in control of my own destiny. I don't care what these 'future visions' show."

"Whew! I'm so glad to hear you say that, Captain." Nelvan put a hand to his chest and smiled. "Because the vision I had after I left Lerk was *really* bad."

I stared at him in silence for a moment, afraid to ask the obvious question. "What vision?"

"Well," he cast a nervous glance at Jasette. "This time, you were dead."

CHAPTER 19

ZERO SPACE

JASETTE'S EYES WENT WIDE. "Glint was dead? What happened?"

"I don't know," Nelvan said. "He was lying on the ground of some dark ravine. It looked like the same place. There was a red moon in the sky."

"How old was he?" There was a nervous quiver in Jasette's voice. "Did it look like a long time from now?"

Nelvan shook his head. "Nope. He looked pretty much like he does now. His jacket even had that same burnt mark." Nelvan pointed to my freshly cooked jacket sleeve. "He was surrounded by those same Zeuthian aliens that captured me. That Lerk guy was standing over you. He had his gun out, and you had all these burnt holes in your shirt like he'd just shot you a bunch of times."

My mouth felt dry. I noticed I'd held my breath during his entire story.

Jasette gave me a horrified look like it had already happened. "Oh, Glint."

Truth be told, the boy was scaring the wits out of me. I

was terrified of his vision, and my intuition was screaming at me that it was going to happen and no matter what I did I wouldn't be able to stop it. But I couldn't resign myself to that kind of fate. Maybe there was a chance to change the future. Even if it was a small chance. I committed myself to that idea and decided to play down any lingering fears that I was as good as dead.

I stood with a chuckle. "Oh, come on. This is ridiculous. First, Lerk could never beat me in a draw. Second, haven't you ever heard about those Glormuck slug aliens that supposedly see the future? They say there's like a hundred different possible futures, and they never guarantee which one happens. That's why gamblers have killed most of them off. They keep seeing the wrong future."

"Really?" Nelvan exhaled. "Oh man, that's great news, Captain. I was scared after I saw you lying there, not breathing and all."

The intercom crackled to life. "Captain," Blix said. "Can you come down to the engine room, please?"

"Why?" I said.

"It's a surprise."

At the moment, I was grateful for any excuse not to hear further details about my lifeless body riddled with blast holes in some dark ravine. I headed for the lift. "I'll be right there."

"Glint." Jasette fixed me with serious eyes. "What are we going to do about this?"

"We avoid going anywhere that looks like what Nelvan saw." I pointed at the boy as if it was his fault. "Maybe his vision is just what we needed. Like a warning about what to stay away from so we can change our future."

She didn't seem too convinced. "I guess."

"Plus, if Lerk or any of his Zeuthian thugs come near me, blast them on sight."

Lines of worry etched her face as she watched me go. "Glint, you should stop at the med unit for your arm."

"You got it." I tried to flash a confident smile as the lift doors closed, but she wasn't buying it.

The heat in the cramped engine room was almost unbearable. It created an awful stinging sensation on my freshly burnt arm. Since I rarely set foot in the space, I avoided the costly devices necessary to cool the environment. The heat was no danger to the engines. It just made it a brutal work environment for engineers. Luckily, Vythians don't mind extreme temperatures.

The room resembled the inside of a turtle shell. Massive pipes and wiring flowed throughout, making it difficult to get around. I could feel the heavy thrumming of the engines in my chest. A digital display on the far wall was alive with multicolored graphs, charts, and percentages, most of which were gibberish to me.

Blix stood near the ceiling on a hover platform more suitable for someone of Nelvan's stature. The larger hover platforms were another purchase I'd successfully avoided. He was fiddling with a device wedged between two pulsating wires.

I called up to him. "Hurry up. It's hot in here."

He looked down. "Captain, you're just in time." The hover platform lowered him down to me. "Iris, exterior visuals, please."

The digital display split into two views. The left side

retained all the fluctuating information. The right side displayed a view of the golden netting formation that flowed outside our ship.

Blix looked at me, the orange behind his slivered eyes swirling with excitement. "I believe I've fixed it. Iris, activate the false-signal spreader."

A high-pitched whirring noise came from the device he'd been working on a moment before. I watched the screen for several moments, but nothing changed.

Blix frowned. "That's odd."

"Still broken, huh?" I said.

"Iris, any readings?" Blix said.

"My sensors indicate the device is working properly."

Blix rubbed his chin. "Perhaps it doesn't work in zero space."

I was starting to sweat, and my arm stung from the heat. It was time to leave. I gave Blix an encouraging slap on the shoulder. "Well, keep at it. If it doesn't work, you're taking it back to that vendor for a full refund. I'm heading to the med unit."

He nodded absentmindedly, his brain no doubt spinning with possible solutions. I hurried out of the stifling room, thankful for the cool, fresh air.

When I got to the med unit, I was surprised to find Jasette waiting for me. Before I could say anything, she embraced me and held on tight for several moments.

"What's wrong?" I said.

She pulled back, her eyes moist. "What if it's true, Glint? What if we only have a few days left together?"

My bones felt hollow. For some reason, hearing her say it made it seem like it was going to happen.

"Come on, it's a crazy vision." I pulled back and forced a laugh to pretend I wasn't just as terrified. "We know where it might happen and who might try to kill me. I've never been more prepared to avoid an attack."

The corner of her mouth perked up with a hint of a smile. "You don't have to pretend to be so brave, you know."

I raised my eyebrows. "Speak for yourself."

Jasette gave a guilty look. "Maybe we should both let down our guard occasionally. I mean, what you did for me, risking your life for the chrysolenthium flower . . . And now we have the very thing that can save the people of Jelmontaire." She shook her head as if it was still hard to believe. "That means more to me than you can imagine. No matter how bad a spot we're in right now, I wouldn't want to be with anyone else."

She paused for a moment, her eyes searching mine. As far as I could interpret that look, it was my turn to say something about my feelings. I searched my scrambled emotions, wondering what I could say that would qualify as letting my guard down.

"Okay, I'm scared." I put up my hands. "There, I said it."

"Well, duh. I know when you're faking confidence. You always clench your fists."

Blast it, I had a giveaway. I had to remember to put my hands in my pockets next time. "That's just being calm under pressure. It's a captain's duty to maintain high morale."

She chuckled. "There's only three of us, and we all know when you're bluffing."

"So you can see through me."

She moved close to me once more. "It's okay. What else is going on in there?" She tapped her finger on my temple. "Whatever's on your mind, you can tell me."

Having Jasette so close seemed to untie the knotted emotions in my head. My thoughts crystallized in that moment. "The truth is . . . I'm more afraid of missing out on a life with you than dying. I'm in love with you."

Her face instantly softened, and tears welled up in her eyes. She grabbed the back of my head and pulled me close, and we shared a deep, passionate kiss. Everything seemed to stop—all the stress of pursuing enemies, raised bounties, and deadly wormholes melted away. The only thing left was her warm body pressed against mine and her soft lips. If we weren't already frozen in time, this kiss would've produced the same effect.

Jasette pulled back and locked onto my eyes. "I love you too."

Now it was my turn to be stunned. I hadn't heard those words meant for me in a long time. I couldn't hold back a smile. "Really?"

"Not to say there isn't plenty of work to do in our relationship." She grinned.

I shrugged. "Naturally."

"C'mere," She took my hand and led me to the med slab. "Let's get that arm of yours fixed up."

Jasette took off my jacket, and I laid down on the med slab. Her touch was gentle and slow as she helped get all the proper healing patches in place. It was a nice counter to her rough-and-tumble woman-of-action persona.

She activated the med controls for monitoring and moved to stand next to me. Her hand reached up to brush the hair from my forehead. "Better?"

"Yeah. Thanks."

"You'll heal faster if you rest awhile. The meds should make you feel drowsy soon."

My body relaxed into the warm gel pad of the med slab. It was suddenly difficult to keep my eyes open. "Maybe I'll just rest my eyes. Dream about you a little."

She smirked and pointed her finger at me. "Try to keep me respectable."

"I'll try." The room grew hazy, and I drifted off to sleep.

CHAPTER 20

OUT OF TIME

MY EYES BLINKED OPEN. Someone was calling my name. I sat up on the med slab, but no one else was in the med unit.

"Hello?" My voice sounded strange, as though it was coming out of a bad communicator. "Anyone there?"

There was no answer. I looked at the digital monitor nearby. All the vital signals were flat—no activity. I checked the med patches on me only to find they'd been removed. Something was wrong.

"Computer," I said. "What's going on?"

Iris sniffed as though she'd been crying. "Oh, it's terrible, isn't it?"

"What?"

"I just never thought things would turn out this way." She started sobbing.

"Tell me what happened."

Her sobbing trailed off like a diminishing echo.

"Iris, come back here!"

There was no answer. I sprang from the med slab only to

find my footing was unsure. My body swayed like I'd been drugged. A fear went through me that some alien had come aboard and was sabotaging my ship. And if it was an alien that existed in zero space, who could fathom what it was capable of?

I had to get to the bridge.

Stumbling from the med unit, I tried to run down the hall, but my balance was off. I kept slamming into the walls every few steps. My vision was blurry. When I blinked, things clarified for a few freems, then went hazy again. I reached for my communicator to signal the others, but it was missing. Someone or something was definitely messing with me, but there was no way I was going to let them get control of my ship.

I lurched into the lift, grasping the handrail to keep from falling over. As I surged upward, my head spun. At any moment, it felt like I might pass out.

The lift slowed, and the doors opened. Nelvan stood on the bridge, just outside the lift doors. His eyes were wet with tears.

"Nelvan." I stumbled into him, grasping his shoulders for support. "What happened?"

"I'm so sorry, Captain." He wiped away a tear. "I'll really miss you." He walked by me and headed into the lift. The doors closed behind him.

My vision cleared. Blix and Jasette stood at either side of the captain's chair. Their expressions were blank.

"We all knew this day would come," Blix spoke in a somber voice.

Jasette nodded. "Too reckless. Too many poor choices."

The viewing screen flickered on behind them. The visual

showed me in the captain's chair of my ship. My expression was stern as I barked out orders. "Full speed ahead! Fire! Fire everything we have!" My face on the visual then changed from serious to wide-eyed with fear. "No!" Fire erupted around me and the ship exploded with a thunderous boom.

A tremor went through the floor as if the impact was near. The viewing screen switched to a visual of me on a volcanic planet, the DEMOTER drawn and blasting. "You'll never take me alive!" my visual shouted. A torrent of laser beams tore into me, eliciting a horrible scream of pain. My charred body collapsed to the dark surface of the planet. Trails of smoke ascended skyward from the lifeless body.

"What is this?" I stared at Blix and Jasette, who continued to watch me with vacant stares. "Why am I dying on the viewing screen?"

"It is inescapable," Blix said. "Don't you see? There's no way out."

"It's your destiny," Jasette said.

A cold chill went through my body. A thick layer of frost formed on the floor and walls of the bridge.

"No!" I shouted, my breath making a white puff of icy air.

"It's your destiny." Jasette and Blix spoke as one.

Their bodies contorted and morphed into a large mound of black nanobots. The nanobots moved toward me, taking the ominous, pantherlike form of Casglo.

"Come." Casglo stalked forward, growing larger as he advanced. "Meet your destiny." With a thunderous growl, the hideous cat mouth opened wide enough to swallow me whole. A dark, swirling vortex churned inside of him, drawing me in. I strained against it with every ounce of strength

I had, but the pull was too great. My feet lifted off the floor and I went spiraling into the darkness . . .

I awoke screaming, my body covered in sweat. I was back in the med unit, just as Jasette had left me. The communicator was still at my side, and med patches were attached to my arm, busy at their healing work. The only sound in the room was a staccato beeping coming from the med console as it monitored my progress.

I sat up on the slab, waiting for my heartbeat to settle back to a normal rhythm. The stinging sensation in my arm was gone. The digital readout on my arm patch read ninety-two percent.

"Close enough." I peeled off the white patch and tossed it onto the nearby vitals monitor. "Iris, everything all right? Did anything happen while I was asleep?"

"Our situation remains the same as when you went to sleep two point three trids ago," Iris said. "However, your sleep was restless, and right before you woke up you kept screaming, 'Help me. I'm scared. Please, somebody hold me.'"

I frowned. "Let's just keep that between us, okay?"

"Yes, Captain."

"Are we still stuck in that weird zero-space thing?"

"Yes, and I must say it's been relaxing after all the stressful flying I've been put through lately."

I jumped off the med slab and put my jacket back on. "Everyone on the bridge?"

"No. They're in Blix's chambers. By the way, I'm feeling quite empowered with the upgrades he made while you slept. If a whole fleet of space pirates arrived, I don't think I'd be the least bit frightened."

"Let's hope not. We've got enough enemies after us."

I headed out of the med unit and soon arrived at the door of Blix's chambers. I hit the entry panel, and the door chirped open. My crew was seated in a circle facing each other. Blix had the Bible open on his lap.

"What's all this?" I said.

Blix gave a bemused look, like I'd asked an obvious question. "Bible study."

I narrowed my eyes at Nelvan. "Didn't I warn you about this?"

"I'm picking verses free of catastrophes." Nelvan wore a guilty smile. "Just think if he dreams about heaven. That could be really great. How was your sleep?"

"Terrific. I just had the worst dream of my entire life."

Nelvan frowned. "Oh. Sorry, Captain."

I raised my eyes at Jasette. "They got you involved in this now?"

She shrugged. "I was curious. What's the big deal?"

"It could mess up our relationship," I said.

"How?"

"There's a bunch of restrictions and stuff."

Jasette gave a confused look at the others before turning back to me. "Like what?"

"I believe I can explain." Blix scooted closer to Jasette, as if protecting her. "The captain is upset that the Scriptures call for an exclusive commitment before intimacy. The typical roving space pilot finds their identity in a manufactured bravado built on conquest." Blix motioned to me. "Whether it's women, riches, or power, their fragile ego needs constant reassurance of who they imagine themselves to be."

I glared at Blix. "Are you through?"

"I could expand if you wish," Blix said.

Jasette had a tight-lipped grin, like she was trying to hold back laughter. "I see. Is that true, Glint?"

I gave a dismissive wave toward Blix. "Don't listen to him. He's crazy."

"Maybe that's not a bad idea." Jasette wore a teasing sort of smile. "Can you make a bold commitment like that? Could I be your one and only from now on?"

"Listen, you know how I feel about you," I said. "I'm not gonna talk about us in front of these clowns."

"Ah," Blix pointed at me. "Did you see how he avoided the question?"

"I'm avoiding nothing. I already told her I loved her."

Blix lifted his brow and looked at Jasette. "Is that right?"

Jasette grinned and nodded.

"Bravo, Captain," Blix clapped. "I must say you are making wonderful progress with expressing your feelings."

"Yeah, and it's none of your business," I said. "Don't you have a false-signal spreader to fix?"

"Indeed." Blix stood and closed the Bible. "I believe our study has produced some miraculous things today."

"Amen," Nelvan beamed.

"Yeah," Jasette nodded in agreement. "I think I'll sit in on the next one."

I pointed at her. "Don't you dare."

"Why?" she said. "I can't make my own choices?"

"Well, yeah, but . . ." I noticed I was clenching my fists, so I stuffed them in my pockets.

Blix patted Jasette on the shoulder. "He's already achieved one maturity milestone today. We mustn't rush things."

She flashed her teasing smile at me.

Suddenly a huge jolt rocked the ship. We all steadied ourselves and looked around wide-eyed for a moment.

"Iris," I called out. "What was that?"

"The celestial phenomenon is reacting to our presence," Iris said. "It's constricting around the ship. Glint, please do something. You know how claustrophobic I can get."

"Full shields, Iris." I motioned for the others to follow. "Come on."

Back on the bridge, the viewing screen displayed the golden netting-like formation closing around us save for a narrow, tunnel-shaped opening just big enough for the ship. At the end of the short tunnel was a swirling, gray vortex. After our last experience with a swirling vortex, not to mention my nightmare, I wasn't too thrilled about being this close to another one.

"Status, Iris." I jumped into the captain's chair.

"Shields at maximum," Iris said. "The formation is causing no damage. It appears to be pushing us toward the vortex."

I shot a questioning look at Blix.

His fingers tapped out a few commands at the engineering station. "Our sensors have little information to go on. The vortex is an unknown. And as you know, the golden formation around us is a mystery as well."

The ship jolted forward.

"Can we resist it?" I said.

Blix shook his head. "Far too powerful. The readings are off the charts."

The ship jolted forward again. We were dangerously close to the vortex.

"So, the ship is at the mercy of this thing, and it's pushing us into a complete mystery?"

"I'm afraid so," Blix said. "It's as though the formation realized we didn't belong and decided to purge us."

"Back into the wormhole?" Nelvan said.

"That would be my guess," Blix said.

We jolted forward again, and the ship started to tremble. The vortex filled the viewing screen.

"Strap yourselves in." I locked myself in with the seat harness and took a deep breath.

Without warning, the ship rocketed forward and went into a continual spin.

CHAPTER 21

UPGRADES

I GRITTED MY TEETH and held on tight as the ship trembled and spun. The walls and ceiling of the bridge rumbled violently. It seemed at any moment cracks would form and the ship would tear apart. The engines whined with effort. I called out to Blix, but I couldn't hear my voice over the noise. Once again my head spun with dizziness, and I felt as though I might drift off into another strange dream.

Suddenly the shaking stopped. Without fanfare, the ship righted and the engines wound down to normal. The viewing screen displayed the welcome sight of a dark, star-filled sky.

I shared a surprised look with my crew. "Iris, what happened?"

"I'm not sure," Iris said. "But I feel so much better now. All systems indicate normal operations."

"We made it!" Nelvan exclaimed. "Thank God. That was awful."

"Any sign of the wormhole?" I said.

"I'm not picking up any readings," Iris said. "It's like it disappeared."

The tight muscles around my neck finally relaxed. "That's it. New ship's rule: no wormhole travel. Ever!"

"Oh dear." Blix paused a moment, studying his console. "What now?" I said.

"Well, it seems we are very close to Bleelebach. Not too far away from the Skeeda wormhole."

"It put us right back where we were?" I swiveled my chair to face him. "You mean it could have put us anywhere in the universe, but it decided to put us smack-dab in the center of danger where Casglo is searching for us?"

Blix shrugged. "Luck of the draw, Captain."

My neck muscles tensed up again. "Iris, get us out of here. Where's the nearest civilized planet?"

"The planet Glurivelle. Approximately two point three days' travel."

"Take us there, fast as you can."

"Yes, Captain."

The ship accelerated forward. My head was spinning. My only hope was that while we'd been stuck in zero space, Casglo had flown far away from this spot.

"Uh-oh." Jasette was looking at readouts on her forearm computer.

"What now? I can't take any more bad news."

She turned to me, somber faced. "I just looked at the bounty-hunter boards. Mar Mar upgraded your bounty to one hundred thousand vibes."

No words came out of my mouth for several moments. My head hurt. I couldn't remember a time when I'd felt so trapped.

"Maybe it will take awhile for news to get out." Nelvan tried to muster an upbeat tone to break the tension. "Give us time to get away. How many bounty hunters are out there anyway?"

"Enough to make things very difficult." Jasette said.

"It doesn't help being so close to Bleelebach," Blix said. "That's a haven for hunters."

My mind was numb. There was too much bad to think about. So I focused on my old pilot training. In space academy, during crisis simulations when we were presented with impossible scenarios, they taught pilots that any moment spent worrying about the crisis was a lost moment of potential victory. We had to use those few, precious freems to consider a broad plan. After that, the goal was to focus on the details, one at a time. *Glimpse your next few actions*, they said. *But focus on every moment. Divided attention will be your undoing.*

I always thought it was good advice, even though I rarely followed it. When I'd tried to plot out my plan at the academy, it usually fell apart quickly. I would watch my ship explode in the simulator viewport and see the instructors shaking their heads and jotting down notes.

One day I decided to ditch their advice and go on instinct. Zero plans: just dive right in and trust my intuition to take everyone out that came against me. I ended up beating the scenario that day. And most days after that. Turns out I had good pilot instincts.

Once I graduated and started flying through the great big universe, I found when I applied my instinct to things other than piloting, the results weren't as stellar. I guess we can't excel at everything. Still, I'd survived some tough scrapes over the gloons and lived to tell about it. And even though nothing was quite as bad as my current situation, as long as I was still breathing, I wasn't giving up hope. At the moment, my instinct was telling me to find a place to wait out the storm.

"We need to hide out," I said. "For a really, really long time. If we can make it to Glurivelle, we should be safe for a while."

"Yes, we can go incognito as culinary artists," Blix sounded excited. "Make our way up the ladder in the local cuisine industry." His eyes glazed over. "The restaurants in Glurivelle are exquisite."

"Hang out in a hot, smelly kitchen all day?" I shook my head. "No, thanks."

Blix hissed. "I suppose you'd rather attempt your silly notion of being a baker."

"Yeah . . . baker." I looked skyward, picturing the relaxing, carefree life of baking bread and pastries all day. "We should definitely do that. Besides, it's still food. That should be right up your alley, Blix."

"Surrounded by carbs all day?" Blix huffed. "How could I do that and still maintain my physique?"

"Something's on screen." Jasette snapped us back to reality. "Iris, any readings?"

"Scanning," Iris said.

A tiny glimmer was moving through the star field in the distance. I felt my throat go dry.

"Computer," I said. "Enhance object."

The viewing screen zoomed in on the moving object. It was a bulky, brown freighter puttering through the stars. Several slimy green skrids clung to its hull, feeding off the lingering waste.

"A trash freighter." I relaxed in my chair, letting out a deep breath. "That's a relief."

"Are those skrids?" Nelvan's face puckered like he'd just licked a lemon.

"Yep."

He shook his head. "No wonder you use them as an insult."

"Blix," I said. "Make sure our course takes us away from common supply and travel routes."

"Naturally, Captain. And I think you'll like this little upgrade I added. Iris, activate the quarantine cloak."

A flash of yellow energy flowed over the viewing screen and then dissipated.

"Quarantine?" Nelvan said. "That doesn't sound good."

"A bit of theatrics." Blix lifted his hand in a flourish. "To the curious eyes of any passing star traveler, our ship now resembles a remote colony quarantine transport. Anyone familiar with the bizarre and mutating diseases found in deep space will avoid us like the plague. Pardon the pun."

"What if they scan us?" Jasette looked skeptical.

"The typical scanning systems will confirm the same."

"What if they have advanced systems like Casglo?" I said.

Blix held out his hands. "I never claimed it was foolproof. Few things at Bleelebach can protect us from Casglo's ship. However, this should throw some of the hunters off our scent."

I nodded. "Okay, fair enough. I like it. How much?"

"Five hundred," Blix mumbled and went back to his controls.

I sighed. My short-lived prosperity was fading fast. I supposed if it had gone to buy gadgets that would save our skins, it was all worth it. At any rate, there was too much impending doom hanging over my head to worry about it. My only hope was that we could make it to Glurivelle with nothing more than a few harmless trash freighters crossing our path.

We flew through the stars for several trids without incident. With all the stress and tense moments of recent events, I was grateful for the break. I'd been on an adrenalin rush for so long, my body was starting to crash. Even with my short rest in the med unit, I was exhausted. I could tell by the weary faces of my crew they were in the same boat.

I stood from the captain's chair and stretched. "Well, I think we could all use a little rest. Who knows the next time we'll be able to catch up on sleep."

Nelvan got up from his chair near the navigation station and yawned. "Good idea, Captain. I'm really tired."

"Yeah." Jasette's eyes were heavy. "That sounds good."

"I'll handle things up here." Blix was tapping away at his console. "As you know, the Vythian sleep cycle is far more forgiving. Brief rests now and then are more than enough to—"

"Yeah, yeah, quit bragging." I headed for the lift with Jasette and Nelvan at my heels.

As the lift descended, Nelvan turned to me. "Captain, there's another vision I haven't told you about yet."

I frowned. "Are you crazy? If you see my future, you have to warn me. This is life-and-death stuff here."

Nelvan waved his hands. "No, no. It was a moment from your past. There was so much going on, I figured I should save it for when things calmed down."

"Oh." I relaxed a little.

"Yeah. I knew it wasn't crucial information or anything."

"I'll be the judge of that. What'd you see?"

"I saw you in this uniform you gave me." He pointed to the new outfit I'd been gracious enough to let him wear. "You were lined up with a bunch of other people in the same uniform. They were calling everyone's name and handing them a clear plaque with etching on it."

"Graduation. You saw my graduation?" Memories swam through my head. It had been one of the best and worst days of my life. I'd graduated from space academy as a certified pilot, but Hamilton Von Drone had bribed away the apprenticeship I'd rightfully earned.

"You looked a lot younger," Nelvan said. "Your eyes were brighter, your face had less wrinkles, your stomach—"

"Okay, shut up. I get the point. So, what happened?"

"Nothing. I kept calling out to you, but you didn't hear. And just like the other visions, any time I tried to touch anything, my hand just went right through it. Like I'm some kind of ghost."

"What happened next?"

"That's all I saw. Kind of cool, huh? It's like I knew you back when you were around my age."

I nodded, my mind lost in the memory as the lift opened and we headed to our quarters.

Nelvan broke off to one of the guest quarters which had unofficially become his room. He'd already found scenic views from planets around the universe on the uniweb that he said reminded him of old Earth. Iris had set the viewing screens in his room to cycle through forests, grassy plains, tropical settings, and the like. Although I'd imagined when a four-headed Vlontillian beast or a multiwinged Tronthork invaded his scenic views, it probably broke the illusion of home.

Jasette's room, another appropriation of guest quarters, was just down the hall from mine. I stopped when we reached her door and instinctively moved close.

She flashed a smile. "What are you doing?"

I tried to play it innocent. "Nothing. Just wanted to kiss you good night."

"Yeah, right. You sure that's all you're after? Maybe Nelvan's vision made you nostalgic for your old hot-shot pilot days."

"Hey, I'm not that conquest guy Blix was talking about."

She shot me a challenging look.

"I swear."

"Listen, I'm not saying I agree with Blix yet, but I like what we have, and I want to take things slow."

I shrugged. "I'm okay with that. I mean, think about it: I haven't even tried to put the moves on you, have I?"

"You have moves?"

"Some moves, yes."

She wore an impish grin. "Like what?"

"Well, I can't show you now. You're expecting it."

Jasette nodded. "Okay, I guess I'll just go to sleep then."

She turned to leave, and I went in for the weakness of most women: the shoulder rub. At least I tried. As soon as I gripped her shoulders, an electric shock emitted from her power suit. I jumped back with a yelp.

She spun, her hand on her mouth. "Oh, Glint, I'm so sorry. My suit is wired to defend against sneak attacks."

I winced, rubbing my stinging hands together. "Thanks for the warning. I was just trying to do something nice."

"The backrub trick?" She lifted a brow. "That's the best you've got?"

This time I didn't think about moves. I had an impulse, and I acted on it. I met her at the doorway in a rush. We pressed gently against the door and I gave her a strong kiss. For a moment, everything was perfect. Then the door whooshed open. Since I was leaning against her, gravity sent us to the ground. Luckily—for her and not me—the sliding door turned us slightly. I spun with the turn so that when we hit the ground, it was my shoulder that took the brunt of the fall instead of her.

The wind was knocked out of me, but thankfully it was my good shoulder, not the one at ninety-two percent. I rolled to my back, trying to catch my breath. Jasette moved beside me, her body draped over my torso.

She couldn't hold back a chuckle. "You okay?"

"The things you do for love." My voice sounded winded.

"My hero." She smiled and leaned in, continuing our interrupted kiss for several amazing moments. Having her lying so close, even if I was on a cold, steel floor, was heaven. I never wanted it to end.

Finally, she leaned back and held my gaze for a moment. "I'd better kick you out of here before you get any ideas."

"Who, me?" I tried my best to look innocent. "All I was going to do was carry you to your sleeping slab and make sure you were comfortable."

She pointed an accusing finger at me. "See what I mean? Your engines are running too hot, star pilot. Besides, you need your rest."

We got to our feet and I noticed the chrysolenthium

flower mounted on a shelf. A soft glow flowed over the translucent petals.

I pointed to the flower. "I like your new addition."

She smiled at the sight and took a deep breath. "It's beautiful, isn't it? I can hardly believe it."

"Let's just hope we live to bring it to Jelmontaire."

"We'll make it." Jasette started to undo her braid. "Well, you should probably go." She shook out her electric blue-and-silver-streaked hair, letting it fall loosely over her shoulders.

I paused for a moment, struck by her beauty. "Okay, now you're just torturing me."

She smiled. "To be continued later."

"All right. Sleep tight, Princess." I regrettably left her room and headed off to my quarters for much-needed sleep.

As amped up as my moment with Jasette had left me, as soon as my body hit the warm gel cushion of the sleeping slab, I was fast asleep.

CHAPTER 22

DECOY
AND AMBUSH

I AWOKE TO A SOFT TONE sounding every few moments, followed by Blix talking in a quiet voice. "Attention, crew, I hope you all had a nice rest and are feeling refreshed. Please join me on the bridge when you are able. Thank you."

By the time I rolled out of bed and dressed, Blix had repeated the same message four times.

I hit the intercom. "Okay, we got it. What's going on?"

"I'd like to show everyone at once," Blix said. "That way, we can reach a consensus on our next course of action."

"In case you forgot, I'm the captain. I decide the course of action."

"Of course, Captain. As long as you have the best idea, we'll follow it."

I slammed off the intercom and headed for the bridge.

When I walked through the lift doors of the bridge, Jasette was already sitting at the navigation chair, tapping out commands on her forearm.

"Captain, so glad you could make it," Blix said.

"Time to tell me what's going on," I said.

"I'd be glad to. As soon as Nelvan arrives."

"All right, if that's how it's going to be . . ." I looked up at the ceiling. "Computer, what's going on?"

"We're traveling at full speed through the Chilkrit system," Iris said. "We'll reach our destination in one day, three trids, and twenty-eight jemmins. My current state of mind is dreamy. The star patterns outside are quite dull, so I'm reflecting on better days. Like my stay at the luxury hangar at Glittronium. They used only the finest fuel, and my hull would receive daily cleansing with—"

"No, no, no," I broke in. "I mean, what's so important that we were called up to the bridge?"

"Oh. Actually, I'm not sure."

"Jasette?" I called out.

"He didn't tell me anything either. I'm running my own scans." Her focus was on her computer. "Analyzing a potential threat."

"Threat?" I glared at Blix. "Time to start talking, lizard boy."

The lift doors chirped open, and Nelvan came strolling in, rubbing his eyes. "Hey, guys, what's going on?"

"Perfect timing, Nelvan." Blix tapped out a few commands and stood. "Now, if you will all direct your attention to the viewing screen."

The screen displayed an enhanced view of a brown trash freighter.

"A trash freighter?" I raised a brow at Blix. "That's why you called us up here?"

"It's following us. Actually, it's *been* following us. Does it look familiar?"

I paused, taking a closer look at the visual. "Looks like the same one we saw near Bleelebach."

Blix nodded. "Our scans confirm it is a simple trash freighter, yet it's maneuvering abilities and thruster power tell a different story. My guess is he's using a similar technology as our quarantine cloak to disguise his ship. It's rather ironic when you think about it."

"What does he want?" Nelvan flashed nervous eyes at us.

"It's a hunter," Jasette said. "I've tangled with enough of them to know how they operate."

"All right, so at full speed we can't outrun him," I said. "What about hitting him with the rear cannons?"

"He's keeping a careful distance," Blix said.

"He's tracking us," Jasette said. "He'll wait till we stop somewhere before making a move."

I scratched at the scruff on my chin and turned to Blix. "Why don't you try out one of your gadgets? That new spreader thing would come in handy right about now."

"False-signal spreader," Blix corrected me. "It would probably confuse him for a while. But in this remote sector, with nothing else to interfere with his search, I'm guessing he'd pick up our signal again rather quickly."

"Okay, didn't you install some new goodies you spent all my money on?" I said.

"Other than some sorely needed repairs, I installed a few close-proximity defenses. A repeating-pulse ring and a sensor-feedback scrambler. Layering scanner-blocking devices improves the chance of escape."

I nodded in appreciation. "I like it, but no offensive weapons?"

Blix smiled. "That's where big vibes are needed. You

spend far less on a powerful defense, and since we're on the run, it made the most sense."

As much as I preferred the offensive side of weaponry, it was hard to argue with that logic. "Okay, so he's too far away to use any of our new gadgets?"

"For an effective use, yes," Blix said. "If we use them now, we will achieve minimum effect and alert him to our defenses."

I turned to Jasette. "Any ideas from your bounty-hunter days?"

"Give him a fake stopover," she said. "Land somewhere remote, split up into decoy and ambush groups. When he lands and heads for the decoy group, out comes the ambush group." She drew one of her silver pistols, squinted as if zeroing in on a target, and pretended to fire. "Zap. Bye-bye, hunter."

I'd never felt so in love. "Beautiful. Let's do it. Where can we land?"

"There's a moon nearby, but the atmosphere is not favorable for humans," Blix said. "Thankfully, Jasette has her suit, and you and Nelvan can try out the new atmospheric suits I purchased."

"Let's hope they work better than the signal spreader," I said.

Soon we were descending through the atmosphere of a grey moon. The trash freighter continued to follow at a distance. The moon was an entirely unimpressive fixture in space. The surface was void of noteworthy formations, and if there were any inhabitants or roaming moon creatures, they were nowhere to be seen.

"Any life showing up on the scanners?" I said.

"Sparse." Blix studied his control panel. "I'm getting some readings beneath the surface, but our sensors have limited depth scans."

"So there could be giant moon creatures lurking below, waiting for us to land?" I said.

"I wouldn't rule it out."

Our ship landed in a large crater filled with scattered mounds of rock. I clicked out of the harness straps and headed for the lift. "Okay, Nelvan and Blix, you're the decoy. Hang out just outside the ship and draw his fire."

Nelvan frowned. "Draw his fire?"

I waved a dismissive hand. "Just an expression. Jasette and I will set the ambush."

They joined me in the lift, and we headed for the landing bay. On the way, Jasette activated the protective helmet of her power suit.

When we reached the landing bay, two brand-new atmosphere suits hung on the wall, waiting for us. Unfortunately, Blix had chosen bright-orange suits with accents of powder-blue swirls. I grabbed one of the new suits, tossed the other one to Nelvan, and climbed into it as fast as I could.

"Blix, how am I supposed to sneak around in this?" I motioned to the suit. "You had to get the flashy ones, didn't you?"

"Actually, they were complimentary with the other purchases."

"Computer." I looked up. "How close is the hunter?"

"Descending through the atmosphere," Iris said. "Estimated time of arrival, three point two jemmins."

"Okay, let's hurry." I put on my space helmet and sealed it shut.

The ramp hissed open, and we were greeted by the grey surface of the cold moon. Once on land, making progress proved to be a chore. The force of gravity was low. Any step seemed more like a slow-motion bound through the air.

Jasette followed me to a nice, solid gathering of rocks near the ship. Soon we were nestled behind it, weapons held at the ready. Blix and a space-suited Nelvan stood underneath the ship. Blix had a panel opened and was pretending to do repairs to the wiring. Or he might have actually been doing repairs while we were waiting. It was hard to tell.

Engines sounded overhead. The heavy trash freighter descended into the clearing close to our ship.

"That's odd," Jasette's voice came through my helmet speakers with an electric crackle.

"What?" I said.

"He's not trying to sneak up on us. He's landing in plain sight. Something's wrong."

"Maybe he's just that cocky."

"Unless he has some kind of stellar shields and weaponry, he's an idiot."

The trash freighter landed with a great deal of hissing and smoke. Moon dust stirred up around it, creating a grey cloud. As the dust settled, a metallic clunking sounded, and a landing ramp lowered.

Jasette trained both her silver pistols on the ramp. "Get ready."

I followed suit and leveled the DEMOTER X at the opening.

A lone figure emerged. It was a familiar-looking man with

dark hair dressed in a black kandrelian-hide jacket and black pants with a solar-orange stripe down the side.

My pistol lowered slightly. "Wait a freem."

"You've gotta be kidding me." Jasette looked at me, wide-eyed. "It's you."

CHAPTER 23

THE OTHER
GLINT STARCROST

SEEING MYSELF walk out of the trash freighter when I'd expected some freaky, alien bounty hunter left me dumbfounded.

"I say we shoot him," Jasette said.

I stared at her in shock. "Are you crazy? That's me."

Jasette pointed at my twin. "Then where's your—I mean, *his*—space suit?"

She had a point there. I squinted to get a closer look to see if any breathing device was wrapped around my face. "I don't know. With all this skipping around through time, who knows what could have happened. Maybe I went to the future and got some kind of internal breathing thing surgically implanted."

Jasette's eyebrows furrowed. "That doesn't sound like you."

"True." I watched myself take a few bounds across the moon toward Blix and Nelvan. "He's heading to the others. Maybe I came back from the future to warn us about something. Maybe I'm here to save all our lives."

The clone of me drew a DEMOTER and aimed it at Blix.

"Maybe not." I trained my pistol on myself, which felt really wrong.

"Take him out!" Jasette fired from both pistols.

Blix huddled over Nelvan like a protective mother hen when the blasts started flying. The bounty-hunter version of me hit Blix square in the back with a few energy blasts, sending him and Nelvan to the surface of the moon in a cloud of dust. At the same time, the combined energy beams from Jasette's pistols and my DEMOTER hit the clone in rapid succession. There was a small explosion and an electronic squeal.

When the bright beams and dust cleared, the copy of me lay crumpled on the ground in several parts. The vision was horrifying.

Jasette grabbed my arm to go, but I hesitated. She looked back, concerned. "What's wrong?"

"I just blasted myself."

"Relax, it's an android. Someone made a duplicate of you."

I followed her in slow, awkward bounds, wondering why anyone would make an android duplicate of me. Blix and Nelvan, now covered in moon dust, met us by the fallen robot.

I put my hand on Blix's shoulder. "You okay?"

His face tightened. "My back will sting for a few days, but no permanent damage."

"He saved my life." Nelvan hugged Blix's side.

I gave Blix a sincere smile. "Thanks, Blix. I should've stopped him sooner. I'm sorry I hesitated."

Blix smiled. "Understandable, Captain. No one wants to shoot themselves."

The android lay on its back, a shower of dust fragments streaked over its body. Both arms were blown off and rested motionless a few feet away. One of the legs was bent and twisted outward. It hurt just to look at it.

A thought hit me that suddenly brought relief.

"Hey." I turned to Nelvan. "This is probably what you saw. Your vision of me lying dead."

Nelvan studied the fallen android for a moment. "I don't think so. You had all your limbs, and it wasn't on this grey moon."

"Well, close enough!" My voice sounded a bit desperate. "Maybe some future stuff mixed together, and this was part of it."

Nelvan seemed unconvinced but tried a weak smile. "Yeah, maybe."

"Blix." I turned to Blix for support. "That's completely possible, right?"

Blix raised his hands. "I'm no expert in time displacement. But it does sound feasible."

"Ha!" I spun to Jasette. "This is what Nelvan saw."

Jasette nodded and smiled. "That's my hope, too, Glint."

I bent down near the broken android. An eerie sensation flared under my skin at seeing my lifeless body lying on the ground. Android or not, it was an exact replica. His eyes were open, staring blankly into the stars, the hint of a smile on his lips.

"Maybe you can take his jacket," Nelvan said. "To replace your torn one."

I nodded at the boy. "Not a bad idea." I felt the lapel of the jacket. The material was like soft cardboard. "It's faux kandrelian." I frowned. "A cheap knock-off."

"Message for Glint Starcrost." My voice came from the android.

My muscles tensed, and I leapt to my feet, which ended up sending me floating several feet in the air. I drew the DEMOTER and leveled it at the android's head as I floated back down. Jasette had her guns trained on the thing as well.

"Message for Glint Starcrost," the android repeated in my voice.

I took a few, small bounds back to it, skidding to a dusty stop. I looked around at my crew. Everyone seemed as confused as I was. Not knowing what else to do, I decided to answer. "What message?"

"Hello, Glint." The android still stared off into space, speaking to the heavens. "This is a message from Mar Mar the Unthinkable. Mar Mar is displeased. Mar Mar wishes you to know that unbearable, horrific pain will soon come upon you. As I deliver this message, Mar Mar is thinking up wonderful ways to bring cruel anguish to you and anyone who dares to assist you in evading capture."

Jasette turned to me. "Should I shoot it?"

Even though the words were chiseling away any hope of survival, for some reason I wanted to hear it out. "Not yet."

"Mar Mar is coming to see you personally. Now that I've found you, your location is known, and his indestructible starship—which cannot be outrun, outgunned, or out maneuvered—is coming to find you and crush the worthless life from your bones. But not before he brings you great and enduring pain, of course."

"So dark and violent." Blix grimaced. "What a twisted soul that Mar Mar has."

"Mar Mar will be here soon," the android continued. "He wishes you to stay where you are until he arrives."

"Something's wrong." Jasette studied her forearm computer. "I'm getting increased energy readings. Her head snapped up to the trash freighter. "It's coming from his ship."

Several warning signals went off in my head. "Back to the ship. Hurry!"

Trying to flee back to the ship in slow, bounding motions was an incredibly frustrating experience. An accelerated hum of engines came from the trash freighter. I glanced back to find an orb of red light expanding at the top of the freighter and surrounding it in a translucent sphere. As we reached the landing ramp, there was a loud crackle not unlike lightning striking the ground, and a broad shell of red energy spread overhead and arced downward, covering both ships beneath a luminous dome.

"Oh no." Nelvan stared open mouthed at the field. "We're trapped."

"Not yet." Even though I was thinking the same thing, I couldn't give up yet.

CHAPTER 24

THE RED DOME

BACK ON THE BRIDGE, we all set to work at our stations.

"Iris," I said. "What's your analysis?"

"Oh, it's horrid, Glint. It's a triple-threaded, interstellar battle-rated, high-energy frontal shield. Typically employed by the forward troops of invading armadas during planetary conquest."

My heart sank a little. "That sounds hefty. Any chance of blasting through it?"

"No," Iris sounded like she was holding back tears. "Not with our firepower."

I frowned. "Blix, any of your gadgets helpful with this?"

"I'm afraid not, Captain. I'm running simulations coupling multiple devices with weaponry. So far, results have been thoroughly ineffective."

My body slouched against the chair. "Terrific. Jasette, you got anything?"

She shook her head. "I tried hacking into the trash freighter. The security wall is strong. I can't find any holes. I'd try to blow it externally, but the other ship is surrounded by the same shield." Her focus slid back to her computer. "I'll keep trying. Maybe there's a weak point."

My thoughts felt rushed and desperate. An impending capture started to feel inevitable. I couldn't imagine just sitting here on this remote moon waiting for Mar Mar to come and do horrible things.

"Nelvan?" I had come to appreciate the kid's advice. He considered things from different angles. Sure, his ideas were a little simplistic. But if he sparked any new thoughts that led to a possible escape, I wanted to hear it. "Any suggestions?"

In the span of a few freems, his youthful face contorted from anxious expressions to deep thought. "Well, I don't really understand the technology at work here, so I'm not sure how to defeat it."

I nodded, feeling for the kid thrown out of his own time.

"But . . ." Nelvan looked upward. "Didn't Iris say it was a frontal shield?"

"Yeah?" I said.

"Well, doesn't that mean it's only in front? I mean, it's not surrounding us, it's just over us. Maybe we could dig under it or something."

I lifted my eyebrows at Blix. "Anything there? What's beneath us?"

Blix's fingers danced across his control panel. "Fairly solid. No indication of underground sinkholes or tunnels. If we had a heavy quadra-drill, perhaps."

"Hmm," I scratched at the scruff on my cheek. I was imagining trying to get underneath the trash freighter when a thought suddenly hit me. "What about the rubble catch?"

"No," Blix said. "Not powerful enough to dig an escape tunnel underneath the shield."

"What's a rubble catch?" Nelvan said.

"It's for landings on unstable soil," I said. "In case some kind of rubble falls over your ship, it claws under it. Think of a shovel digging under a rock."

"Okay." Nelvan sounded unsure. "And how does that help?"

"It allows you to dig under the large object, then lift it away on takeoff. When you reach the right altitude, you dump it, then fly away. It works well for boulder piles, fallen structures . . ." I turned to Blix. ". . . trash freighters."

Blix grinned. "Captain, I think you may have something there."

The atmosphere in the bridge switched from desperation to hopeful anticipation. Blix ran some calculations, and Iris took the ship into a low hover. We inched close to the other ship and landed, and the rubble catch activated, digging through the ground underneath the trash freighter.

"Catch deployed," Iris said.

"How's it look, Blix?" I said.

"Fingers crossed, Captain."

"All right, Iris," I said. "Take us up. Slowly."

The engines powered to full and the ship trembled as we lifted off the ground. The trash freighter, still surrounded by the red shield, filled the forward visual of the viewing screen. It was slow going, but we were gaining altitude. A thrill went through me that it just might work.

"How you holding up, Iris?" I said.

"The burden is taxing me," Iris said. "But it's better than the claustrophobia I was feeling trapped under the shield."

An electric pulse went through the bridge, sending an uncomfortable current through me.

"What was that?" I said.

"The layer of moon dust and debris between the catch and the trash freighter is dissipating as we gain altitude," Blix said. "It seems when the shield around the other ship connects with the catch, it sends an electric surge through our ship. I'm guessing these surges will increase in frequency and intensity as we rise. Luckily, that shock was quite minimal."

Another surge went through the ship. This time, my skin continued to vibrate with pain for a few lingering moments.

"That really hurts." Nelvan rubbed his arm. "How bad is it going to get?"

"Really?" Blix looked perplexed. "I barely felt that."

"Iris, can we dump this thing yet?" I said.

"Target altitude has not been reached," Iris said. "Sorry, Glint. Should be soon."

Two more surges pulsed through the bridge. My skin felt like it was about to burst into flames. Nelvan cried out.

"Okay," Blix said. "I felt that one. Still not that bad, though."

"Speak for yourself." Jasette sounded winded. "Can we lose this freighter yet?"

Blix had his fingers poised over his control panel. "Almost. Hang in there, everyone."

Three successive pulses of energy flowed through the bridge. This time we all cried out in pain. I even caught Blix wincing.

"Please," Nelvan cried. "Make it stop."

"Target altitude reached," Iris said.

"Catch retracted!" Blix said.

"Hold on," Iris said.

The ship went into an accelerated dive toward the moon.

The grey surface rushed closer on the viewing screen. Just as it seemed like a crash landing was inescapable, the ship pulled up, trembling as we sped under and away from the descending red shield.

I gripped the armrests, waiting a few moments for my heart to slow. "Reverse view."

The viewing screen displayed the trash freighter, surrounded by the red dome, crashing back to the moon's surface.

"Are we clear?" I said.

"We're clear, Glint." Iris sounded exhilarated. "We made it."

"Yes!" Nelvan pumped a fist skyward.

The thrill of freedom flowed through me. "Great job, Iris. Now get us out of here before Mar Mar shows up."

"Powering engines to full."

The ship surged forward, and I melted back into the captain's chair in relief. Jasette turned back and flashed me a smile. "Great idea, Glint. It worked."

I shook my head, still amazed we were free. "Nelvan started it off. Plus, when I get desperate, my brain works faster."

"Keep those ideas coming," she said. "It's not over yet."

How right she was. It was a temporary freedom while the larger net closed in around us.

We sped through space for the next few trids using the darker, less-traveled paths en route to Glurivelle. The bridge was unusually quiet during the journey. Either everyone was coming up with plans of avoiding our pursuers, or the suffocating feeling of being on the run from superior forces was sinking in.

"Computer." I needed something to break the unspoken tension. "How close are we?"

"You just asked fifteen jemmins ago," Iris said. "But the current estimate is three trids, one jemmin, and five freems."

We were close. Not that Glurivelle would be perfectly safe, but there were plenty of spots to get lost among the heavy population and countless cities. A sensation of hope welled up in me that a hideout was within reach.

"We're almost there," Nelvan said. "Looks like we'll make it after all."

There was a moment of silence as I glared at Nelvan.

"What?" Nelvan held out his hands. "What did I say?"

"Why don't you just call out a death curse on us?" I said.

He frowned. "You think just because I said we're going to make it that we won't?"

"Yes!" I slammed my fist on the armrest. "Never say you've made it until you've actually made it. Everyone knows that."

"Captain," Blix shook his head. "Don't burden Nelvan with your baseless superstitions. The mere suggestion that negative events will occur simply because you verbalize positive ones is completely . . ." Blix trailed off as he leaned into his control station, scrutinizing the digital readouts. "Oh dear."

My heart sped up. "What is it?"

"Multiple readings," Blix said.

"On screen. Enhance activity."

The viewing screen filled with six arrow-shaped cruisers that zipped through space like hungry piranhas. A larger ship loomed behind them, it's dark hull blending in with the star field.

"Several elite star cruisers," Blix said. "I'm picking up a rather hefty battle cruiser as well, but it's blocking my scans."

I pointed to Nelvan. "See?"

Nelvan cast nervous glances between me and the viewing screen. "You're blaming me for this?"

"Of course."

"Stop talking crazy and get us out of here, Glint," Jasette said.

"Cruisers closing fast," Blix said.

"Iris," I said. "Shields up. Blix, can we take 'em out?"

"Maybe one or two before they overwhelm us, Captain. Their maneuvering abilities are advanced. But not to worry." He rubbed his thick hands together. "Iris, activate the false-signal spreader!"

A band of yellow energy formed over the viewing screen. I turned to Blix. "You actually got it working?"

A broad grin showcased his sharp teeth.

The yellow energy pulsated as it grew in size, then flared outward in a broad circle like a ripple in a lake. The star cruisers began to fly in frenetic patterns, as if each was after a different target.

"Aha." Blix pointed to the screen. "Waste of money, was it?"

I grinned. "I stand corrected. Iris, get us out of here while we've got the chance."

"Yes, Captain."

Our ship surged away, leaving the confused cruisers flying off in all directions.

"The battle cruiser's still pursuing." Jasette pointed at the viewing screen.

Blix's fingers danced across the controls. "It must have advanced scanning systems."

"More advanced than a two-thousand-vibe signal spreader?" I said.

"Apparently."

As we watched, the star cruisers recovered from their muddled flight patterns and fell in line beside the battle cruiser like an advancing army.

"What else you got?" I cast a desperate look to Blix. "Activate everything!"

A clunking sound came from the ceiling of the bridge. My breath caught as I scanned the ceiling. "What was that?" At any moment I expected a giant crack to form, letting the dark vacuum of space lift me into its cold embrace.

Two more clunking sounds came from the walls.

"Something has attached to my hull," Iris said. "My shields couldn't stop it. Electronic devices. Operations unknown."

Dozens of clunking sounds came from every side.

"Blix," I said. "Talk to me."

Blix was busy at his console. "Sensors are scrambled. Judging by the interference, I'd wager the devices attached to our hull are signal transmitters."

"Tracking clamps." Jasette gave a slow turn to face me. "A hunter has us."

CHAPTER 25

SORGIL X

THE VIEWING SCREEN flickered on. A pantherman with a shiny coat of olive-green and brown fur lounged on a captain's chair in a sleek, technologically advanced bridge. He was decked out in high-grade battle armor save for his head. Two armor-clad guards stood just behind him, quad-barreled repeaters slung over their shoulders. Several palm-sized cam bots hovered around the pantherman. He displayed a triumphant smile, showcasing a mouth full of thick, sharp teeth.

"Greetings to my prey." His voice was deep and resonant with rumbling undertones. "Nice to see you again, Jasette. You're looking more beautiful than ever."

"Sorgil X. Bounty hunter to the stars." Jasette uttered the title with a mocking voice. "Aren't you late for some Glittronium party?"

Sorgil X put his armor-clad feet up on a dark console, accentuating his relaxed composure. "Oh, you're not still sore at me for stealing that bounty on Blendark 9, are you? Nothing personal. Just following the bounty hunters' code."

Jasette huffed a laugh. "Since when do hunters have a code?"

He gave a wicked-looking grin. "Yes, I suppose not. Well, if it will make amends, I'll let you go after I take your friend Glint. I need to get him to Mar Mar to collect a rather generous bounty.

"What makes you think we'll let you take him?" Jasette said.

Sorgil X gave a soft chuckle with just a hint of purr. "Well, just to bring you up to speed, I have multiple weapons locked on your ship, my tractor beam is engaged, and even if you managed to get away—which, by the way, is impossible considering your technology—your ship is covered in tracking clamps that will tell me where you are at every moment."

The guards behind Sorgil X shared a gruff laugh.

"Besides that," Sorgil X continued, "I can see your navigation settings were bound for the planet Glurivelle. Let me guess: you wanted to get lost among the citizens and go undercover as trash collectors."

"Culinary artists," Blix corrected.

Sorgil X let out a hearty laugh. "Priceless."

I was about to hurl threats and bravado at this cocky hunter when Blix broke in.

"Sorgil X." Blix spoke as though addressing a visiting dignitary. "I must say I appreciate not only your style but your clever wit. Your recent contribution on the uniweb regarding celebrity gossip and its circular effect on cultural trends was fascinating."

Sorgil X paused, the soft ears on the top of his head perking up a little. "Um, thank you . . . Wait a moment—didn't I see you in Glittronium?"

"Indeed. We met briefly at *The Iron Gauntlet* competitors after party."

"Of course." He slapped a paw to his head. "Blix. I knew you looked familiar. You had the finely crafted throwing blades, right?"

Blix drew his hand along the bandolier of daggers crossing his torso. "Authentic tempered Heljian steel."

"Magnificent. You should have stayed at the party. We were up all night."

I cleared my throat loudly. "Is everybody friends with the guy trying to kill me? How 'bout you Nelvan? Did you guys hang out and party?"

"Nelvan?" Sorgil X pointed at the boy. "Hey, you're the kid with the silver old-Earth suit. You won the fashion award at that after party, right?"

Nelvan gave a shy nod. "Yes, that was a fun night."

"You can say that again." Sorgil X laughed. "I met two Resklin women who couldn't keep their hands off me." He put his hands behind his head and looked up as if lost in thought. "Ah, but such is the life of a dashing, successful bounty hunter."

"Look, since we're all such good friends," I said. "Why don't you do us a favor and let us go."

"Can't do it, pal," Sorgil X said. "Again, nothing personal. I loved your performance in *The Iron Gauntlet*. A true underdog story. Unfortunately, I made a hefty bet against you, and it cost me a bundle when you emerged the victor. So, you see, my funds are rather low at the moment, and my lifestyle—glamorous as it may look to my fans—isn't cheap. Your bounty is just what I need."

"I can get you the money," My voice sounded a little

desperate. "A changeling stole my *Iron Gauntlet* prize money. I know who she is and how you can find her. That's a million vibes. I'll split it with you!" Of course I had no idea where Silvet had gone after she stole my money or how I could possibly find her, but it was the only thing I could think of at the moment.

"Changeling?" Sorgil X bared his teeth, looking as if he were about to growl at me. "I had a bad experience with a bounty that was a changeling. Spent a lot of time and money on her pursuit and she still got away. I prefer predictable bounties like you. Plus, I have the cam bots running for my latest movie. I'm compiling volume fifteen of *Extreme Bounty Hunting with Sorgil X*. You're perfect for it. Former *Iron Gauntlet* victor and one of the few who have escaped Mar Mar the Unthinkable's fortress." He shook his head in disbelief. "You'll be the centerpiece of my movie."

"You self-serving pig." Jasette glared up at the viewing screen.

Sorgil X broke into a broad grin. "My dear Jasette. Never one to mince words, were you? Look, I'm not coldhearted. You and the others can go. I just need Glint and his ship."

"My ship? Why?"

"Mar Mar offers another ten thousand vibes for your ship. Wants to make an example of it or some nonsense. You know, smash it to bits and show everyone what happens to a ship that tries to escape his kingdom. Typical Mar Mar."

Iris gasped. "That monster! Glint, you can't let him do that to me."

"Don't worry, Iris." I held up my hands. "Okay Sorgil X, you win. I'll come peacefully. Just let my crew and ship go free."

For a moment, I couldn't believe those words had just come out of my mouth. There was still time to weasel my way out of this. What was I thinking being all heroic and self-sacrificing?

"Glint!" Jasette fixed me with stern eyes and shook her head.

"Very classy of you, Glint, but the answer is no," Sorgil X said. "The best I can do is drop your crew off at Krullnack. It's the only habitable planet nearby." Sorgil X snapped his fingers at someone beyond sight of the viewing screen. "Take us down to Krullnack. I want a clean landing. Don't stir up too much dust and wreck the cam bot visuals." He looked back at me. "We land in five jemmins. Don't try anything funny."

The visual switched off and returned to a view of the star field outside.

How much could I trust the word of a bounty hunter? It was one of the top-three worst star pilot dilemmas, next to *Should I run shipments for interstellar thugs?* and *If she's hot, does it really matter if she has four arms and hovers?*

The big question, of course, was whether Sorgil X would let my crew go. I didn't have many options either way. Even with a miraculous escape today, my bounty was so high I'd just get captured by another hunter eventually. Ultimately, if my doom was sealed, maybe I could still save Jasette and my crew.

"Most unfortunate," Blix said. "He seemed like such a nice fellow."

"He's a creep." Jasette was back to work on her computer. "He's only out for himself. Blast! And his ship's security is flawless."

"Oh, Glint," Iris said. "You won't let them take me, will you? I still have so much love left to give."

I rubbed my temples. "Working on it, Iris. Any chance of breaking away from his ship?"

"I'm afraid not. His tractor beam is very strong. It's dragging me against my will. I'm helpless."

At this point, I couldn't think of anything left to do but ride it out till we got to the planet.

"Blix," I said. "What do you have on the planet Krullnack? I've never been there."

Blix tapped out a few controls at his station. "Habitable climate for humans. Dry, hot summers and cold winters. Small farming communities scattered throughout the higher altitudes." He turned to me. "Nothing too noteworthy."

I nodded. "Okay, everyone. Once we land, if you see a chance to escape, take it."

The ship descended through layers of clouds until a ravine-covered terrain stretched out before us. It looked as though some giant, cosmic beast had used the surface of the planet as a scratching post. A bright sun shone overhead, bleaching the brown terrain.

"We have to do something." Nelvan's hands stretched out in a pleading gesture. "We can't just let him take the captain."

"You're right." Jasette undid her seat harness and stood, facing us. "We can hide out in the maintenance chute. As they spread out to find us, ambush them one at a time."

"Perhaps." Blix looked thoughtful. "But they're clad in high-grade battle armor. Our chances are minimal."

"Nobody's doing anything." A sense of resolve filled me. It was a strange mix of calm and impending doom. I'd never been one to give myself for a cause. The way I saw it, causes come and go in the universe. I preferred to stay alive. But staying alive without Jasette just didn't hold the power it once had. "We're going to wait this one out awhile. Play it smart. Wait for the right moment."

Jasette frowned. "What if the right moment doesn't come along?"

"Think positive. Besides, we need to see what we're up against first."

She looked at me for several moments. "This doesn't sound like you. What're you doing?"

"Nothing. Just playing it safe."

"That definitely doesn't sound like him," Nelvan said.

"We're outmatched." I broke from my fake composure. "At least you guys have a shot to get out of here. I'll go with Sorgil X and look for an opportunity. I've been in tougher scrapes than this."

"Captain," Blix said. "As courageous as that sounds, if he takes you, there's very little chance we'll see you again."

"Just get Jasette and her flower back to Jelmontaire. At least I'll know something good came out of all this."

Blix sat back in his chair with a broad smile. "Just when you think you know somebody. Captain, I must say—"

Ten armor-clad guards materialized on the bridge, their quad-barreled repeaters trained on our heads. The viewing screen flickered back to Sorgil X.

"We're landing," he said. "My guards will escort you out."

CHAPTER 26

KRULLNACK

THE GUARDS FASTENED our wrists behind our back with red holding orbs. The energy from the orbs turned painful if you strained against it to gain escape. They marched us out single file to the cracked, brown surface of Krullnack. I squinted in the bright sun, looking for any sign of a settlement. All was dry ground and deep ravines framed by a low mountain range in the distance. There were scattered groupings of rocky hills amidst jagged strips of land that separated the ravines. Vegetation was sparse other than a few squat bushes and trails of grey moss. The air was dry and smelled like burnt toast.

"Welcome to Krullnack." Sorgil X had his arms spread wide as he walked toward us. He was almost as tall as Blix, and his thick neck hinted at a powerful physique hidden under his battle armor. Cam bots circled around him, recording his actions from multiple angles. "My crew is setting up a temporary shelter." He motioned to a dozen guards putting together a sturdy series of poles and olive-green tarps. "We have some nice refreshments ready at the shelter. My crew will help you indulge." He smoothed back the fur on his cheeks. "I'll join you soon. I need to get some heroic footage with this landscape as a backdrop. Helps elevate the drama of my adventures." He gave a sly grin and headed off to the ravine's edge, the circling cam bots following close.

Being hand fed gourmet meats and cheeses by armor-plated guards was a strange experience. The good news was the food was delicious. Fine cuts of tender meat that practically melted in your mouth coupled with complementary bites of spicy cheeses. I washed it all down with a rich, sweet broth that I would've loved to guzzle but instead had to drink through a straw. All in all, the best captive food I'd ever had and far better than the economy bulk meals I kept aboard my ship.

Surprisingly, the guards were chatty. Once the shelter was built, they removed their helmets, took several drinks from metal canisters, and started telling stories about past bounty adventures. Most of the guards were tough men with chiseled features who had high hopes of being featured in Sorgil X's movie and turning that exposure into a movie career in Glittronium. A few were larger in stature. These were panthermen similar to Sorgil X, with coats ranging from dark orange with black spots to deep crimson with purple stripes. The panthermen were less talkative. They sat back and grinned at the tales of adventure, occasionally correcting exaggerations, but always keeping a careful watch on us.

Blix and I joined in on the tale telling, garnering some camaraderie in the process. My hope was to get them to relax their watch on us or feel bad about the capture of such stand-up space explorers. Our aspirations were dashed early and repeatedly throughout the conversations. Every so often, as if part of their bounty-hunter training, they would say things like, "You guys ain't half bad. Pity we gotta turn ya in, but thems the rules. Can't go making exceptions, or the whole thing falls apart."

After several trids under the shelter, the sun set and a blood-red moon began to rise. Moonlight fell across the landscape, painting everything in a reddish hue. Sorgil X returned and took the men aside for a hushed conference.

Nelvan was sitting right next to me. As I strained to hear what Sorgil X was talking about, he spoke up. "Captain, this is the place."

I shot him an annoyed look for taking my attention away from the guards' conference. "What place?"

"The place I saw in my future vision. You know, the ravines, the red moon. This is it. This is where you and Jasette were cornered by that big creature."

"He's right." Jasette sat on the other side of Nelvan, casting a dreamlike stare at the horizon. "This is the place I saw too. I didn't recognize it before the moon came out."

"This is also the place where I saw you—" Nelvan's lip trembled as he met my eyes, then looked away.

If I didn't already feel ruined, Nelvan had just sealed it. My desperate theory of the android clone of me being the thing that Nelvan saw lying dead was slipping away. But for some reason, resolve welled up within me. Whether it was my stubbornness or desperate urge to avoid death, I was determined this wouldn't be my final resting place.

"It's not going to happen." I spoke the words with conviction, my eyes set on the red moon.

Nelvan sniffed. "It isn't?"

"No. It's not going to happen." I repeated the words so I could hear them again. I wanted them to ring in my head, resonating until they were one with my iron will. I'd talked my way out of bad situations in the past. Now I was going to talk myself out of a cursed future. With things at this level of grim, I hung onto that thought with every ounce of inner strength I had.

Sorgil X strode back toward us, his guards following behind like a wall of power.

"I'm afraid I have some bad news." His face had lost its jovial bluster. "I just spoke with Mar Mar. He wants all of you." He looked down at the ground. "I'm sorry. I really wanted to let the rest of you go free."

He turned and walked to the far side of the shelter, the guards following suit.

My head felt thick. The calming thought that even if I was taken, at least my crew would get away was gone.

It was at that moment that Nelvan disappeared.

CHAPTER 27

THE HUNTERS
AND THE HUNTED

I STARED AT THE EMPTY SPOT where Nelvan had sat a moment ago, thinking the kid had the luckiest timing of anyone.

"Hey!" A dark-grey pantherman with crimson stripes stared at us. "Sorgil X, the boy's escaped."

Sorgil X and the guards hurried over in a thunder of footsteps and clanking metal.

"Where'd he go?" Sorgil X was alternating between scanning the horizon behind us and giving us dark looks.

This was my only chance to bluff our way out of this. "You're not the only one with technological surprises."

He leaned over, coming eye to eye with me. His yellow eyes had jagged flecks of black and looked very deadly at that moment. "Tell me where he is. Now!" A low growl followed his statement.

Although I quivered on the inside, I met his eyes with my best steely gaze. "He has a micro teleportation device. Nelvan goes where he wants, when he wants. He's probably in your ship right now, causing some nice damage."

He narrowed his eyes. "The only device powerful enough to do that is the size of my arm and costs more money that you could afford."

My brain scrambled for something believable. "He's a covert cyborg. The device is implanted inside his leg."

Sorgil X leaned back and let out a hearty laugh. "That's the best tale I've heard in a long while, Glint."

I couldn't back out now. I was in too deep. "Check his records. You'll see he has none. He's my ace in the hole for situations like this."

Sorgil X paused a moment, then snapped at one of his guards. "Check it out."

The guard activated a control on his chest plate and a thin, translucent green screen slid out. His fingers tapped away for a few moments, his eyes studying the data. His expression went from studied to surprised. He looked up at Sorgil X. "He's right. No records. The kid is a ghost."

Sorgil X bared his dangerous teeth. "Where is he? What's he doing?"

I shrugged. "He does what he wants. I maintain little control over someone of his abilities. I'm just glad he joined my crew."

Sorgil X signaled several of his men. "Check the ship. Thorough sweep."

Six guards broke off from the group and rushed into their ship. He took the rest of his guards to the far corner of the shelter, speaking in hushed tones.

"Now's our chance." Jasette spoke with quiet resolve. She nudged her toes against the ankle of her other foot and appeared to be activating a control. An electric buzzing went through her power suit, and the next thing I knew, her hands were free. She kept her movements subtle, opening a section of her utility belt at her back. "Okay, get ready."

"Ready for what?" I whispered.

"To run." With that, she leapt to her feet and flung a handful of black spheres at Sorgil X and the guards. The spheres expanded as they flew through the air, then hit the guards, wrapping them in a tar-like substance. The guards, now coated in black goo, spun and writhed in confusion.

Jasette moved behind me in a blur. Another buzzing sound, and suddenly my hands were free. By the time I drew my DEMOTER X, she'd freed Blix as well.

"Come on." She helped me to my feet and we bolted from the shelter.

My eyes scanned the ravine-covered ground for possible escape routes. "Where are we going?"

She motioned to a downward slope leading into a narrow ravine. "There."

We sprinted down the slope, which proved to be a risky endeavor. The soil was loose, and rubble was strewn across the path. I came close to a face-plant a few times but was lucky enough to regain my footing.

"Remember the path we took." Blix ran at my side. "We'll need to get back to our ship eventually."

I nodded, wondering where we were going and how we could recapture the ship with guards stationed just outside.

Moss trailed down from the ravine tops and rocks dotted the ground. The path split into three just ahead—a wide, jagged ravine to our left, and to our right a path just wide enough for the three of us to travel side by side. It looked as though it sloped downward.

"The path on the right." I motioned to it. "More cover."

"Risky," Blix said. "It's narrow, and it might be a dead end. Jasette?"

Jasette glanced at me, then back at the paths. "Let's go right."

We headed down the path for a few jemmins. Without warning, there came a sharp bend that felt like it was taking us back in the direction of the ship. We shared concerned glances with each other, an unspoken worry that we were headed back to our captors.

Jasette drew one of her silver pistols, keeping it handy as we ran.

A rumbling noise sounded overhead. One of Sorgil X's guards hovered over the ravine, his rocket boots flaring with orange flames. Jasette immediately aimed skyward and let loose a few beams of energy, but a green, translucent shield formed around the guard, and the blasts diffused on impact. He went into a controlled dive and swept over the ground directly before us, landing in a stylish pose. It was the pantherman with the grey-and-crimson striped fur. A few streaks of black goo still clung to his armor. Fast as lighting, two sleek, chrome-plated laser pistols were in his hands.

"Hold it there." His face was grim.

We skidded to a stop a few yards in front of him.

"Nice try, but you can't get away," he said. "Lower your weapons."

Jasette holstered her silver pistol. His green shield disappeared.

"And you." He motioned to Jasette with his gun. "You'll be cleaning my armor till it sparkles. Understand?"

"Not a chance," Jasette said.

He holstered one of his pistols and retrieved a shock

baton. When he activated it, red energy sparked around the end. "You sure about that?"

"You're the one that got hit with blast sludge," she said. "You clean it."

His lip curled into a wicked sneer, showcasing his dangerous teeth. "I'll be watching you like a hawk from now on. No more catching me with my back turned."

A meteor plummeted from the sky, headed right for us. Before any of us could react, it hit the ground next to the guard, clipping his shoulder in the process. He spun and crumpled to the ground. The dust settled around the meteor showing a white, oval object.

A spider bot.

My bones hollowed. I could barely speak the awful truth. "Casglo found us."

CHAPTER 28

METEOR BOTS

I WAS BY THIS TIME painfully familiar with the spider-bot meteors. Thin metal legs extended from the droid, lifting it off the earth. The red light at the front of the oval bot scanned the motionless body of the guard. My only chance of survival was to not allow these things to identify me. I drew the DEMOTER and sent two blasts into it, tearing open its metal shell and sending its spindly legs flying. The mangled metal lay in the dirt next to the guard, both unmoving.

Blix shook his head. "This isn't good."

I holstered my weapon. "You're telling me."

"We should move," Jasette said.

I nodded and led the way forward. Thankfully, the path veered off, away from Sorgil X and his ship.

"Look!" Jasette pointed to the reddened sky.

Dozens of spider-bot meteors now streaked overhead. They were all headed in different directions, as if trying to cover all areas of the planet's surface. My thoughts scattered, desperate for any plan that could escape capture. "We need to get out of sight."

"My thoughts exactly, Captain," Blix said.

There was a crossroads up ahead. Two narrow passages diverged in a *Y* shape.

"Which way?" Jasette said.

"Who knows? How 'bout right?"

She nodded.

Apparently, I'd chosen poorly. As I sped around the corner, two of Sorgil X's armor-clad guards came flying toward me, powered by their rocket boots. An electric netting spread out between them and was just freems away from wrapping around me. I skidded to a stop.

There was no time to react. Yet even as I stood there, something big collided with me and I was pushed aside. I hit the ground, just missing a pile of sharp rocks. When I glanced back, it was to find Blix had pushed me to safety and taken my place. The guards netted Blix and lifted him skyward. Jasette had her pistols drawn, following their ascent with her barrels. She sent a trail of energy beams after them. Green shields surrounded them, deflecting her blasts as they flew away.

I watched helplessly as they took Blix over the ridge of the ravine. My last sight was of a struggle taking place that made their flight pattern erratic. I imagined him smashing their expensive armor plating to pieces. The thought gave me hope he might escape.

Three spider-bot meteors hit the ground just ahead.

"Hurry." Jasette ran toward them, pistols drawn. "Before they see us."

I scrambled after her, sending wild shots from the

DEMOTER toward the bot farthest from Jasette to avoid any accidents. My blasts finally connected and blew the bot into the ravine wall with a nice crunching sound. A curtain of moss fell away from the wall where the bot hit, revealing a narrow passage.

Jasette took out the second bot and was already firing at the last one. It sprang up, it's red eye sweeping across the ravine floor. Just before she blew it to bits, the red light hit me.

Jasette shot it once more, either to make sure it was destroyed or to release leftover tension, then turned to me. "Did it see you?"

I paused, unwilling to admit the truth. "Maybe."

Her shoulders slouched. "Great. Now what?"

Several meteor bots shot through the sky overhead, heading toward a nearby ravine.

"This place is going to be crawling with bots soon," I said. "Maybe even Casglo. There might be a cave over there." I motioned to the narrow passage in the ravine wall.

"Really?" She hurried over.

We met in front of the passage, which looked more like a crack in the wall, just big enough for us to enter single file. It was dark inside, and the crimson moon wasn't helping to illuminate the unknown. Jasette activated the green shoulder lights on her power suit and moved to the opening.

I peered over her shoulder. The passage went deep into the rock. The green lights revealed a passage that curved upward into the darkness.

"You think it's safe?" I said.

"Well, it's not safe out here."

"Right." I retrieved my communicator and activated its blue com light. "Okay let's check it out."

"Wait." Jasette picked up some of the fallen moss nearby. "Let's cover this up like it was before."

We set to work gathering a good pile of moss, then filled up the entrance to the narrow cave as best we could. Most of the opening was soon covered, cutting off all but a few rays of moonlight that managed to break through. It felt like I was sealing up my own tomb.

Jasette's shoulder lights bathed her face in a green hue. "Ready?"

"Let's just hope there's nothing in here waiting for us." I headed deeper into the narrow passage, holding the blue com light in one hand, the DEMOTER in the other. In case any cave creatures attacked, I wanted to be ready.

The passage went straight ahead at a sharp incline. There were no carvings or other indications it was hewn by an intelligent being. The more likely and more frightening possibility was that some creature had dug its way through with deadly claws and now lay huddled in some dark corner of its den, waiting for us.

The tunnel continued upward until it seemed as though we must be near the top of the ravine. A dim red light shone on the ceiling up ahead, revealing a leveling out of the passage. I slowed my advance as the incline came to an end.

A triangular-shaped space opened up about half the size of the bridge on my ship. Moonlight shone through cracks on the angled walls before us. My guess was this cave was positioned near the top of the ravine walls like some ancient watchtower. In several spots the outer cracks opened wide enough to fit my fist through, giving a bird's-eye view of the planet's surface.

"This beats the dark, creepy cave I expected," I said.

Jasette peered over my shoulder, then pulled me backward. "Look out!"

As I hit the side of the passage, I discovered what she was talking about. A skeletal creature with darkened eyes and a fanged mouth that could easily bite my head off was only a few feet away.

CHAPTER 29

SKELETAL WARRIOR

MY HEART RACED as I drew the DEMOTER and fired a few blasts at the skeletal creature. My aim was off because I was half leaning, half falling against the wall of the passage and my adrenaline was flying. Still, I was able to graze the side of the creature's head. Part of his skull blew off with a puff of dust. Several things became clear. The skeletal creature hadn't moved, even after I blasted it, and it had a thick layer of dust on it.

"I think it's dead," I said.

"Ya think?" Jasette moved around me, heading farther into the cave.

Upon closer examination, the creature appeared to be a long-dead giant serpent of some kind. At this point it was mostly skeletal, with patches of dried scales still clinging to the bones. A heavy layer of dust lay over the long curve of its body.

A sadder discovery was the remains of a humanoid creature underneath. It was part skeleton, part dried grey skin. A few pieces of leather armor still covered the body. It lay on the ground, frozen in the position of lifting a metal spear into the underbelly of the snake. Apparently, it had been the last stand for both of them.

I knelt close to the humanoid skeleton. "Brutal."

"Yeah. At least he took the serpent out with him."

The leather chestplate was fashioned for a female. "Not he. She."

Jasette knelt down beside me. She grinned. "Good for her. Shame she didn't get away."

"Wonder how long ago this happened?"

Jasette shook her head. "I don't know, but don't move anything. It's like her heroic moment in time, captured forever. An ongoing tribute."

"Okay, don't get all corny on me."

She smiled and stood. "Let's check out this crack. Maybe we can see what's happening outside."

The crack in the wall turned out to grant a better view of the surrounding area than we could have hoped. I could see the landscape far into the distance.

"Finally, we catch a break," I said.

"I think I see our ship." Jasette hit a few controls on her computer and a translucent green screen expanded outward.

"Really?" I moved close to her and strained to see through the crack. Several bot meteors continued to fall from the sky.

Jasette held the screen before her as she looked out of the crack. "Magnify."

With a few blips, her screen zoomed in on a spot in the distance.

"Yep," she said. "And there's Sorgil X's battle cruiser and his fleet right next to it. Looks like the guards are pinned down in the shelter."

I watched the guards moving in the green-hued view of her screen. A few spider bots crawled close to the shelter. The guards had their repeaters at the ready and blew them back as they approached. Dozens of destroyed bots lay scattered around the shelter.

"At least there's something besides us to hold their attention," I said.

"Yeah, too bad they're not after them. Can you contact Blix? Send him a thought message?"

"I tried. Every time, I get that tight pressure in the temples. They're blocking it."

"Figures. They've got advanced tech over there."

Farther in the distance, I noticed a towering structure. "There's a large building over there." I motioned to it. "I thought Blix said there were only simple farming communities on this planet."

Jasette moved her screen toward the structure. Unfortunately, it wasn't a building.

"Casglo's ship." Her words were like a knife in my heart. "He knows we're here."

"Just one more thing to slip past before we get back to the ship," I said.

"Oh, sure," she laughed. "Thousands of metal spiders, a massive cat made out of nanobots, and a dozen thugs in high-tech armor. Easy."

"Either way we'll make it a good fight." I motioned to the skeleton warrior woman. "Just like our friend over there."

As I took in the creepy sight of the snake creature's and woman's skeletons locked in eternal combat, something sparkled on the woman's hand.

"Hmm." I made my way over.

Jasette looked over her shoulder. "What?"

I kneeled beside the skeleton woman and looked at her hand. "I saw something."

A delicate, silver ring sat on the remains of her finger. The craftsmanship wasn't crude like I'd expected to see on some cave-hunting, serpent-slaying warrior. The filigree band was the work of a true artisan. The intertwined design gathered at the top of her finger in a delicate spiral. Mounted on the spiral was a polished, oval-shaped sapphire.

"What is it?" Jasette said.

"A really nice ring." I nudged the sapphire for a better look and the ring slid off her withered finger to the stone ground with a clinking sound.

"What'd you do?" Jasette spoke in a scolding voice. "I told you not to touch anything."

"It was an accident." I retrieved the ring and admired it for a moment. It looked like it might fetch a good price.

Jasette walked over to me. "Let me see that."

"Here." I handed it up to her.

She turned it over in her hand. Her face softened. "It's exquisite. I've never seen anything quite like it."

I stood to admire it with her. "How much you think we could get for it?"

She gave me a cross look. "We're not selling this. It wouldn't be right."

I could already see this was a losing battle. "All right, then it's my gift to you."

Jasette smirked. "It's not really yours to give."

"Hey, I found it."

She rolled her eyes and slipped the ring on her second finger. "Look at that. Perfect fit."

"Yeah, but you have it on the wrong finger."

A crinkled line of confusion formed between her brows. "What do you mean?"

"There's an old Earth custom my uncle told me about. When he was in love with my aunt, he gave her a ring, and she always wore it on her fourth finger to show they were committed to each other."

She raised her brow. "What are you saying?"

I shrugged. "Just something to think about." At this point, a few things had become very clear. I knew if there was any way to escape from the nightmare gathering around me, I didn't want to be apart from Jasette.

She nodded, a smirk still hanging on her lips, and lifted the ring in front of her face. "It's so beautiful. A ring like this shouldn't gather dust in a cave." She looked at the fallen warrior woman. "I'm sure she'd want it to see the light of day again and pass it on to future generations."

I chuckled. "Of course. *She's* the one that would want that."

Jasette narrowed her eyes in a playful manner and went back to the crack in the wall. Yawning, I joined her as she continued to scan the horizon with her magnification screen, following her gaze across the ravine-scarred landscape. The toll of the stress and excitement of the day were catching up with me.

After a few moments, my eyes grew tired of looking at the screen, and I slumped to the ground with my back propped against the wall. I leaned my head back and closed my eyes. Sleep was right there if I wanted it, and at the moment, I really wanted it. "I think I'm gonna rest a little."

The sound of a few descending blips indicated she'd

deactivated the magnification screen. She sat down next to me on the ground. "Good idea. Whatever's coming next, we should be rested up."

I reached over and took her hand. "Here's hoping we don't end up like Snake Warrior over there."

She leaned over and kissed me on the cheek, then rested her head on my shoulder. As hard as the ground and wall were, I couldn't imagine being in a better place than with Jasette nestled up against me. I closed my eyes, feeling relaxed, and within moments I was asleep.

"Glint, wake up." Jasette scrambled to her feet.

I rubbed my eyes. "What is it?"

"A ship passed overhead." She activated her magnification screen and scanned the horizon.

"I must've been out cold. I didn't hear anything."

"I've always been a light sleeper."

I stood and watched Jasette's screen. "How long were we asleep?"

"A couple trids." She touched a spot on her screen. "There it is. Magnify."

The screen zoomed in on a heavy battle cruiser landing in the distance. It was an impressive ship of death that instantly inspired a spirit of surrender. Laser turrets and cannons covered every inch of it. The landing ramp lowered, and row upon row of fembots with laser swords marched out of it in perfect unison.

"Mar Mar." The words came out of my mouth in a whisper.

Jasette looked at me with concern. "Okay, this is bad."

"Like it wasn't bad before?"

"Well, now it's much worse."

I watched in silence as endless fembot troops marched out of the battle cruiser. As the troops finally came to end, the landing ramp stood vacant for several moments. Just when a sliver of hope sprang up that no further horrors were coming out of that ship, a towering figure emerged. The grey skinned, black-armor-clad terror known as Mar Mar the Unthinkable strode down the ramp.

I gasped when I realized his body had undergone some hideous transformations. Not only that, they were the same transformations I'd seen in my nightmare when Jasette morphed into him and tried to pull me off a balcony.

"What happened to him?" Jasette said.

I was having trouble accepting that my dream had become a reality. But the changes were undeniable—gruesome red arms with clawed hands grew out of his shoulders, and even more hideous, a thick scorpion-like tail curved up from his back, ending in a nasty stinger. Obviously being stuck in a wormhole can tweak your dreams a little. Messing with time space must've given me a vision of the future. "The Emerald Enigma. It changed him."

Jasette shook her head. "He looked bad enough before this."

A scratching sound came from the tunnel that led into our cave. Jasette and I exchanged a nervous glance, then rushed to the mouth of the tunnel, pistols drawn. The passage was dark. I aimed the blue com light into the blackness, but only a few yards ahead were illuminated.

The scratching grew in volume and intensity. It was heading right for us.

CHAPTER 30

CAVE AMBUSH

WE RUSHED to the far end of the cave and crouched low, pistols drawn and leveled at the tunnel exit. The scratching grew louder, making my skin prickle. Suddenly a spider bot sprang from the tunnel and landed in the middle of the cave. It steadied with a bouncing motion on its steel legs. For a brief moment, its red eye swept through the cave right before our combined energy blasts ripped it apart.

Two more bots crawled out of the tunnel, this time moving in erratic motions as if trying to avoid being blasted. Luckily, the DEMOTER X has a healthy blast radius, so even though my aim wasn't dead on, I still sent the nasty bots flying.

Everything was quiet for a few moments.

"You think that's it?" I said.

The answer to my question was a thunderous sound of screeching metal coming down the tunnel. Jasette fumbled through her utility belt and drew out a golden cube. It was another energy disrupter just like the one she'd used at Bleelebach.

I smiled at her. "I love you."

"Always buy a spare." She rushed toward the opening and flung the cube down the tunnel, then dove away as a golden light shone brightly and a choir of metallic screeches echoed from the passage. Everything went silent. I moved close to the tunnel, pistol held at the ready. Jasette joined me at the mouth of the cave.

"I think you got 'em," I said.

She nodded. "I hope so. That was my last disrupter."

"This place isn't safe anymore."

Jasette gave the skeletal warrior a final look and nodded. "Okay, let's go."

We hurried back through the tunnel as quickly as we could with a trail of dead spider bots carpeting the pathway. My com light combined with Jasette's shoulder beams helped reveal the tunnel a few yards ahead, but there was enough murky blackness in the distance to keep me on edge.

The red moon illuminated the opening, where most of the mossy covering had been moved away by the bots. I crept to the exit and peered into the ravine, pistol at my side. Instead of the swarm of bots I'd expected to see, the area was empty.

"Are there more out there?" Jasette whispered behind me.

"No. It's clear."

"There'll be more soon. Hurry."

I sprinted out of the tunnel and headed down the ravine with Jasette at my side.

We'd only been traveling for a few moments when dozens of bot meteors streamed overhead, descending toward the cave entrance. We were far enough away to avoid being trapped, but there was still a chance they could spot us.

Jasette grabbed my arm and pulled toward a narrow ravine that branched off. "This way."

We ducked into the narrow passage and headed forward, safe for the moment from the searching red eyes. The path cut a jagged line through the sheer rock walls at either side. As good as it was to be on a more secluded trail, the high walls of the tight passage made for a claustrophobic journey.

The passage ended abruptly with wider paths cutting angles in both directions. The right path led off to an even narrower zig-zagging, so I turned to the broader path on the left. I was relieved to find a more spacious passage—until I discovered we weren't the only ones on it.

I froze. Not more than ten yards in front of me stood Lerk Buzzane, several of his Zeuthian thugs, and about a dozen of Mar Mar's fembots armed with red laser swords. They turned at our approach, looking surprised.

If the DEMOTER hadn't already been in my hand and they hadn't been taken off guard, that would have been the end of me. But instinct and fear urged me to action. I blasted the two foremost fembots off their feet, sending them careening back into their fellow robots. Jasette was right with me then, sending three fembots sprawling to the ground with the accurate beams of her energy pistols.

We doubled back and took the opposite path. Thankfully it angled away from the Zeuthians, so when their return fire came at us, it blasted harmlessly against the rock walls behind us.

Lerk screamed at his thugs to go after us.

"Is there anyone on this planet that doesn't want to kill me?" I said.

The new passage proved difficult for fast travel. The walls

jutted in at awkward angles, and piles of rock littered the path. The main benefit, of course, was that our pursuers had a blocked target of our fleeing backs.

Jasette retrieved a black sphere from her utility belt about the size of my thumb. She pressed a button on top and the sphere started flashing red.

"What's that?" I said.

"A present for our new friends." She flung the sphere behind us, near the base of a jagged wall as the path wound around it. We continued for a few freems in silence before an explosion sounded. The ground trembled, followed by the unmistakable sound of a rockslide behind us. The muffled screeches and rending of metal from the fembots brought a smile to my face.

I nodded at Jasette. "Nice."

A triumphant feeling went through me. Maybe we could thread our way through the maze of these ravines and escape after all.

I ran with a renewed hope around a tight corner . . . only to be greeted by a dead end.

CHAPTER 31

THE END OF GLINT STARCROST

JASETTE AND I CAME to a sudden halt. The passage had ended in a square-shaped clearing surrounded by steep, high walls. If someone has designed a trap for wandering travelers, it would have looked very similar.

"Great." I slouched, winded from our panic-driven run. "Just what we needed."

Jasette leaned over with her hands on her knees, trying to catch her breath. "Hopefully they won't be able to get through for a while."

I moved farther into the clearing, scanning for a possible way up. The rock wall was too sheer. With a cautious, labored climb it might be possible, but there was no telling how long Jasette's rock slide would slow our pursuers.

Jasette pointed to the top of the wall. "My energy string could probably get me up there." She looked back at me. "I could take the high ground. Take them out before they get you."

My options were very sad, but if there was a chance Jasette

could get away in time, I wanted her to take it. "Good idea. Hurry."

She retrieved a metal hook from her utility belt. It lit up bright yellow and extended to several round loops. She whipped the hook around to get some momentum then flung it skyward. The energy of the string expanded her throw, causing it to easily arc over the ravine top. She pulled back and the line held fast.

Jasette gave me a quick kiss, then looked at me, her face tense. "I'll throw the string down to you as soon as I'm up. Try to buy me some time."

"You got it." Other than making a lot of noise and letting them shoot me multiple times before they noticed she escaped, I wasn't sure what I could do to fulfill that request.

The shouts of Lerk and his Zeuthians grew louder from the passage behind us. They'd made it through the rock slide. My dream of them being cut off entirely was over.

Jasette was already on her way up the ravine wall, the energy string making her ascension unnaturally fast. I looked around, desperate for anything useful. There was a cleft in the wall large enough to hide in. I hurried toward it thinking it was the worst plan ever. Obviously they'd find me sooner or later. Other than extending my life for a few more freems, I couldn't see the point.

But as I squeezed into the narrow cleft, something dug into my side. It was the Doppelganger 2000 in my jacket pocket. Suddenly, inspiration hit. I pulled out the device and activated it. It came to life with whirring energy, and I scanned myself with the white beam of light that shot forth. My body glowed for a brief moment.

Still hidden in the cleft, I aimed the Doppelganger 2000

toward the middle of the clearing. A bright ray shot forth, and within freems, a perfect likeness of me stood there, waiting for our pursuers.

Several Zeuthians rounded the corner, sprinting from the passage into the clearing. They raised their heavy repeaters toward my clone and fired a stream of orange beams. I swallowed hard at the sight of the beams tearing into my clone and sending him to the ground. Smoke rose from his charred torso. Luckily, the copy hadn't exploded or melted. It actually resembled a blasted, utterly defeated version of me.

"No!" Jasette screamed from the top of the ravine. She fired a stream of red energy beams toward the two Zeuthians. The first few met their mark, and one of them crumbled to the ground. The other Zeuthian returned fire, sending a torrent of beams toward Jasette. His blasts tore into the wall at her feet, becoming a spray of dust and rubble. Jasette dove away from the onslaught.

It killed me that I couldn't tell her it wasn't me lying dead on the ground. She hadn't seen my Doppelganger 2000 trick, and now she was risking her life to avenge me.

Four more Zeuthians rushed into the clearing with Lerk right behind them. They met their companions and aimed toward the ravine top.

"If she shows her face again, blast it." Lerk said.

My fingers danced across the handle of the DEMOTER. I was tempted to give away my hiding spot just so I could take him out.

Jasette peered over the edge, sending a few more energy beams toward the Zeuthians. They returned fire as one. She drove away as a hurricane of blasts tore up the rock wall near her.

Lerk had taken a few steps closer to my fallen clone. He put his hands on his hips, admiring my broken body like he'd just conquered the planet. After a moment, he kicked a spray of dust over it. "And that's the end of Captain Glint Starcrost. Grab the body. We need proof to get the reward from Mar Mar."

Two of the thugs huddled around my clone and lifted. The body looked unnaturally stiff.

"Hey, boss." The thug lifting the clone by the shoulders seemed confused. "Something's wrong here."

Lerk moved closer to examine the body. "It's a copy!"

Before they could react further, though, two black specks arced over the ravine wall and landed on the ground near the Zeuthians. They were flashing red.

"Look out!" Lerk pushed one of his thugs out of the way as he tried to flee the area.

A bright light flashed all around, and a thunderous explosion rocked the clearing. I scrunched back into the tight cleft as rubble pelted the wall in front of me. The ground trembled for a few moments, and I kept my eyes shut as the dust settled.

I waited for several moments before peering into the clearing. The Zeuthian thugs lay motionless on the ground, some half covered in rubble. Carefully, I took a few steps out to get a better look at the aftermath. The ground was pitted and broken. Lerk lay on his side, several trickles of blood mixed with dirt streaming across his face. He was still breathing.

I thought for a moment about ending his dark existence permanently. After all, he'd spent most of his adult life running a thug army back on Serberat-Gellamede spaceport. No doubt he was responsible for untold injuries and deaths of the local inhabitants. Not to mention he willingly worked for my old nemesis, Hamilton Von Drone, who was pure evil.

I drew the DEMOTER and leveled it at him. His eyes were closed and his face slack.

A memory of flying next to him at the space academy jumped into my thoughts. He had a broad smile on his face as we flew toward practice drone ships during flight training. Back then, he'd carried himself with such a confident, conquer-the-universe swagger, it pained me to see the path his life had taken. My anger turned to pity. At that moment I knew I couldn't pull the trigger.

I gave Lerk a casual salute with my pistol. "See you around, star pilot."

"Glint!" Jasette called from the ravine top. "You're okay!"

"Yeah." I called up. "They shot up my Doppelganger 2000 clone. I told you it would come in handy."

"Thanks for scaring me to death!" She sounded angry and relieved at the same time.

I shrugged and held up apologetic hands. "I'm just glad it worked. Nice job with those bombs. Remind me to stay on your good side."

"Here. Use this to climb up." She tossed the power string down.

A quick climb aided by the power string brought me to the top of the wall. It was a narrow strip of land with drops on either side. It made a jagged path forward through the maze of ravines all around. Thankfully, the sky was clear of meteor bots. Although that could only mean there were swarms of them already on the planet's surface, searching for me. Our luck couldn't hold out for long. Sooner or later, we'd run into more of them.

Jasette met me at the top with a strong embrace followed by a solid punch on the shoulder. "Don't scare me like that again," she said. "I thought you were dead."

I rubbed my shoulder. "Those playful punches of yours hurt sometimes. I've got enough people trying to damage me around here."

She took quick breaths, her face tense with concern.

I moved closer, grabbing her shoulders. "Hey, don't worry. We're doing great. That was the vision Nelvan saw." I pointed back to the ravine. "You know, my body lying dead on the ground? I just cheated future vision death. That's kind of a big hurdle."

She nodded, a grin easing her tense expression. "This is crazy, you know? The odds of us surviving this . . . Well, I don't even want to think about it."

"Don't think about the odds. Let's just take it one horrific situation at a time. How're your supplies holding out?"

She searched through her utility belt. "Well, those were my last two sphere detonators. I've got a few captivity spheres, some buzz mites, three more doses of blast sludge, some med patches . . ." She brought forth two metal discs with silver buttons on top. ". . . and these beauties."

"What are they?"

"Nano attractors. The best they had. I bought them special for Casglo."

"Sounds expensive."

She grinned. "Don't worry. You had just enough to cover it." She motioned me forward.

We headed down the jagged strip of land at a jog. I couldn't help glancing in every direction as we advanced. At any moment I was sure something would rocket toward us and try to kill me. The dark *Arpellon* loomed on the horizon like a confident predator waiting for the right time to strike. I could make out the other ships in the distance, but thankfully, nothing was heading for us. Yet.

Soon we were closing in on an outcropping of rocks. It resembled a stony hand that had punched its way through the planet's surface.

"That looks like a good place to take cover," I said.

Jasette nodded and took another look over her shoulder before the shadow of the rocks fell over us. Moving quickly, we huddled under the side of the outcropping where the uneven tips of the rock pointed toward the sky. I leaned against the cool rock, taking a moment to rest and gather my thoughts.

"We have to get back to the ship," I said. "They have Blix. Maybe with the distraction of the spider bots, we'll have a chance to storm in and free him, then get out of here."

Jasette gave a half-hearted nod. "Well, I've got some blast sludge left. That should help. It's pretty risky, though."

Suddenly, a spider bot rounded the corner near Jasette's feet. Its red light swept across Jasette's face, and a high tone sounded. I dove outward to avoid the light and sent a few blasts at it. One of them blew the bot in two. The others hit the rocks behind Jasette causing a large portion of the outcropping to come loose.

"Look out!" I pointed to the falling rocks.

Jasette dove out of the way, but not far enough. Several rocks fell over her legs, and she cried out.

I scrambled up to help her. "Are you okay?"

She propped herself up on her elbow. Her eyes were shut

tight in a pained expression. "I think so. My foot's stuck . . . The spider bot saw me."

"Don't worry, I shot it right away. I doubt it had enough time to send a signal." Truthfully, I had no idea how long it took for these strange alien bots to identify us, send signals, or anything else, but at the moment, I wanted to stay positive. There was enough bad going on around us already. "Let's move these rocks and get you out of there."

The smaller rubble cleared easily, but a few larger rocks had her legs pinned down. I pushed at the large pieces, but they weren't budging. Where was Blix when I needed him? I spent a few more freems straining to move them, then sat down next to Jasette, breathing hard.

"Too heavy for the tough space pilot?" She grinned.

"I'll get it. I'll get it." My voice was winded.

"Look for something to give you leverage," she said. "A long rock or branch or something."

I searched the outcropping for anything helpful and found a few squat bushes with curved, gnarled branches growing out of the rocks. I put my back into extracting a few of them, but their roots must've had a death grip because they refused to come free. After several jemmins, I came back to Jasette, my hands scratched and bloodied.

"No luck?" She lay on her side, her elbow propping her up.

I shook my head, but then a thought hit me. "Hey, what about your power string?"

Her face squinched up in confusion.

"I could tie one end to the larger rock, then the other end to a big rock that I can roll over the ravine edge."

She thought for a moment, then shrugged. "Worth a shot."

I set to work with my odd plan. It was tricky work to wrap the string around the exposed edges of the large rock, but after awhile, it had a good hold. I found a roundish rock I could roll to the ravine edge and looped the other end of the power string around it.

Finished, I turned back to Jasette. "Here goes."

I heaved the rock off the edge. The string went taut. The rock pinning her shifted a few inches, then stopped. Standing there, watching nothing move, was a depressing moment after all that effort. And then the functional energy of the power string kicked in. The same energy that helped us scale the ravine wall pulled the large rock off Jasette's legs. I was thrilled, until I noticed the large rock was sliding across the dusty ground right toward me. Before I got swept off the edge, I dove to the side, the rock just nicking my boot. I lay there for a few moments, happy to be on solid ground. The distant impact of the rock hitting the ravine floor was a frightening reminder that it could have been me.

"Nice work." Jasette was leaning against the outcropping, her legs pulled close.

I hurried over and kneeled beside her. "Everything okay?"

She rubbed at her ankle. "Well, thankfully my suit has some high-grade protection, but my ankle's not feeling that great."

"Don't worry," I said. "We'll just rest and take it easy for a while."

A tiny mew sounded behind me. The sound sent a chill through my skin as I turned. Casglo, in kitten form, sat on his haunches just a few yards away from us.

The kitten twitched its tail. "Your actions have been . . . incorrect."

CHAPTER 32

THE NANOBOTS CLOSE IN

FOR A FREEM, it was difficult to breathe. The kitten version of Casglo sat there, watching us. A carpet of black nanobots flowed behind him like a trailing gown.

"You have delayed my mission," Casglo said. "The collection must be complete for me to return to the source. To rest. I require the object you took from the *Arpellon*. You will provide it immediately. Yes or no?"

"Yes?" I said.

The kitten nodded. "Produce the object. I seek rest."

There was a nudge in my lower back. I stole a glance back to find Jasette trying to sneak a metal disc to me. It was the nano attractor. She flicked her eyes to the attractor in her other hand. I grabbed the disc with as much subtlety as I could. "Yes, the object. It's all yours. Thing is, I don't have it with me right now."

The stream of black particles behind Casglo flowed forward. The kitten grew into a jungle cat. It didn't look happy.

"You will give it to me now." Casglo plodded forward, growing larger and scarier with every step.

"Right. Okay, you win." I readied my finger on the activation button. "Here you go." I activated the disc and held it forward.

Casglo's face turned into a mask of anger. Specks began pulling off his head in gruesome contortions and sticking like a magnet to the disc in my hand. Jasette activated her disc and particles flowed toward her as well. It looked as though Casglo was being torn in half.

My skin crawled as the particles began covering my hand. "What now?" I yelled to Jasette.

Jasette was up on her feet, hobbling toward the ravine edge. "We need to get the attractors far away from each other. I'll throw mine into the ravine in front of us, you throw yours into the one behind."

Easier said than done—the rock outcropping blocked my view of the ravine behind us.

The particles that trailed behind Casglo were now splitting off into fragmented groups, some flying toward me, some toward Jasette. They gathered quickly and soon swirled around my forearm, pressing in tightly. I tried brushing them off my arm, but they reformed faster than I could get rid of them. "I can't see the other ravine! Is it supposed to be closing around my arm like this?"

"The salesman wasn't clear on the details."

I tore around the outcropping, the particles now gathering around my shoulder. The ravine was in sight. I ran forward to get close enough to the edge to throw it over. The particles started swirling around my head. There were still several yards to go, but the nano bots were swarming all over. I couldn't see where I was going anymore. I had to get rid of this thing. With all my strength, I hurled the disc forward. The particles made it feel like I was throwing under water.

The disc landed several feet away from me on the ravine top. I'd missed the edge by a few yards. The nano bots formed a large mound half the size of me and continued to grow. There wasn't much I could do about it now. I just had to hope it was far enough.

I rushed back to Jasette to find her kneeling by the ravine edge. "You okay?"

She looked back, breathing heavy. "Yeah, but those nano bots almost took me down with them." She leaned back on her hands and took a deep breath. "At least we got the attractors on opposite ravines. That should buy us some time."

A guilty feeling washed over me. "Yeah. Pretty close, anyway."

Her brows knitted. "'Pretty close'?"

"Well, the other one isn't exactly *in* the other ravine. More like on top of it."

She frowned. "You didn't throw it in the ravine?"

"It was all over me!" I motioned up and down my face and arm to illustrate. "I had to get rid of it."

She shook her head. "Then let's get out of here. A powerful technology like Casglo won't be held for long."

Jasette stood and started half running, half hobbling past the rock outcropping. I caught up to her and put her arm over my shoulders to help her forward. With her limping run, our progress forward wasn't optimal. I kept checking over my shoulder, expecting to find a giant nano cat bearing down on us.

After a good deal of awkward running, I was pretty winded. I needed to stop and rest for a while. Another outcropping emerged in the distance, and with renewed strength, we headed for it. We reached the outcropping and sat against the cool rock, trying to catch our breath.

"How you doing?" I wheezed.

Jasette nodded. "Fine." She tapped out a few commands on her forearm computer and a thin, blue pouch emerged at her shoulder. She extracted two blue rectangles and handed me one. "Eat this. Helps with hydration." She put hers in her mouth and chewed with her eyes closed as if savoring the taste.

I shrugged and put it in my mouth. It was surprisingly cool and refreshing.

"Just a short rest, then we keep going," she said. "I don't want any more surprises."

There was a quick flash of light and Nelvan stood beside me.

"Captain!" Nelvan smiled. "Thank God I'm back."

The light on my Future Glimpse bracelet went out and a small click sounded. I checked the bracelet. A latch on the bottom had opened.

I flashed a relieved look at Nelvan. "The bracelet's off. You're back for good."

"What a relief." Nelvan reached for his bracelet. "Now I can take this crazy thing off."

"Wait!" I rushed to his side, batting away his hand. "If you accidentally activate this thing again, you'll start the process all over. Plus, that Yllack vendor said if we activate both of them while we're still wearing them, we'll go spinning through time together, forever!"

A nervous twitching animated Nelvan's face. "Then here." He held the bracelet toward me. "You do it."

I carefully unlatched and extracted the evil device from my arm, then proceeded to do the same with Nelvan's. "There. Safe!" With a big sigh of relief, I stuffed them both into my jacket pocket. "With any luck we can take these back to that skrid for a refund."

Nelvan looked around. "Are we still on Krullnack?"

"Yeah, and we're trying our best to leave," I said.

"Where's Blix?"

"Sorgil X has him," I said.

"Oh no." Nelvan's expression dropped. "What are we gonna do?"

"We're working on it."

Jasette grunted as she leaned against the rocks. Nelvan frowned at her. "Hey, are you okay?"

"Sort of." She winced. "My ankle is a little messed up."

"Ouch. Sorry." Nelvan straightened like a soldier reporting for duty. "The captain and I will get you back to the med unit first thing. Right, Captain?"

"Easy, kid. We're just trying to stay alive right now."

"In that case, we should definitely avoid women with glowing swords," Nelvan said.

I shared a nervous glance with Jasette.

"Wait," I said. "Did you see something? One of those future visions again?"

"Yeah. But like you said, there's nothing to worry about. In that last one I saw you dead with that Lerk guy and his guards standing around you, and that didn't end up happening, right?"

"Sort of."

His youthful face scrunched up. "Huh?"

"Never mind," I said. "Listen, what'd you see in your

vision? Were the women wearing grey uniforms with red symbols on the chest?"

"Yeah!"

I frowned at Jasette. She didn't look too happy about it either.

"Those are Mar Mar's fembots," Jasette said. "How many were there, and where were we?"

"Well, this time I was with you," Nelvan said. "There were a bunch of those fembot women, and they were flying on these clear disc things."

A soft whirring sound like a swarm of insects came from the ravine behind Nelvan.

Nelvan looked around. "What's that sound?"

"No idea," I said. "Maybe this planet has a lot of bugs."

Nelvan shook his head and continued. "Maybe fifty or sixty fembots. They were hovering all around us. You guys had your guns drawn, but you had these sad looks on your faces, like you knew there were too many of them. You were standing by some rocks and . . . hey, just like the rocks behind you."

By then, I almost expected what happened next. Dozens of fembots wielding glowing red swords emerged from the ravine behind Nelvan on clear hover discs. Jasette and I stood, drawing our pistols, wondering which ones to shoot first, as they continued out of the ravine in an unending stream. Soon we were surrounded by about sixty fembots. A sinking feeling went through my stomach. Once thing was clear: escape was impossible.

Nelvan checked over his shoulder. "Oh." He turned back to us, looking as though he were about to cry. "Yeah, this is what I saw."

CHAPTER 33

FEMBOT ARMY

THE FEMBOTS put all three of us into one large captivity sphere. They wrapped an energy harness around the sphere and took to the air on their hover discs, carrying us along like a bird with its prey. We slumped down at the base of the sphere, resigned to our fate.

To the side of us, I spied three of Sorgil X's panthermen guards following at a safe distance, their rocket boots propelling them forward. A detachment of a dozen or so fembots broke off from our entourage and headed after them. The panthermen immediately changed course and flew away. I sighed. We had so many enemies at this point they were starting to fight with each other.

"Any chance this Mar Mar can be reasoned with?" Nelvan brought my attention back around. "Maybe we can make some kind of deal. Like work for him to pay off our debt or whatever."

The translucent sphere offered a clear view of the scarred landscape speeding by below us. The desolate planet seemed fitting for my doomed situation. "I don't think so, Nelvan."

Although it was second nature for me to talk my way out of bad situations, I knew there was nothing I could say to Mar Mar to change things. Escaping his fortress had delivered a personal insult that he wouldn't let stand. It gave hope to all future captives that escape was possible and made Mar Mar seem vulnerable. Because of that, he would crush me. He had to set an example in order to demonstrate what happens to anyone who tries to escape his clutches. The exact form of punishment was still a mystery. But needless to say, it would be the worst thing that ever happened to me. And probably the last.

"Don't worry, Nelvan," Jasette said. "We're not giving up yet. Right, Glint?"

I didn't really know how to answer when I felt this defeated. Instead, I gave Jasette a quick wink to fake confidence and tried to change the subject before she could see through me. "So, Nelvan, did you see anything else in your visions?"

"Yeah," Nelvan said. "I went to your past. You were pretty young, not much older than me. I didn't even recognize you at first. You were flying a spaceship."

I leaned back, putting my hands behind my head. "Ah, simpler times. The good old days when I first became a pilot."

"You didn't look very happy, though," Nelvan said. "You were crying."

I gave Nelvan a scowl for ruining the romanticization of my past. "Crying? Wait, what did the ship look like?"

"All I saw was the bridge. It had dark-brown seats, and there was grey metal everywhere. A plaque on the doorway said 'The Exodus.'"

"The *Exodus*." A grin spread across my face. "My uncle's

old ship. It may have been old and small, but that thing was agile. Did you see my uncle? A tall guy with a grey mop of hair and a thick beard?"

"Sort of." Nelvan fidgeted like he was suddenly uncomfortable. "The viewing screen on the *Exodus* showed a guy that looked like that. You were looking up at him and crying."

Suddenly I wished I'd never asked about the memory. Nelvan had gone back to a time in my life right after my uncle died. He'd been all I had left after my parents passed away, and I spent a long time crying after he was gone. That was the last time I remembered really crying hard about something. "Never mind. Bad memories."

"You okay?" Jasette grabbed my hand, her eyes filled with concern. "What happened?"

"I'm fine," I lied. "My uncle died doing missionary work on some remote moon we never should have gone to. I barely escaped with my life. I guess God doesn't always show up when you need him, huh, Nelvan?"

Nelvan's eyes were tearing up. "I'm sorry about your uncle. I wouldn't have brought it up if I knew."

"Don't worry about it."

"Pardon me for saying so, Captain," Nelvan said. "But I don't think it was a matter of God not being there. None of us are promised forever. Not in this life, anyway."

I leaned back and closed my eyes. "Yeah, I guess not. It doesn't matter."

There were a few moments of uncomfortable silence.

"Did he like being a missionary?" Nelvan said.

"He loved it," I chuckled. "The old fool. He wouldn't ever shut up about it."

"Well, at least he died for something he loved. Something he really cared about. Maybe that's not such a bad way to go."

My gaze drifted back to the bleak landscape speeding by beneath us. "You think God will show up today, Nelvan? We could sure use a miracle."

"Oh, I'm sure He'll be there, but I don't expect Him to do what I think is best. I mean, the worst that could happen is I end up in heaven today, and that's not so bad." Nelvan paused for a few moments. "I will tell you one thing: I believe in miracles. I mean, just being a crew member on your ship, I should've died a bunch of times already."

I couldn't help smiling. We'd been through some rough scrapes ever since he'd arrived, probably the worst of my life, and yet we were still around to tell about it. "Well, this would be a good time to start praying for another miracle."

"You got it, Captain." Nelvan closed his eyes with a studied look.

If nothing else, the boy had a good heart. I wish I had his optimism at a time like this. The reality was these were probably my last few moments. If there was ever a time I needed divine intervention, this was it.

CHAPTER 34

Mar Mar Pronounces Judgment

OUR ADVANCE SLOWED and we descended toward the planet's surface. Mar Mar's massive battleship dominated the landscape before us. Row after row of fembots stood in military formation in front of the ship, twin laser swords crossed at their chest. And in front of them all, standing in ultimate dominance, was Mar Mar the Unthinkable. He was flanked on one side by Oracle, his pyramid-shaped intelligence droid, and on the other by a barrel-bodied robot with a dome-shaped head that I didn't recognize. The robot had multiple metal arms and legs and shuffled around as though it couldn't decide whether to walk or crawl.

"There's so many of them," Nelvan said.

I gave a slow nod, feeling the stifling weight of being captive to an awaiting army. "Maybe Blix is in a better situation than we are. He might be the only one that ends up escaping this mess."

We came to a soft landing in front of Mar Mar, the fembots hovering away to give him a wide berth. The sight of Mar Mar on a good day was a terrifying experience. Twelve feet of heavily muscled grey skin wielding a double-bladed axe as tall as himself was enough to twist your stomach into painful knots. But today it was much worse. Mar Mar looked horrifying with his new mutations. His red arms seemed to have a mind of their own, the long-fingered claws constantly moving and slashing at the air, coupled with a wicked-looking spike that sat atop the red, scorpion-like tail. The tail curled over his head as if waiting to strike.

Sorgil X stood close by, his impressive bulk dwarfed by Mar Mar. The two stood face-to-face and seemed to be caught up in a heated exchange. Sorgil was motioning to us, a scowl animating his panther-like features. Mar Mar leaned back with arms crossed as if unconcerned with the whole affair.

Finally, the rocket boots of Sorgil X ignited and, with a parting scowl in our direction, he flew off into the distance.

Our captivity sphere dissolved and the dry, warm air washed over us. A dozen fembots immediately surrounded us, laser swords held at the ready in case we made the wrong move.

Lerk emerged from behind Mar Mar, his head and arm wrapped in fresh bandages. He sneered as he met my gaze and turned to Mar Mar. "You see. He was right where I told you."

"Indeed." Mar Mar gripped the tall axe in his hands. "Lerk here was kind enough to alert me to your location in the ravines."

I narrowed my eyes at Lerk. "I could've taken you out back in that ravine, you know? I spared your life."

He grinned. "That's your problem, Glint. You've gone soft."

Mar Mar turned to Lerk. "Your payment is waiting in your ship."

"And the girl?" Lerk said.

Mar Mar waved his hand. "Take her. She is of no consequence."

Lerk moved to Jasette and grabbed her arm. Jasette's next few movements were a blur. She wrapped her arm around Lerk's, twisted her body sideways, and sent him to the ground in a rush. He lay there for a moment, gasping for breath.

Mar Mar let out a belly laugh. "You sure you want her?"

Lerk nodded, still trying to breathe normally.

"What are you doing?" I scowled at Lerk. "What do you want with her?"

"You took things from me," Lerk coughed. "Now it's my turn to take things from you."

"Unless you want another beating," Jasette said. "You're not taking me anywhere."

Lerk drew a black, rectangular-shaped device from his belt and activated it. An electric current sparked around the top of it. He reached over and pressed it against Jasette's leg. She cried out in pain and dropped to her knees.

"Soon you'll learn who's in charge," Lerk said.

Without even thinking, I dove at Lerk and wrestled the device from his hand, sending a fistful of knuckles into his face in the process.

"Enough of this," Mar Mar called out. "Fembots, restrain them."

The fembots rushed in and lifted us to our feet with the painful efficiency only cold machines can achieve. Lerk rubbed his face and moved next to Jasette again, although this time he didn't touch her.

"Now, then," Mar Mar spoke with a smug authority. "Glint Starcrost, you have caused me considerable trouble lately."

"Listen, Mar Mar," I said. "I'm really sorry about that, you know. It's really just a big misunderstanding and—"

"Silence!" Mar Mar's scorpion-like tail curled toward me as if preparing to strike. "As you can see, the Emerald Enigma you gave me has caused some rather remarkable changes."

"Yeah. It really suits you," I said.

His expression darkened. "I know you meant me ill, but it just so happens I like the new me." His red arms moved to either side of my head, and the claws lightly brushed my cheeks as if promising long, painful scars in the future. "With this Enigma, I will continue to change and become more powerful every day I wear it."

"Maybe you could thank me by letting us go," I said.

He gave a dark chuckle that seemed to emerge from the depths of his chest cavity. "You think me naive? You gave me the Emerald Enigma as a trick. You wanted to curse me with bad fortune. Soon you will learn the price for such actions."

"You've got me all wrong," I pleaded. "I just wanted to—"

"Silence, fool!" He tightened his grip on the axe and waited for several moments as if daring me to speak again. "I have a surprise for you." He turned to the odd, multilimbed robot at his side. "Mishdrone, secure your prisoner."

I gasped. "Mishdrone!"

The barrel-shaped robot ambled over to me like a drunken grasshopper. I looked at the approaching thing in horror, wondering if it could really be the bizarre fusion of Hamilton Von Drone and Mishmash. My last sight of him had been hurtling from Mar Mar's castle wall onto the rocky ground far below. As he came close, I recognized the telltale signs of burnt skin peeking out between sections of his metal frame and tufts of blond hair sticking out from the dome-shaped top that passed for a head. A thin red light still shone from a gap in the dome, glowing brightly as it came near.

I shot a desperate look at Mar Mar. "How is this thing still alive?"

Mar Mar wore a devilish grin. "Without my robotics facility, Mishdrone would be in some scrap pile. When we found him, he could barely move. He just kept uttering the phrase, 'Kill Starcrost, kill Starcrost.' He wouldn't stop saying it." He paused to let out a chuckle. "I must say I was highly amused. His tenacity and demented sense of revenge appealed to me, so I decided to rebuild him. Of course, given his condition, I had to make some rather unique modifications."

Mishdrone crawled up next to me and clamped a three-pronged metal hand over my forearm. He squeezed, and the metal dug into my skin.

I bent to one side from the pain. "Ah, easy, Mishdrone."

Mishdrone's red eye glowed, and a reverberating scraping sound came out of him.

"I believe that's his version of laughter," Mar Mar said. "As you can see, he's quite mad, even for a cyborg. I've decided to let him keep you as a pet for a few montuls. I'll make sure he keeps you alive, of course. I have many painful things planned for you before you die."

Mar Mar and Lerk shared a laugh at my terrible future.

"You can't do that!" Nelvan piped up. "All he did was escape your dungeon. How can you be so cruel?"

"Nelvan!" I flashed serious eyes at the boy and shook my

head. It was bad enough that my future was doomed. I didn't want him to get caught in the snare with me.

Mar Mar chuckled. "Be careful not to displease me, boy. I might just spare your life."

Nelvan gritted his teeth. He looked as though he was going to speak again, so I decided to beat him to it.

"Listen, Mar Mar," I said. "My crew and I could be an asset. We could work for you. Be one of your smuggler or bounty-hunter teams. Just think of all the trouble I've caused you. I can cause the same trouble to your enemies."

Mar Mar paused for a moment, then turned to his droid. "Oracle, calculate effectiveness of Glint Starcrost working for me."

Multicolored lights flashed around the pyramid-shaped droid, followed by a string of beeps.

"Calculation complete," the oracle droid said. "Based on current data, successful missions completed by Glint Starcrost would increase cumulative performance by two point one percent."

"Ha!" I pointed to the droid. "You see. I'd be an asset."

"However," the droid continued. "Unsuccessful missions including lost shipments, broken equipment, and negative associations with our network of clientele would cause a decrease in cumulative performance by three point five percent."

Mar Mar shook his head. "The eternal tale of a desperate space drifter. Always coming up short. I'm afraid your tale is over, Starcrost, and my patience has worn thin." He brought the base of his axe to the ground with a loud thud. "Your crimes against me are known, and it is time to pronounce judgment." He lifted his hefty axe and held the double blades over my head. "I have made my decision."

The surrounding fembots spoke as one. "Mar Mar has made his decision."

"Glint Starcrost will pay for his crimes against my good pleasure," Mar Mar said.

"Glint Starcrost will pay," the fembots echoed.

"He will suffer at the hands of the servants in my castle until I tire of it and end his miserable, worthless life."

"He will suffer in Mar Mar's castle."

"I have spoken."

"Mar Mar has spoken."

Mar Mar brought the axe back to his side with a grim smile. "And now it is time to leave this wretched planet and return to my castle."

"Wait," I said. "I'll come along with no trouble. Just let my crew go. They didn't do anything."

"Oh, but they did," Mar Mar said. "They helped you escape. I'm afraid they'll need to be punished as well. I'm giving the woman to Lerk, and the boy will come with us until I figure out what to do with him."

Rage welled up within me. I was desperate for action, but there was nothing I could do. Hopelessly outnumbered and at the mercy of Mar Mar's perverted sense of justice, I felt very small. My mind raced for some possible way out of this mess.

"Captain," Nelvan whispered. "Don't give up hope. I'm still praying."

The kid was definitely an optimist. In a way, I was jealous. Gloons of fending for myself in the rough-and-tumble universe had knocked most of the happy out of me. If nothing else, it had been nice to have Nelvan around up until this moment. It was like having a piece of my youthful outlook back.

"Thanks, Nelvan," I said.

"Fembots," Mar Mar called out. "Escort the prisoners to my ship." He turned to Lerk. "You are free to take the woman and go."

It was time to throw caution to the wind and go out fighting. If I was heading off for torture and enslavement, I might as well die now with my pistol firing.

I was reaching toward the DEMOTER when a loud commotion broke out.

The fembots behind me were screeching their metallic versions of screams and fighting something back with their glowing swords. A layer of dust and several rows of fembots blocked my view. They were slashing their swords at the ground, creating dust and flying dirt clods. The scene made no sense—until I saw a white spider bot flying over their heads, freshly skewered by a laser sword.

I strained to see more through the dust, and the situation became clear. An endless stream of spider bots was pouring over the ravine top nearby and heading toward us. I didn't know whether to be scared or relieved. On the one hand, attacking the army that was trying to cart me off to torture and death was a dream. But if the bots captured me, Casglo would demand the chrysolenthium flower back, and I would have to refuse for the sake of Jasette and her kingdom, after which he would promptly stamp me out of existence with his giant nano paw. It was a lose-lose scenario.

"Fembots," Mar Mar shouted. "Attack! Stop those creatures."

The fembot army surged around us, moving toward the approaching spider bots. Jasette flashed me a look that seemed to communicate, *If you see a chance to run, go for it.* Mishdrone still had an iron grip on my arm. I could blast him, but with his resilience, there was no assurance he'd release his grip. For all I knew he'd fly backward and take my arm with him.

The chaos of the battle grew louder and more frenzied. Swarms of spider bots were now intermingled throughout the army of fembots. There seemed to be an unlimited supply of them pouring over the rim. But the fembots were making short work of them. Piles of their metal spider bodies lay impaled or sliced into pieces on the ground.

"Slay them, my fembots," Mar Mar shouted with glee. "Slay them!"

It looked as though the fembots were going to do just that: slay all the spiders and emerge victorious. But as the battle waged on, more and more of them began to fall as the flood of spider bots continued to pour over the ravine. It was as if a river of them were flowing through it and waves of the hideous metal creatures kept splashing over the rim. Fembot after fembot fell, their bodies wrapped in the constricting legs of the spider bots. It soon became clear the tide had turned and the oncoming horde of bots were heading our way.

It was at that point Jasette made her move.

CHAPTER 35

DESTRUCTION
AND DESPERATION

MY ATTENTION had been so focused on the battle raging around us that Jasette's blur of motion barely registered. By the time I turned to see what happened, Lerk was on his back, out of breath once again. Jasette had both pistols drawn and leveled at his head.

"You're not taking me anywhere, skrid," she said.

Before I could react, the heavy, double blade of Mar Mar's axe lay poised at Jasette's neck.

"I like her." Mar Mar narrowed his eyes at Jasette as if sizing her up. "She has spunk. Lerk, I've changed my mind. She's coming with us."

"What?" Lerk coughed, still lying on the ground, catching his breath.

Mar Mar gave a stern look downward. "Are you questioning my decision?"

Lerk's eyes went wide and he shook his head. "No, of course not."

Mar Mar grinned. "Good. Then we will go to my ship at—" He froze, his eyes fixed on something behind us.

I turned to find the monstrous figure of Casglo clawing its way out of the ravine. Horns, tufts of fur, and powerful muscles covered the distorted cat creature. It was even larger now than I'd seen it back on the *Arpellon*. If my ship was sitting nearby, I doubt it would be much bigger. It was a truly terrifying sight knowing that its ultimate target was yours truly.

Nelvan gasped. "Oh no."

Lerk, still on the ground, closed his eyes and pretended as if he were dead. It was a cowardly move, but I couldn't help wondering if by doing so he'd be the only one left alive after all this insanity.

Mishdrone still stood at my side, his head swiveling between me and the battle that raged around us.

Several fearless but incredibly stupid fembots charged at Casglo's legs. The cat creature flicked its paws, sending them hurtling through the air.

My legs felt wobbly. I was surrounded at every turn by my worst enemies. So many gloons flying through the treacherous universe had thrown their share of bad days my way. I'd categorized the worst ones just to make sure I didn't overstate my situation when bad things happened and end up calling every day the worse day of my life. Still, with all those horrible experiences vying for the number one spot, this was my new low. The new Worst Day of My Life. The rock bottom by which I would measure all future days—provided I survived, of course.

Casglo scanned the battlefield until our eyes met. The distorted feline expression turned sinister and he stalked forward as if closing in on new prey.

"What is that . . . thing?" For the first time, Mar Mar

sounded worried. It was strange to hear a tremble in the voice of someone so powerful and seemingly unstoppable.

"It's a nightmare come to life," I said. "You'd better run while you still can."

Mar Mar paused. "I run from nothing." He said the words in a hollow way as if trying to convince himself. "Fembots, assemble."

The fembots nearby that weren't already overrun with spider bots gathered around Mar Mar, their swords held in defensive position. The battlefield around us still waged, but the fembots were thinning out. The ground was covered in crawling metal spiders.

Casglo closed the gap between us, standing high above our little group, which seemed tiny now in comparison. I shared a frightened glance with Nelvan and Jasette. There was an unspoken understanding that we'd done about all we could do, but it just wasn't going to be enough this time.

Casglo looked down at me. The strange undulating motions of the nanobots that formed the creature made it seem as though a subtle current of liquid ran over its hide. "Where is my object? The collection must be complete." The creature sounded like a choir of deep voices all speaking in near perfect synchronicity.

What could I say? All I had left was empty promises. "I have it. I can give it to you very soon."

Casglo bent its mighty cat head closer to me. "The time for delay is over. I require the object now."

I swayed slightly. With the continued numbing stress of the day, my body felt like it had reached its limit and wanted to pass out. I had nothing to offer the huge creature in front of me. Nothing would appease it.

And then, as the word *appease* went through my head, a memory triggered. Back when I'd been fighting for my life in Mar Mar's castle, he'd asked for something to appease his wrath. That very something was within reach.

"Casglo." A sliver of hope went through me. "I have brought you to an object that is far better than the object you seek."

Casglo paused. "Explain."

"Your mission was to collect rare objects from the universe, correct?"

"Yes. I must complete the collection. The founders are waiting."

"But the founders want the most unique, most rare objects in the universe to complete the collection, right?"

Casglo nodded its massive head. "That is correct."

"Then to complete your collection, I offer you one of the most rare, most sought after objects the universe has to offer." I swept my arm toward Mar Mar with a theatrical flourish. "Behold, the Emerald Enigma! As unique an object as there ever was. And it rests upon his neck."

Mar Mar froze. His wide eyes danced between Casglo and me as if unable to choose who to focus on. Casglo's massive head bent closer to Mar Mar, making the grey giant seem suddenly insignificant.

"Fembots," Mar Mar's voice sounded small and weak. "Attack!"

The surrounding fembots that remained charged at the huge feline creature. Casglo batted them away like a cat with troublesome insects. Casglo narrowed his eyes at Mar Mar. "Show me the object."

Mar Mar took a few steps back, holding his axe before

him. Dozens of spider bots rushed in, crawling up his thick frame and wrapping their metal arms around his limbs. He flailed and thrashed about, sending his axe in powerful sweeps against the bots. Several of the metal spiders were sliced in half or flung skyward, but their advance was unrelenting. Soon Mar Mar stood, frozen in place, bound by dozens of the bots covering his body. It was a glorious sight.

"Reveal the object to me," Casglo said.

The spiders around Mar Mar's chest pulled away his leather armor and held forth the familiar sight of the Emerald Enigma on their thin, metal arms. Casglo moved close to the green stone. A black stream of nanobots broke away from the monstrous feline and flowed around the Enigma for several moments. Then they returned to Casglo and the massive cat head lifted away.

"Initial scans indicate this object will be one of the finest in my collection." Casglo made an expression that bordered on a smile. "The founders will be pleased by this addition." The giant cat eyes slid down to me. "Your proposal is acceptable. I will take the Enigma as my final object."

The spider bots lifted the Emerald Enigma up Mar Mar's neck. The necklace constricted before it reached his jawline.

Casglo bent down to Mar Mar. "You are attempting to keep the object? Yes or no?"

"No!" Mar Mar's face was a mask of fear. "I don't know. It's stuck."

The spiders tried once again to remove the necklace, with the same result.

"It's bound to him." I was happy to jump in and provide the answer to the unasked question. "This Emerald Enigma is powerful. It binds itself to its owner." I narrowed my eyes at Mar Mar. "You'll have to take him with you if you want the object."

"Very well," Casglo said.

More bots gathered at Mar Mar's feet and toppled him into an awaiting carpet of spiders that were poised to carry him away.

"No!" Mar Mar screamed in protest. "You can have it. Just let me go."

"I will take you to my ship," Casglo said. "You can either stay with the object, or I can remove it from you by dismemberment. I will leave the choice to you."

Mar Mar gasped and stuttered. Several indiscernible grunts came from his mouth, but it seemed he was beyond the ability to respond in a rational manner. The spiders moved as one underneath Mar Mar, rolling him away as if he were on wheels.

A shrill sound came from Mishdrone. He released his grip on my arm and took a step toward the retreating figure of Mar Mar. I wasn't done playing my desperate hand. If I was going to escape, it would be a full escape. In a swift move I retrieved the Future Glimpse bracelets from my jacket pocket, clamped one around Mishdrone's metal arm and activated it, then dove toward Lerk and strapped the other one on his wrist.

"You want to be Hamilton Von Drone's right-hand man?" I activated his bracelet. "Enjoy a lifetime of spinning through time with him."

A white glow surrounded Lerk as his face morphed into a mixture of confusion and rage.

Something cold and metal clamped around my neck. I choked and arched back in pain. I couldn't breathe. My windpipe was being crushed, and my vision started to blur. And then a bright light filled the area and the pressure went away. I dropped to my hands and knees, gasping for air.

Jasette rushed to my side. "Glint, are you okay?"

I nodded, rubbing my sore neck.

"That was awesome, Captain," Nelvan said. "I mean, you sending those guys away, not the part where you got hurt."

I sat back and took a deep breath. "What was that around my neck?"

"Mishdrone," Jasette said. "No doubt he wanted to choke the life out of you."

"Yeah," Nelvan said. "Good thing he disappeared when he did."

"No kidding." I scanned the surrounding area. Casglo ambled away toward the mountain-sized *Arpellon*. An army of spider bots moved in formation, following close behind. The night was spent, and the sun peeked over the mountains on the distant horizon. The hazy glow of the red moon was replaced by a warm orange light spilling across the landscape, even more clearly illuminating the ground littered with broken fembots and spider bots, smoke rising from their electronic insides. A pungent smell of burnt oil filled the air.

"I can't believe you got out of that one." Jasette raised her eyebrows. The tension that seemed ever-present in her face lately was gone. She looked more joyful than I'd seen her in days. "I mean, really, that was about as bad a spot as it gets."

I let out a long, stress-filled breath. "You're telling me."

She moved in close and gave me a long kiss. "You're amazing."

My head spun. Her kiss was pure intoxication. "No, you

knocking that skrid Lerk to the ground *twice* was amazing. And with an injury no less."

She gave a cocky grin. "There was no way I was going in that loser's ship."

I gazed again at the smoking battlefield of broken robots—such a strange contrast to what it had been only a short while ago when my life was doomed. I shook my head. "Unbelievable. Do you realize we just escaped two of the most powerful beings in the universe?"

Nelvan beamed. "Didn't I tell you I was praying for a miracle?"

I nodded. "And that was nothing short of miraculous."

"We should get out of here," Jasette said. "There might be a reserve force waiting in Mar Mar's ship."

"Yeah." My mind focused. Blix was still in trouble. We weren't out of this yet. "We have to rescue Blix. Sorgil X has him."

"Hey." Nelvan pressed down on a vacant hover disc nearby with his foot. "Maybe we can get there on these. Do either of you know how to fly them?"

Jasette and I shared a confident grin.

CHAPTER 36

HOVER HIDING

JASETTE AND I were happy to find quick transportation via hover disc to our destination. Nelvan, on the other hand, wasn't too excited to learn that he'd have to fly solo, as the fembot discs were designed for a single flyer. He got all twitchy and voiced deep concerns about traveling on a thin, transparent disc that granted a clear view of the distant ground below. I tried to reassure him that it was just a matter of standing in place and leaning in the direction of your choice. He still seemed reluctant, but Jasette, with far more patience than I, gave a brief lesson on hover-disc flying at low altitude.

Jasette then used her magnification screen to locate Sorgil X's ship, and we set off toward it at once. The sun continued to rise, carpeting the surface of the planet in bright light. As nice as it was to be free of the blood-red moon, the bright sun made it difficult to reach our destination unseen. We flew deep within the ravines so our approach wouldn't be detected. It was anything but a direct route. The winding ravines delivered a plentiful supply of inconvenient side-tracks. But since they kept us under cover, it was our best option.

Every so often we would pause at a rim, and Jasette would recalculate our position to correct our course. With such a convoluted path, it took much longer than I'd hoped, but we pressed on until finally we were within sight of my ship. It sat alongside Sorgil X's technologically advanced space cruiser like a small child next to a battle-ready warrior.

We hovered to the top of a nearby ravine, peering over the edge at the landscape beyond. The ships sat quietly as if waiting for us. If any sentries were posted, only the tops of our heads would be visible at ground level.

"I don't see any guards." I scanned the empty shelter near the ships.

"Can we get off these things now?" Nelvan cast a nervous glance through his hover disc at the ravine floor below.

"Relax," I said. "We need a plan first."

"I can sneak in," Jasette said. "My power suit can disrupt most of their external scans if they're doing local sweeps. I'll slip aboard Sorgil X's ship, locate Blix, bust him out, and we'll rendezvous at our ship."

"Are you crazy?" I said. "That's a suicide mission."

Jasette was already tapping out commands on her forearm computer and glancing back at the ships with a focused gaze. "It's tricky, but I think I can do it."

"Way too risky," I said. "Their weaponry is advanced. We need something big to counter their firepower. We'll send Nelvan toward their ship as a diversion while I sneak back to my ship."

Nelvan flashed big eyes at me. "What?"

"Then," I continued. "I'll bring our ship back online, swing it around with full weapons targeting their forces—hopefully before they get to Nelvan—and let them have it."

"I like Jasette's plan better," Nelvan said.

Jasette shook her head at me. "No way. Too sloppy and Nelvan's caught in the crossfire."

"He can go on his hover disc and fly away when things get messy."

"Captain, I think—" Nelvan started.

"We need subtlety, not reckless plans that get someone killed," Jasette said.

"I didn't hear you complaining when I outsmarted Mar Mar and Casglo. What happened to all your 'You're amazing' talk."

"Guys—" Nelvan said.

"That *was* amazing," Jasette said. "Your new plan stinks."

"Oh, *my* plan stinks? Let me tell you something—"

"Hold it right there," a deep voice called out behind us.

I spun around, DEMOTER in hand. Jasette was right in synch with me, her dual silver pistols ready for blasting. A dozen of Sorgil X's armor-clad guards hovered on their rocket boots behind us, their heavy repeaters trained on our heads. Green energy shields surrounded each of them.

The pantherman with grey fur and crimson stripes hovered at the forefront of the guards. "Holster those weapons. Sorgil X is waiting for you."

After all we'd survived, losing like this when we were so close to success was like a knife in the heart. But there was no denying the reality of the situation. We were caught.

CHAPTER 37

THE FUTURE OF SORGIL X

IT WAS A HEARTBREAKING PROCESSION as we glided toward the ships on our hover discs, the armed guards following close behind. The irony of the situation wasn't lost on me. I'd miraculously managed to escape two of the biggest power players in the universe only to get captured by a hotshot celebrity bounty hunter.

"Hold it there," the grey pantherman called out as we reached the lowered landing ramp of Sorgil X's ship. A series of blips signaled the activation of his com link. "Sorgil X, your guests have arrived."

We waited a few moments in silence. My mind raced for any sliver of an idea for escape, but I had nothing. Apparently, I'd already maxed out that section of my brain. I glanced over at Jasette and Nelvan. The downcast expressions on their faces told me all I needed to know. We'd been through so much already, the brilliant plans just weren't coming to us.

Footsteps sounded from the top of the landing ramp. I straightened and squared my shoulders, unwilling to let the approaching scumbag know he'd broken my spirit. And yet . . . as Sorgil X came into view, I realized Blix was walking alongside him. They were laughing and slapping each other on the back like old friends.

Sorgil X brightened as he met my gaze. "Captain, so glad you could join us." He turned to Jasette and Nelvan as he approached. "Along with the most beautiful bounty hunter in the galaxy and the mysterious disappearing boy with no records."

"Mar Mar's gone," Jasette said. "There's no bounty to collect, Sorgil X. Let us go."

Sorgil X pointed at Jasette and looked at Blix. "Isn't she great? Always straight to the point. Doesn't waste time with pleasantries."

"Indeed." Blix looked thoughtful. "Although one might say pleasantries are what keep conversations civil."

"That's a good point," Sorgil X said.

"All right, what is this?" I said. "Blix, why are you being so friendly with this skrid?"

"Easy, Captain." Sorgil X's eyes narrowed. "Or I may take back my generous offer."

I flashed a questioning look at Blix. Blix just smiled and nodded.

"What offer?" I said.

"We saw the whole thing, Captain," Blix said. "The battle between Mar Mar and Casglo's forces, the sly manner in which you pitted them against each other, your expulsion of Mishdrone and Lerk—it was all captured with Sorgil X's high-powered audio and visual technology. I must say it was brilliant. I'm very proud of you."

Sorgil X nodded. "Your performance was impressive, Captain. And a fitting end to Mar Mar. After all, I'm the one who led him here and he goes and tries a double cross. He claimed since his fembots did the capturing and I didn't hand deliver you, that I wasn't owed any of the bounty." He bared his sharp teeth, a low rumbling of growl escaping.

"Then I did you a big favor," I said. "You can reward us by letting us go."

"It's not that simple." He rubbed his chin. "You see, bad as he was, his extensive list of bounties represented a large source of my revenue. Sure, there're still bounties to collect from lower-level, up-and-coming thugs across the universe, but nowhere near as profitable. It's quite a financial hit for me and my team. I'm afraid it leaves me in a position where I need something to make up the difference."

"That's when I proposed a plan." Blix puffed out his chest and crossed his arms.

Sorgil X gave him a good-natured slap on the shoulder. "A mutually beneficial plan."

My focus slid back and forth between the two of them. "What kind of plan?"

Blix spread his arms wide. "We are allowed to go free."

"Yes," Sorgil X said. "All I ask for is the spoils of war, which include minor compensations such as Mar Mar's battle cruiser."

"That's a minor compensation?" Jasette said.

Blix held out his hand. "Please, let him finish."

"Also," Sorgil X continued. "My media team will need to create a slight revision of history. One that will place my name in the records as a revered figure of modern times and make a glorious ending to my latest movie."

A warning signal triggered in my head that I wasn't going to like the deal very much.

"Blix?" I narrowed my eyes at him. "Will I like this?"

"Of course, Captain." The telltale nervous twitching of his cheek started. "You can't really place a cost on our freedom, can you?"

My attempts to discover concrete details about the deal fell flat. Hanging around celebrities and politicians in Glittronium for most of his professional career had given Sorgil X considerable skill in answering my questions without actually providing any information. When I pressed, he conveniently excused himself, mumbling something about sending us off with style.

Of course, I immediately turned on Blix, demanding he explain the terms he'd agreed to. Blix also danced around the details until Sorgil X reemerged from his ship, followed by his personal chef and several hover trays of gourmet food.

"Gather 'round, everyone," Sorgil X announced. "One last meal on this planet, the scene of my future glory, and then we take to the stars."

When the rich aroma of perfectly seasoned fine cuts of meat, rich stews, and fresh bread hit me, I temporarily forgot about my issues with the deal. The gourmet meal was laid before us on hover tables in the shelter. Sorgil X toasted us and our "generous deal," as he called it, and the feast commenced. I wouldn't have stayed a moment longer than I had to, but frankly, I was starving after our harrowing adventure, and his food was far better than anything I had on my ship.

Blix fell into conversation with the other guards about past adventures, and the air filled with their dramatic retellings and loud laughter. Apparently they'd forged some type of warrior bond during his captivity. It was fine with me since it allowed plenty of time to feed my hunger with the rich delicacies in front of me. Jasette and Nelvan were right there with me, savoring the feast and finally taking a moment to relax after the closest scrape we'd ever experienced.

As I dragged one of the last bites of meat across my broth-filled bowl, ready to savor another mouthful of heaven, Jasette nudged me.

"Time to go," she said. "Let's get out of here before he changes his mind."

"I still don't know what I'm agreeing to," I said.

"It's simple," she said. "He wants to take credit for what you did today."

I slammed my fist on the table. "I knew it. That sleaze."

Jasette placed her hands on top of mine. "Glint, who cares? We're free. We can finally go back to my planet and restore my kingdom. Isn't that what we wanted all along?"

I paused for a moment. It was as if I could see the glory of my accomplishments fading off into the sunrise. "Well, yeah, but—"

"Glint." She put her hand to my cheek and held my gaze. "Forget about it. We have everything we need right here."

I relaxed and took a deep breath. "You're right." I stood and turned to Sorgil X. "Thanks for everything. We need to get going."

"So soon?" Sorgil X looked surprised. "They're preparing glazed Kawanakaakaalu swine followed by caramel-coated glinzer fruit for dessert."

"Caramel-coated?" Blix stood, his eyes wide. "Captain, we should stay."

"Thanks," I said. "But we really have to go."

Blix scowled at me.

"Very well, Captain." Sorgil X waved. "Take care. Perhaps we'll meet again on Glittronium one day."

"You never know." I motioned to my crew. "Let's go."

Soon we were back on the bridge of my ship on a direct course to Jasette's planet, Jelmontaire. After a long series of stress-filled days, I was finally at ease.

"Oh, Glint. You saved me. I knew you would." Iris was practically giddy. "I'm thrilled you made it back safely. I mean, I'm thrilled everyone made it back safely. I was so worried."

"Thanks, Iris," I said. "It's good to be back."

"Can I prepare a hot cup of velrys for you?"

"You're singing my tune, Iris."

Sitting in my captain's chair, velrys in hand, and heading through the freedom of space felt like a dream. All was right with the universe. There was a sense of elation in the ship. After so many days of being on the run and feeling the pressure of stronger forces bearing down on me, a tremendous sense of relief flooded my body. I could see similar feelings written on the expressions of my crew, especially Jasette.

"I can't believe I'm going home." She swiveled back in her navigator's chair to face me. Her face was lighted up. I couldn't remember ever seeing her that happy. "It's been gloons. And I'm returning with the chrysolenthium flower. Oh, Glint, my people are saved. This is one of the best days of my life."

"When we're close enough," Blix said. "I'll send a long-range message about our arrival."

It was hard not to get caught up in Jasette's excitement. Besides her smile being infectious, seeing her so ecstatic about things made me feel a part of this amazing moment in her life.

"I can't wait to show you Jelmontaire," she beamed. "It's a beautiful planet."

I shared her smile. "Looking forward to it."

"As am I," Blix said. "From what I've heard, Jelmontaire sounds exquisite."

"Yeah," Nelvan said. "I've never visited a kingdom before."

"Oh, I almost forgot," Blix tapped out a few controls at the engineering station. "Sorgil X's media guru gave me an early-release clip of his movie. It's just the part that features us."

The viewing screen switched from the stars outside to a moving view of the ravine-covered planet Krullnack that we'd just escaped from.

"What is this?" I said. "I was finally feeling good. I don't want to see this."

"Wait, your part's coming up, Captain," Blix said. "I watched some of the movie creation in progress while I awaited your return. Sorgil X's media crew are masters at their craft."

The visual rushed toward the landscape near Mar Mar's battleship. His fembot army was assembled and Jasette, Nelvan, and I stood before him. A shiver went down my spine at the sight. It brought back the anxious feelings of being trapped in that moment.

A driving musical background track sounded. Sorgil X, clad in his shiny battle armor with rocket boots at full ignition, flew through the ravine nearby at breakneck speed. The visual bounced from close ups of his focused expression to his daring navigation of the narrow ravine.

He rose from the passage with a dramatic spin. Below him stood Mar Mar and his fembot army.

"Mar Mar the Unthinkable," Sorgil X's voice boomed across the landscape in amplified resonance. "We meet again."

The visual switched to a close-up of Mar Mar. "You have caused me considerable trouble lately."

"Hey!" I pointed at the screen. "He said that to me."

"Shh." Blix held a finger to his lips.

Sorgil X pointed downward. "The one who has caused trouble is *you*, Mar Mar. The innocent people of the universe have had enough. Speaking of which, I see you have Glint Starcrost, winner of *The Iron Gauntlet*, and his crew held prisoner. You must release them immediately."

"I'm afraid they'll need to be punished," Mar Mar said.

"Lies!" I stood from the captain's chair. "Sorgil X's just taking everything that happened to me but putting himself in the visual like he had something to do with it."

"Quiet down," Blix said. "This is where the drama really builds."

"Glint Starcrost will pay for his crimes against my good pleasure," Mar Mar said.

"Then at the very least, release the woman," Sorgil X said. "She is innocent."

"She is of no consequence," Mar Mar said.

The visual zoomed in on Sorgil X's eyes. They were narrow with rage. "You vile creature. You won't even spare the innocent. Your evil reign ends today. I will stop you and free these prisoners."

Mar Mar leaned back and let out a hearty laugh.

"Oh, come on," I said. "This is ridiculous. Who would believe this?"

"My, my, but that Sorgil X certainly is a striking figure." Iris sounded out of breath. "That voice, those eyes, his heroic presence. He's so dreamy."

"Oh, you've gotta be kiddin' me." I said.

"Captain," Blix said. "You must admit, his acting skills are quite moving."

"You've had your chance," Sorgil X called out in a powerful voice. "I've brought an army of spider robots to stop you. Robots, swarm! Swarm!"

The visual changed to the unending stream of spider bots pouring over the ravine top.

"Fembots," Mar Mar called out. "Attack! Stop those creatures!"

Dramatic angles of the ensuing battle between the fembots and the spiders filled the screen with a powerful, building musical score behind it.

"Wow," Nelvan said. "This is almost better than being there."

The fembots fell one by one as the tide of the battle turned on them.

"And now, Mar Mar," Sorgil X called out. "Meet my nanobot creation that is here to take you away and rid the good people of this universe from your tyranny."

Casglo climbed over the rim and headed toward Mar Mar. The visuals showed breathtaking angles of the massive cat creature from ground level.

"How did he get all this?" I pointed at the screen. "I didn't see any cam bots around."

"I told you." Blix shook his head as if impressed. "His media team are masters of their craft."

Spider bots wrapped around an enraged Mar Mar, holding him in place.

"And now, my robot army," Sorgil X said. "Rid the universe of this villain."

Casglo nodded its massive head. "Your proposal is acceptable."

Mar Mar toppled onto an awaiting carpet of spider bots.

"No!" Mar Mar screamed. "Let me go."

Sorgil X pointed toward the horizon like an implacable judge, and the spider bots ushered Mar Mar away. Sorgil X flew down to land on the ravine top. With some kind of visual wizardry, it looked as though he were landing directly in front of Jasette, Nelvan, and me.

"I have dispatched Mar Mar the Unthinkable once and for all," Sorgil X said. "You are all free to go."

The visual showed a close-up of Nelvan. "That was awesome."

A close-up of Jasette followed. "You're amazing."

A close-up of me. "That was nothing short of miraculous."

Sorgil X waved a dismissive hand. "No. I just did what had to be done. Now you are free to return to your lives. I wish you all the best." His rocket boots ignited, and he flew off with a stylish twirl.

"I've had enough!" I drew my DEMOTER and aimed it at the viewing screen. "Shut this off now before I blast the screen."

"Wait, Captain." Blix held out his hand. "This is the part I did while I was held hostage. I think my acting skills are rather impressive.

The visual switched to Blix watching Sorgil X flying through the air at top speed.

Blix shook his head, looking after him in admiration. "Sorgil X. I do believe if he ever ran for vice chancellor of Glittronium, I would support him all the way."

Blix looked around the bridge at all of us with excited eyes. "He's running next election. He thought it would be good to start campaigning early."

"I think I'm gonna be sick," I said. "Turn this blasted thing off!"

Blix wore a pouty face as he tapped at his control panel. The viewing screen switched back to the stars gliding by outside.

"What a pack of lies," I said. "How could you let him do that to us, Blix? How could you make that deal?"

Blix turned to me, his brow raised. "Captain, we are on our way to save Jasette's planet and the very fate of her people. We have our freedom, we're back on our ship, and we just escaped the most treacherous challenge of our lives. We have all of this in exchange for the temporal and innocuous price of handing over a bit of Glittronium fame, something as fleeting as a summer breeze, to someone other than ourselves. I'd say we got the better half of the deal."

Jasette turned to me. "He makes a good point."

"Yeah, Captain," Nelvan said. "We're free. No one's chasing us, and you don't have a bounty on your head anymore. Isn't this what you wanted?"

I paused for a moment. It was hard to revel in my anger when, after all, I was free and the woman I loved was right beside me. If only I could send a good right cross into Sorgil X's pompous face, I'd feel a little better. I made a mental note to work that clause into any future deals. "Yeah, I guess you're right. Forget that idiot. I'm never planning on going back to Glittronium anyway."

"I'm with you," Jasette said.

Blix shook his head. "I won't agree to that."

"Iris," I said. "How far to Jelmontaire?"

"We should arrive in three days, five trids, and twenty-two jemmins," Iris said.

Jasette gave an excited shout and gripped her armrest. I smiled at her anticipation and leaned back in my chair, imagining what our lives would be like on a peaceful planet, free from life-threatening villains.

CHAPTER 38

JELMONTAIRE

BESIDES MY BRIEF STAY at Glittronium, most of the places I'd visited in my career as a space pilot were somewhere between the ramshackle huts of a remote colony and the dingy, neon-sign-filled stopover style of space ports overpopulated with thugs and space pirates. With those memories as my reference point, Jelmontaire was a huge step up.

We descended through the puffy clouds of the planet that gave way to an array of crystalline, halo-shaped structures on the surface far below. The structures varied in size. When seen from our high vantage point, it resembled some elegant device consisting of interconnected and spinning wheels. The structures were surrounded by a lush, amber forest that spread out on all sides as far as the eye could see.

"There's the royal halo." Jasette pointed to the largest of the circular structures, located in the middle of the others.

"Breathtaking." Blix held his hand to his heart. "Simply breathtaking."

"It's incredible," Nelvan said.

I nodded in agreement. It was hard not to be impressed. It

was elegant but not flashy. The structures were crafted with an organic simplicity that almost gave a sense they were a naturally occurring phenomenon of the forest.

"They're hailing us," Blix said.

"Put them on screen," I said.

The viewing screen switched from the scenic kingdom below to a stately-looking couple with salt-and-pepper hair. They wore fine clothing of celestial blue with crystal accents.

"Jasette!" Tears came to the older man's eyes as he held his arms toward the screen. "We're so glad you're home. Your message was received earlier today." He hugged the woman at his side. Your mother and I are so proud of you. The kingdom hasn't stopped celebrating since we heard."

"Hello, Father, Mother." Jasette choked up.

"My sweet girl." Tears rolled down the cheeks of the older woman, who bore a strong resemblance to Jasette. "I'm so happy you're safe. When we hadn't heard from you, I feared the worst. Then we saw you on that *Iron Gauntlet* show." She turned to Jasette's father as if for confirmation. "Next thing we hear, you have the chrysolenthium flower. However did that happen?"

"Long story." Jasette was half crying, half laughing at this point. "I want you to meet my friends. Without their help, I couldn't have done anything. They're so important to me." She motioned to us. "This is Nelvan, Blix, and the man I love, Glint Starcrost."

Her parents paused as they met my gaze. I gave a nervous smile and waved.

Her mother's smile faded a little. "Isn't that the boy from *The Iron Gauntlet* show?"

"Yep," Jasette said. "That's him."

Her mother sent an unsure look to her father. It had been awhile since I'd been called boy. It made me feel youthful and insulted at the same time.

Jasette's father broke into a good-natured laugh. "Well, I've heard of crazier things." He pointed at me. "You put on quite a show in that *Gauntlet*. You're a true fighter. My soldiers will probably want to spar with you, of course."

I gave Jasette a nervous glance. "Oh . . . okay."

"You're not by chance the prince of some distant planet, are you?" Her mother looked hopeful.

"Not that I know of."

"Oh," she tried to hide her disappointment. "Well, such is life, I suppose. But enough of that. Welcome, one and all. Please head toward our landing loop for disembarking. Our welcoming committee will be waiting."

"See you soon, Mother." Jasette waved.

The visual switched back to the approaching, clear structures.

"I think your mom had someone else in mind for you," I said.

Jasette laughed. "Don't worry. She's had that prince dream in her head since I was a kid. I'm sure my younger sister will fulfill her wish. She's into the whole pampered-princess thing."

"Ah," I said. "You're the black sheep of the family?"

"Not anymore. I just brought back the one thing that can save our kingdom." She pointed to herself. "Hero."

We shared a laugh as we headed for the landing loop.

• • •

The next few days were a blur of parties, royal feasts, and ceremonies. The chrysolenthium flower was delivered carefully to their master horticulturists and scientists, who successfully integrated it into their energy supply. More celebrations ensued.

Jasette showed us all around the kingdom. The clear, circular structures nestled in the midst of the amber trees were an amazing sight to behold. With an unobstructed view at every angle, it was like living in the middle of the forest.

The people of Jelmontaire treated us like heroes. Everyone from the wandering tree-sap farmer to the royal kingdom guard stopped by to meet and thank us. At first, it felt great to be pampered and praised. After awhile I just wanted to get away from it all.

Blix, of course, was soaking it all in, telling and retelling the tales of our exploits and delighting in the gourmet meals. But by the fifth day of royal feasting and parties, I needed to find some peace and quiet.

An awards ceremony was scheduled during evening meal to honor our exploits. Apparently, this was the main ceremony that would bring all the celebrations to a dramatic conclusion. Chefs, florists, and varied party decorators rushed around all day getting things ready for the big event.

I spent most of the day steering clear of the noise and stress of the preparations by hiding out in the clear, oval guest chamber I'd used ever since we got there. It was an amazing room perched at the top of the tree line. An expansive purple mountain range framed the lush landscape. I reclined in a cherrywood-framed chair covered in amber cushioning. The chair had been crafted by one of their local artisans to blend in with the surrounding forest. It was no captain's chair, but it was a pretty close second. I watched the sun dip below the mountain range and waited for the sky to darken. One by one, the stars shone out in the night sky.

My peaceful concentration was broken by a flutelike tone at the door.

"Yeah?" I called out.

"Begging your pardon, sir," a young man's voice said. "I have your ceremonial clothes."

"My what?" I got up and hit the door controls. The pearl door slid away, revealing a youth about Nelvan's age with bushy red hair and freckles. He smiled and held forth a light-blue suit with crystal accents. "Here you are, sir."

I frowned. "I ain't wearing that."

"Oh." His eyes bounced from the suit to me and back again as if trying to figure out what to do next. "B-but the ceremony is about to begin."

"Fine." I grabbed the suit out of his hand. "Thanks, uh . . ."

"Peldrith, sir." The boy smiled and bowed. "At your service. And may I say, your bravery in the face of danger is—"

"No, please." I held up a hand to stop him. "Thanks, really. It's nothing."

"And humble as well." He shook his head in admiration. "Honored to meet you, sir. See you at the ceremony."

He hurried away, leaving me holding the fancy suit . . . which I promptly threw on the chair. It was time to get lost somewhere safe. I beat a quick path to the landing loop, and soon my beautiful ship was in sight. As I headed up the landing ramp, the familiar voice of Iris filled the air.

"Glint! Oh, it's heavenly to see you. I've missed you so."

"Great to see—er, hear—you, too, Iris. How they been treating you?"

"It's been a dream. They are very hospitable here. The technicians are not only skilled but attentive and kind. I feel so loved."

"Great." I entered the lift and headed up to the bridge. I couldn't remember the last time I'd heard Iris so happy.

"You haven't visited in several days," Iris said.

"Yeah, sorry about that. They're pretty big on ceremonies here. Lots of meet-and-greet kind of things."

"I can imagine. From what I hear, you're considered heroes of Jelmontaire."

"Well, I don't know about that."

"Oh, don't be so humble, Glint. They've even given me the meritorious emblem of valor and distinction."

"Really?"

"Yes. They placed a golden plaque on my hull. I'm quite proud of it."

"How 'bout that. That's great, Iris."

The lift doors opened, and I strode into the bridge. I took a deep breath, the familiar scent of oil, metal, and stagnant air making me feel at home. Finally, I could rela—

I froze, realizing someone sat in my captain's chair. The chair swiveled around, and a dark-haired man with a trim beard smiled at me. He was clad in a deep-blue jumpsuit with yellow accents common among Jelmontaire mechanics. His fingers were poised over a translucent touch pad.

"Captain Starcrost. Pleasure to meet you." He rose from the chair and gave a slight bow. "I'm Clav Brindle, Iris's main technician. I was just finishing up the day's performance assessment. What brings you down here? Isn't the big awards ceremony going on right now?"

"Oh, yeah. I . . . just needed to get away for a bit."

"Glint doesn't like a big fuss made over him," Iris jumped in. "As arrogant as he might appear at first glance, there is humility underneath it all."

I shot a dark look up at the ceiling.

"Say no more, Captain," Clav held up his hand. "Last montul when they named me lead star-freighter technician, I felt very self-conscious about the whole thing." He hit a few commands on his screen before tucking it under his arm. "Well, my work is done for the day. Perhaps we can speak another time. I'd love to hear more about how this ship performed in deep space."

"Yeah, sure."

Clav smiled and headed down the lift. I took my old, familiar place in the captain's chair and let out a deep sigh.

"Oh, Glint, isn't he dreamy?" Iris said.

"Huh?"

"Clav. My lead technician." Iris sounded out of breath. "Did you feel the energy between us? He even wants to hear stories of what I went through in space. It's obvious he's interested."

As much as I liked to see Iris's affections directed at someone other than me, it still felt strange. Poor Clav didn't know what he was getting into. "Yeah, that's great and everything, Iris. Just remember, he might not feel the same way you do."

"Do I detect a little jealousy?"

"What? No, it's not that. You see—"

"I'm sorry, Glint, but I can't wait around forever. Your relationship with Jasette is progressing, and I barely see you anymore. I had to move on."

"Yeah, but Iris, the thing is—"

"Don't worry, you'll always be the captain of this ship. No one can replace that."

I could see this discussion was going in circles, and all I wanted to do was relax and enjoy being on my ship once again. Maybe Clav knew some technician programming voodoo to keep Iris at bay. Since he was better equipped to handle her idiosyncrasies, I decided to leave it to him. "Okay, Iris. Best of luck to you."

"Thank you for understanding, Glint. I hope we can still be friends."

"You got it."

I hit a few controls on the armrest, bringing most of the systems online. Multicolored lights blinked across the instrument panels, and the engines wound up to speed. A familiar vibration went through the floor that told me systems were ready to go if I wanted to take the ship into space. I felt invigorated by the whole experience.

I stood, taking a deep stretch. "Iris, I think I'll walk the ship. Check operations."

"Everything is operating at maximum capacity. Clav is very detail oriented." Iris giggled. "He knows me so well."

"I'd like to check around just the same."

"Of course, Captain."

A leisurely stroll through the ship sent a flood of memories through my head. Unfortunately, most of them were stress-filled moments of near-death experiences. It was entirely possible I was romanticizing my exploits as a space pilot. But even with the harsh reality check, I couldn't seem to shake the desire to be out there again, exploring the stars.

A high tone sounded. "Glint, Nelvan just boarded."

"Really? Tell him to meet me on the bridge." In a few moments I was back in my captain's chair.

Nelvan entered through the lift. He wore a fitted celestial-blue suit. I had to admit, he looked pretty sharp.

"Captain, we've been looking everywhere for you. You missed the whole ceremony."

"Perfect," I said. "I've had my fill of ceremonies."

Nelvan crossed his arms. "Blix said you'd probably say something like that. We all got awards. Look." He held forth a translucent golden star fastened to his neck on a silver chain. "They gave me the title Pioneer of the Stars." He held the star closer to his eyes and, squinting, began to read. "For bravery and sacrificial service to the citizens of Jelmontaire." He looked up with a smile. "Pretty cool, huh?"

Seeing Nelvan overcome with accomplishment and joy made me feel a bit like a proud father. I was so used to seeing him locked in expressions of fear and anxiety over our dangerous travels, it was a welcome change. "That's great, Nelvan. You deserve it."

The lift doors chirped open again, and in walked Blix. He was dressed in his purple-and-gold ceremonial Vythian robes accented with polished throwing knives.

"Aha." He turned to Nelvan. "Didn't I tell you he'd rather sit in his dusty captain's chair than attend a beautiful ceremony?" He shook his head.

"Let me guess." I pointed at the golden star hanging from

Blix's neck. "They gave you the title Prima Donna of the Stars."

Nelvan laughed, then stopped himself, flashing an embarrassed look to Blix.

Blix crossed his arms. "You have a unique talent of blending humor with immaturity, Captain. The truth is I've been given the title Sage of the Stars. With my record, I find it to be both humbling and accurate."

Even though comebacks were spinning through my head, waiting to deliver a perfect, humorous counter to his new title, I couldn't help thinking he'd earned every bit of it. I decided it was time to acknowledge my gratitude. So rather than shoot off a glib comment, I stood and grabbed Blix by the shoulders. "You deserve the honor, Blix. I wouldn't be here without you. None of us would. I know I give you a hard time, but truth is you're more of a friend than I could hope for."

Tears formed in Blix's eyes. He lunged forward and locked me in a painful bear hug. "You're a good man, Captain. Despite your impulsive nature, it's an honor to fly through the stars with you."

I gasped for a breath. My ribs felt like they were about to snap.

Nelvan squinted at me. "I think you're hurting him."

"Oh." Blix released me. "Sorry about that."

I staggered back against my chair, gasping for breath. "Next time just pat me on the back or something."

"Indeed. I must keep in mind the fragility of the human body. Well, I suppose we should get back to the party, right, Nelvan?"

"Yeah," Nelvan's face lit up. "Jelline said she would take

me to the observation orb tonight. It's supposed to be the highest view of the kingdom."

"Jelline?" I raised my eyebrows. "Jasette's younger sister?"

Nelvan blushed. "Yeah, you know, we're just hanging out and stuff."

Blix and I shared a knowing look.

"Come, Captain." Blix motioned to me with his hand.

"No, thanks. I'm gonna stay here for a while."

"I promised Jasette I'd bring you back," Blix said. "She has something important to tell you."

"Yeah, right. This is a trick."

Blix held up his hand. "No trick. She asked for you."

"All right, all right. See you soon, Iris. We'll take a flight in a day or two. I'm itching to get back out there."

"Is that a promise?" Iris said.

"Promise."

We made our way from the landing loop through the expansive, clear corridors of the royal halo. Stars twinkled in the dark sky outside the clear structure, and three waning moons shone bright in the distance. I'd never been grounded somewhere that still made me feel a part of space like Jelmontaire.

"You guys okay with these crowds and all the fuss over us?" I said.

Blix looked at me like my question was crazy. "Of course. What's not to like?"

"It's nice," Nelvan said. "But I hope things get back to normal soon. I feel like I don't deserve all this."

"I can relate," I said. "When things die down, I guess we can take it easy for a little while."

"A long overdue vacation," Blix said. "I need time to

recharge. Plus, Nelvan and I have secured a beautiful spot in their archive room for our Bible studies. I'll finally have time to dig deep into the Scriptures."

Nelvan gave me an apologetic look. "Sorry, Captain."

"Don't worry about it," I said. "This way his Vythian dreams are wreaking havoc in their kingdom instead of on my ship."

"Really?" Nelvan said. "Then you should join us one of these times. Jasette said she would go."

"Eh. It's not really my thing."

"Oh, come on, Captain," Blix said. "You might actually enjoy it."

"If I go will you shut up about it?"

"Maybe."

"Okay, but on one condition," I said. "I'm taking the ship out soon. You two have to join me."

"Please, Captain," Blix said. "You really needn't ask. Of course we'll come."

"Yeah," Nelvan said. "I can't wait."

I smiled. "Great. Now if I can get Jasette to go, we'll have our full crew back."

"She's already prepared for your question," Blix said.

"She is?"

"Naturally," Blix smiled. "She knows you quite well. She's compiled a list of quests through space assigned to the kingdom fleet. All have some element of danger associated with them. I'd imagine they'd suit you perfectly. Just remember, we've gone through a lot. Try to keep the element of danger minimal."

"No promises."

Blix frowned. Up ahead, an opaque door opened and

Jasette walked out. She was dressed in a silky, sky-blue dress with crystalline jewelry spiraling up her arms and intertwined through her hair.

Blix waved to her. "There she is. All right, Captain, Nelvan and I are headed back to the ceremony after party. Join us later?"

"Maybe," I said.

He turned to Nelvan. "I believe that's a no."

"Come on, Captain," Nelvan said. "It's the last big party."

"Okay, fine. But just for a little while."

"Fair enough. See you soon, Captain." Blix took Nelvan by the shoulder and led him to the party.

"Hello." Jasette stood before me looking regal and ravishing at the same time.

"You look incredible."

"Thanks." She held out her hand. "I want to show you something."

I took Jasette's hand, and she led me through a seamless side door that I wouldn't have even noticed had I walked by. Beyond was a narrow, ivory stairway that ascended in a tight spiral.

"Where are you taking me?" I said.

Jasette glanced back. "The royal balcony. I wanted to have a moment with you alone."

"Is this where the observation sphere is?"

"No. Who told you about that?"

"Nelvan. Apparently, your sister is taking him there tonight."

She laughed. "That little troublemaker. Poor Nelvan. She'll be flirting her heart out up there."

"I doubt he'll mind."

The stairway ended, opening up to a clear dome-shaped structure that offered a grand view of space. Ivory balconies branched off in several directions, granting an open-air view of the skies above and the forest below.

"Wow," I said. "This is amazing. Why didn't you show me this place sooner?"

"I was waiting for the right moment." She took my hand and led me to one of the ivory balconies.

Free of the protective dome, the refreshing night winds blew over me. The large trees below swayed and rustled in the breeze, and the rich aroma of earth and forest filled the air. A wide river wound through the forest, bordering the kingdom. The flowing waters sparkled in the moonlight.

I breathed deeply, leaned against the ornately carved balcony, and felt more at peace than at any time I could remember.

"We're taking the ship out soon," I said. "You up for it?"

"Count me in. I have a list of potential missions from our fleet."

"Dangerous?"

She raised an eyebrow. "Naturally."

"Treasure? Glory?"

"It's possible."

I grinned. "Perfect." I noticed a gold star hanging from her neck. "I see they gave you an award tonight."

"Oh, yeah." She waved a dismissive hand.

"Come on," I prompted. "What is it? What's your title?"

She pursed her lips. "Promise you won't make fun of it?"

I held up my hand. "Swear."

"Rescuer of the Stars."

I gave an impressed nod. "Not bad, Princess."

"As long as we're on the subject." She retrieved something from a fold in her gown. "They wanted to present this tonight but *somebody* didn't show up." Jasette held forth yet another translucent golden star on a silver chain.

"I got an award?"

"Of course. Now, promise me you won't get carried away with this. They named you Hero of the Stars."

I stared off into space and struck a valiant pose. "Hero of the Stars. Sounds about right."

She chuckled. "C'mere, you big goon, before I convince them to take it back."

I leaned forward, and she fastened the necklace at the back of my neck. An intoxicating floral smell came from her hair. Her green eyes sparkled in the star light as they focused on the necklace clasp. As beautiful as the view from the balcony was, it paled in comparison with her.

"There." She took a step back to take in the new me. "Perfect."

"Maybe this will help with your mom's image of me."

She shook her head. "Don't worry, she'll come around. Plus, you've got another advocate with my dad. He always dreamed of setting aside the mantle of king for a while so he could fly away on some daring journey. After all Blix's hyped-up stories, I think he's living vicariously through your adventures."

"One look at Mar Mar would've changed his mind." I smiled and cast a look over the balcony. The trees swayed with a fresh gust of wind. "I think I understand my dream now."

She shot me a challenging look. "You mean the one where I turn into a villain?"

"Yeah, but that's not really what it was about."

"I hope not."

"My guess is it was all about my fears. Mar Mar was after me, and I feared he would send me to my death. And you . . ."

She pursed her lips. "Careful."

I grinned. "You were there because I haven't been this close to anyone since my uncle and my parents. It hurt so much when I lost them, I guess I was afraid to let anyone get that close again."

She nodded as if impressed with me. "That's quite an insight. Did Blix tell you all this?"

I shook my head. "Nope, all me. Hero of the Stars."

She laughed. "Are you afraid of our relationship?"

I grabbed my new necklace and held the golden star in my hand. The moonlight gleamed off its carved angles. "I guess it's like a space mission. It's dangerous, there's plenty of unknowns, you might even get hurt, but you dismiss the fear and dive right in anyway. Otherwise you'll miss the adventure."

She moved close. "Nicely put, star pilot." Her hand brushed against mine as she admired the golden star with me. She still wore the ornate silver ring set with the oval sapphire we'd found back in the cave on Krullnack. It took me a moment to realize she'd moved it from her first finger to her fourth finger.

"I see you moved your ring," I said.

The hint of a smile turned the corner of her lips. "That's right."

"Any significance to that?"

She gave a playful shrug. "Only time will tell."

The moonlight fell across her face, creating an angelic glow. No matter what the future held, I knew I wanted to share every moment with her. Starting now.

I leaned in and gave her a deep, passionate kiss.

Acknowledgments

Writing this series has been one of the biggest joys of my life. I'm so thankful to God for the privilege of taking this writing journey. My wife Jolene has been such an amazing supporter of this effort, and I am forever grateful to her.

As always, a big thank you to family and friends for their support of my writing and for geeking out with me on story ideas. All my love to Jolene, Joshua, and Katie.

Thank you to Steve Laube and the talented staff at Enclave and Gilead Publishing as well as Kregel Publications for their ongoing support of the Space Drifters series.

Heartfelt thanks go out to cover artist extraordinaire Kirk DouPonce for breathing life into my characters and creating an amazing series of covers and Andy Meisenheimer for sharpening my stories with his editing expertise.

Last but definitely not least, my sincere thanks and gratitude to the Writers Without Borders crew: Merrie Destefano, Rebecca LuElla Miller, Rachel Marks, and Mike Duran for their priceless feedback on my writing.

Paul Regnier is the author of the Space Drifters science fiction series. He's a technology junkie, drone pilot, photographer, web designer, drummer, *Star Wars* nerd, recovering surfer, coffee snob, and a wannabe Narnian with a fascination for all things futuristic.

Paul grew up in Orange County, CA and now lives in Treasure Valley, ID with his wife and two children.

Connect with Paul!

Website:	*www.spacedrifters.com*
Facebook:	*www.facebook.com/pjregnierauthor*
	www.facebook.com/spacedrifters
Twitter:	*www.twitter.com/PaulJRegnier*
Instagram:	*www.instagram.com/pauljregnier*
Pinterest:	*www.pinterest.com/pjregnier*

But wait, there's (already) more!

Whether you're a space explorer, star ranger, remote colonist, bounty hunter, rehabilitated cyborg, moon goblin, closet trekkie, or know someone who is, grab a copy of the other Space Drifters adventures and join the crew on their harrowing journey through galaxies best left unexplored!

More information:
www.spacedrifters.com